Obsidian Series – Book 1

The Labyrinth Wall

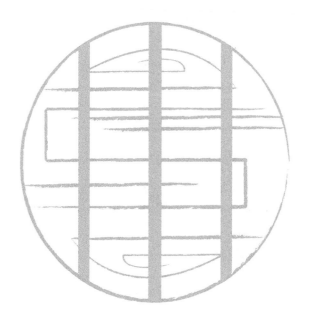

Emilyann Girdner

ISBN: 978-0-9915312-6-4

The Labyrinth Wall

Fourth Edition (Map Edition), November 2017

Edited by Nicole Zoltack and James Allen, Sr.
Text type set in Garamond
Cover Art by Emilyann Girdner

This book is in memory of my Grandmother:

Mary Elizabeth Peavy Allen

Thank you, Grandma, for your encouragement,
your support and your unfailing love.
You read me Blueberries for Sal, Mother Goose,
and other exciting tales that helped me to love stories.
You and these stories will always be in my heart.
I love you.

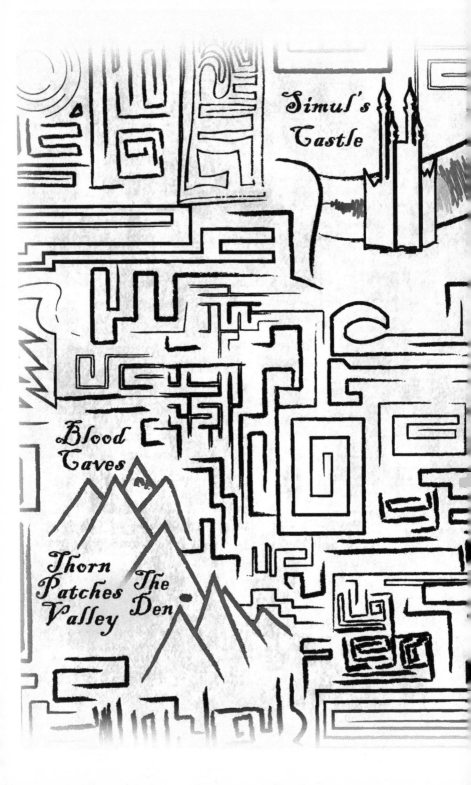

Table of Contents

Chapter 1
The Man in White

Bouncing off the walls of this wasted dark labyrinth, the slimy words leaking from Simul's mouth carry no authenticity. Consuming green grapes to fill his large stomach, he stands high in his tower. Looming above thousands of us, his creations called the Mahk, he spouts his typical lecture. "We, your Creators, deserve respect. We gave you life, the opportunity to live long, and serve well." His knack for being a bad liar is transparent as he says the words, "we treasure each of you," before limping closer to the guard rail. The condition of his soul likely mirrors that of his tough and leathery skin. Perched on his balcony railing, the proud man goes on speaking, but the empty words mean nothing to me.

Beads of perspiration coat the back of my neck, so I sweep my curly red hair up into a knot and steady it on top of my head using the butt of my dagger. I glance around at the large crowd. Like tiny pebbles that gather at a river bank, we coat the barren landscape sweeping out in front of the castle, only to be dissected at its edges by the openings of labyrinth passageways. The dark cylindrical fortress stretches far above us like a snake looming over its prey, Simul's words are the venom it sprays. We're all enemies to each other by the Creators' design, competing for food that only comes to us at the Creators' mercy. Loose skin hangs on the lanky middle-age man beside me. Like most of the Mahk, he's clearly on the brink of starvation. Though they only brought me into existence two years ago, if I had to compare my body to a Creator, I'd guess I look like a seventeen-year-old, give or take a year.

My fidgeting hands find menial entertainment in adjusting my baggy green pants that close in tight around my ankles. All Mahk wear the same bottoms, patterned sashes around our waists, form-fitted shirts, and sleeveless orange shrugs. The Creators might dress us all the same because it's easy, or to remind us that none of us are special; we're easily replaced. Either way, the little rebellious details on almost every person are impossible to miss. One woman wears a small ring she either found or made on her own. Another man has cut his pants to just below his knees. Small details like those are proof we aren't programmed little creations meant only to provide obsidian to our Creators.

It's not long before we're all forming a line, then offering our obsidian taxes. Yawning, the guard withdraws a small cracker from his food satchel. *"Cracker,"* like every other object and every word since my creation, I just know what it is. I never have seen one, never have eaten one, but that's a cracker. All Mahk have been created with knowledge planted in our minds.

"Number," the tall, heavily armed guard demands in a gruff voice as a crumb rolls off his beard.

"Araina, P329111." Our names are an interesting thing, our only semblance of unified rebellion against the Creators; confirmation of our identities beyond their simple number system.

His gaze navigates a piece of parchment. Then he marks on it with a writing utensil, which is fancy. It has a colorful fluffy feather waving about as he writes with the other end. He pushes me on toward the next guard. No "thank you" or even an instruction to keep going, only a shove.

My offerings are slim, three slick opaque obsidian shards and some kimberlite.

They give me only three potatoes, a dead rat, and two canisters of water. With a quick cram, the items enter my bag, out of sight. My stomach growls angrily. Frustration would love to bare its teeth about now. Like all the Creators, the distributor is plenty well fed. He clearly suffers no shortage of soft clean clothing each day.

"That's all we got this week, Blue," I whisper to myself as if she's beside me. It's my moments with gentle Blue that make me think it's not necessary to kill to survive. She may not take Mahk or Creator form, but there's more soul under those feathers than in Simul's whole being.

Eagerness to reach my secret spot and see Blue propels my quick departure. It only takes about thirty minutes to reach Sikla, the one volcano in our land. Compared to the monotonous miles of twisted trees lining cracked black walls that make up most of our world, this volcano is a brilliant jewel. Bright orange lava flows down its conical form and occasionally it coughs ash into the atmosphere.

Entering back into a labyrinth passageway, the sound of dingy rocks crunching beneath my feet swims in my ears. A cowering stone statue greets me at the corridor opening. It's one of many in the labyrinth. The breathless stone remnant of what was once a living Mahk represents yet another unhappy way to die in this place. Sporadic dimples and lines form intricate detail in the jagged walls. My eyes follow the climbing cracks in their surface, but their towering tops stretch out of sight.

A map of the labyrinth is clear in my mind, because I've traveled its paths a million times. Aside from a couple of select places that few dare to enter, like the Blood Caves or the Rotting Pass, I've been everywhere. There could be some turn left unexplored, but it's unlikely. Not that long ago, it seemed rational to hope there was more than the hostile life this place offers. Eating what's provided, when it's given by the Creators, or fighting amongst ourselves for scraps is the Mahk way of survival.

"This is my world," I confide to the walls; they're as good as friends in this place. "I'm a puppet and the Creators pull my strings."

Grating faintly sounds ahead, bringing me to a halt. Silence follows.

Dagger now retrieved from my hair and gripped tightly by my side, I inch forward. A break leading to another corridor lies close ahead. Pressure heavy in my chest, my body scales the wall, sneaking toward the opening. Still no more sounds.

Ready for the worst, I peek around the corner. The lonely passageway stretches beyond my sight, no threat to be found.

That's a relief. My walk toward my hiding spot with Blue can't pass fast enough. Though not many Mahk venture this far away from the castle or Sikla, there's always a chance of being followed. Hunger consumes every moment of Mahk existence, so Mahk will take food if they have to. It's happened to me many times, some of which I've barely survived. Other times, I've been the taker. You do what you have to do.

Rapidly paced footsteps interrupt my thinking, just before pain thunders in my lower back. Air thrown from my lungs, I try to catch my breath as my body falls violently into the dirt. Someone is trying to yank away my bag; my food.

An angry-eyed girl about my age scratches at my arms, screaming at me.

"Get away," I screech.

Dagger still in hand, I swing at her pale shoulder. Quicker than a blink, her leg kicks at my hand, dislodging my weapon. It flies across the corridor, landing near a twisted stump. Again she reaches for my bag. This time, I let her get close, waiting for just the right moment to pull out of reach. She stumbles, which was the plan. An extra shove sends her flying, head smacking into the sooty wall. Her body drops to the ground. Her eyelids twitch, but she seems unconscious. No sense in waiting around to verify. *She's out, but for how long?*

My feet can stand to carry me away faster, but the back pain is taking a toll. I check her position every few strides. She hasn't budged. Finally, my turn is in view, and I slip out of the corridor.

That one was sneaky. Exercising more caution wouldn't have hurt. The sound tipped me off. Impatience was what cost me.

Thanks to my recklessness, an uncomfortable pain throbs in my lower back from her attack. Focusing on the discomfort won't help. Only fifteen or so minutes until I reach Blue, reach home.

The branch poking through the wall above the boulders comes into view. Joy washes through me. I've almost reached our hiding spot. Upon my arrival, the climb up the boulders is faster than usual. Maneuvering too hastily across the branch and through the small hole in the wall causes me to nearly fall from the tree.

"Blue?" I drop to the ground, surveying the small space. "Blue? Come here." My eyes scan the twisted black bushes and walls filled with my drawings.

She croaks but is still nowhere to be seen. After a few minutes, she emerges from behind some thorny bramble. Blue's slender body rushes to my side, her tall skinny legs jerking to a halt before she nudges my cheek.

Fingers dancing through her blue feathers, I'm unable to resist the smile that spreads across my face. "Okay, okay."

Standing at my height, her big gold eyes bat at me.

"What were you doing back there?"

She fluffs her wings as if to gesture confusion.

My thumb grazes the little scar above her eye where my dagger nicked her face the first time we met. She still loves me despite the pain I inflicted on her. Even now, I tell myself if I had no obsidian to pay my taxes, if I had absolutely nothing left to eat, I could… Cringing, I push the thought far away.

She prances back behind the thick, tangled black bushes. She likes to play in them, but their giant thorns are unsettling to me. Her feathers must protect her.

Evidently she's busy. I shrug, preparing to pull out a rock and draw on the wall. Images in my mind scream to be released. That girl who attacked me and her angry eyes need a place in my drawings.

Splashing sounds from Blue's direction. She croaks bleakly.

"Blue?" My arms are pushing through the tangled branches. What could she possibly be splashing in? Water that isn't provided by the Creators isn't safe. My heartbeat drums in my ears.

When I finally reach her all the way at the back of the shrubbery, a scream rings from my lips when her long legs submerge in acidic water. Nerves twitch under my skin. Countless times I've suffered burns from the water around here.

"Blue, no!" I dash toward her.

She disappears into the dangerous liquid of a small pool extending from the base of the wall.

Without hesitation, I dive in. The cool water wraps around me. It doesn't burn or blister my skin at all. The water isn't acidic like the other river or pools near which my fingers dig for obsidian. My eyes open to see Blue a few feet ahead of me, swimming beneath the wall to the other side. Gliding through the water on her trail, I realize this pond might be the source of the Creator's clean water.

Swimming is a new experience. Invading my ears and my nostrils, the liquid is at first unpleasant. Within moments, my thoughts move on to the relaxing cool temperature and the satisfying pressure grazing each arm with every stroke forward. Glimpses of smooth multicolored pebbles resting on the mud catch my eye. Lovely chartreuse plants rise up from beneath us. Smooth texture greets my hands when they touch their green tips. The plants might even be edible.

We emerge on the other side of the wall into an expanse of emerald grass and brown trees. Lush blades of healthy greenery stretch far into the distance and little wild flowers bloom throughout. Unlike the twisted, barren dark trees of the labyrinth, these are bushy with big oval leaves. Some are growing pink and red fruit on them. Each the size of a fist, they cause the branches to dip toward the ground. Everything is displaced from the ebony trees and volcano I've always known.

The cleansing water has made my skin a shade lighter. I'm no longer covered in soot. Blue prances around the field happily. It's tempting to join her, but this place, though lovely, doesn't feel safe. My gut suggests something isn't right about our surroundings and as I wave her back over to me, another figure breaks from the surface of the water.

Darith emerges soaking wet and jumps to his feet. We can't be more than fifteen feet apart. He probably doesn't even know who I am, but I'd be a lot happier if he wasn't always beating me to the punch. He's either a better thief than me or he reads my thoughts and then acts before I get the chance. He's cost me so many meals I've lost count.

Getting rid of him has been tempting in the past, but there's never a right moment. That's how the world works. You eat to survive and you kill to eat. Operating life like everyone else would make living a lot easier: take what you need and don't put much thought into the repercussions. Though I've taken food in desperate times, I've never killed to do it.

Arms hanging limply, eyes wide open, I'm frozen for a moment as we observe one another. Then his gaze shifts to Blue. My body comes to her protection as I dash between them before he has a chance to strike her down with his curved black sword.

"You want to kill her? You're going to have to get past me."

Surprise sweeps through his green eyes and his face tightens. Within a second, his sword is clutched in his grasp and ready for an attack.

"Araina, I never would have guessed ya would have such a big secret. How long have you been protectin' this nice large meal? Why don't we split it?"

To hear anyone else acknowledge my name out loud is startling. "Araina" only ever comes from my lips. The guards never say it back. It sounds venomous on Darith's tongue, but what bothers me most is that he has the nerve to make an assumption about what I would or wouldn't be likely to do.

"You guessed wrong!"

He attacks and misses. I dart behind him strategically and he stumbles, attempting to dodge my agile movements. Terror rises in me at the feeling of his sword almost grazing my hand. A slice across his shoulder should slow him down. He's taken aback by the exposed raw flesh and retreats a few feet. We dance like this a couple more times, aiming to kill, but finding ourselves evenly matched.

When his weapon slices my leg, Blue croaks from behind me. Nausea swells in my stomach at the sight of my blood staining my green pants, but I push past it. My grip on the dagger becomes less steady as sweat invades my palms. The sharp edge of his ebony sword is swinging toward me, but he's not quick enough. My position is perfect for a good stab into his side.

"The wall! What's happening?" The color is draining from his face. The labyrinth wall is rippling and a man bursts right through.

Darith and I do a double take, our gazes fixed on the stranger across the field. A man just came through a wall. This was different from the branch coming through the wall above the boulders. This time, the wall seemed to wave as he jolted through. There was never an actual opening.

In the next moment, he's on his feet as his head darts about in confusion. His tall, skinny body jolts frantically, facing one direction then another, trying to determine which way to go. Deeply drawn eyebrows shelter the man's brown eyes that scream fear. He must be running from something. Goosebumps rise on my skin when his gaze lands on me and he charges in my direction.

The tall brown man with matching hair trips on his loose white pants as he sprints across the field toward us. He screams at me, "Raiyla."

That word has no meaning to me. Maybe it's "help" in his language.

I've been so off guard, I barely notice Darith preparing to take another blow at me. My body ducks down and I draw back.

"Friend of yours?" he questions.

"None of your concern, but no."

He resumes his murderous attempts on my life, despite the potential threat of the approaching stranger. I'm overwhelmed by the situation. It's becoming difficult to dodge his charges, which prevent me from keeping an eye on the man in white.

If the mystery man is aiming to attack me, I'm as good as dead. Giving up isn't an option, not in my book. The longer that sword is in Darith's hand, the likelier chance it will end up striking me. Energy summons from every corner of my being into one punch to his face. He looks dizzy. Next my leg kicks his arm, nearly dislodging his weapon. Retaliating with a shove, he almost knocks me to the ground.

A brief moment passes as we race to collect ourselves. I have to be first. A swift kick from my foot hits Darith in the chest and knocks him back into the pool of water. As I turn to take note of the other man's position, he's now upon me and he grabs my injured leg with both hands. My body jerks with fear, my leg kicking him.

Everything is happening so fast there isn't enough time to process it all: a new place within the labyrinth, an attack on mine and Blue's lives, and now a man emerging out of a wall. *How did he come through that wall? From where?*

My hand signals Blue toward the bushes to take cover so we can regroup. As we make our way, I notice the pain in my leg is dying down. My skin is mending itself. My eyes fall on the man in white who is attempting to regain his composure.

Did he do that? Was he trying to heal me? Is that even possible?

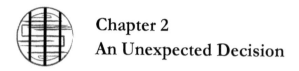

Chapter 2
An Unexpected Decision

Two more figures emerge through the rippling wall. They look like Creators, a man and a woman. One points to the man in white before they chase him across the field. He runs in a different direction, like he doesn't want them to know I'm here.

Loud splashing interrupts my thoughts as Darith jumps out of the water and gasps for air.

Seizing the moment of his vulnerability, I hasten out of the bushes toward him, hoping to take him by surprise.

"That was new and different," he announces, already aware of my approach.

Coming to a halt, I roll my eyes. My dagger is snug in my grip. Here comes another round.

"Put that away," he sputters as he shakes his head. Water sprays from his hair all over me.

Darith's record of killing for food beats a camel's record for spitting, yet he's standing ten feet away from me with his sword sheathed.

Approaching me calmly with his hands in the air, he's acting like I can trust him, like I should have any reason to.

"Look, I wasn't ever gonna kill ya anyway, little Araina," he mutters.

A solemn expression masks my fear, my confusion. My legs start to waver a little, but my inner strength takes control. Rapid rhythm pounds in my ears to the beating of my heart. It's crucial to stand strong. This is the moment I've been waiting for. So many times he has unnecessarily killed. He's taken so many meals from me. I could kill him in a second.

He straightens to his full height after he's finally rung his hair out to his contentment. He stands about a foot taller than me with an eyebrow raised. Aside from our matching green eyes, we have almost nothing in common. His olive skin and chestnut brown hair are a contrast from my bright red hair and pale white skin. I've never been close enough before to study him so thoroughly. A small scar resides on his cheek and a string hangs around his neck that disappears under his shirt.

Little Araina? He doesn't know the first thing about me...or so I thought. He knew my name, though. The moment has now passed for me to take him down fast and off guard. The longer he stands there, completely defenseless with his sword tucked away, it becomes impossible for me to make an attack on a helpless victim.

"I don't understand." My arm drops down to my side.

"I mean I was plannin' to maim ya a little and take off with the bird. Wasn't gonna kill ya, though," he offers, as if that's some comfort to me. He then walks off toward the wall from which the man and guards appeared.

Blue is still in the bushes and I'm standing about thirty feet from the pool of water.

"Oh, okay, just maim me," I mimic him sarcastically. "That's great to know. Not that I believe a word coming from your mouth, but why weren't you going to kill me? You kill everyone else you meet."

He continues walking.

Finally, I follow him curiously. "What are you doing anyway?" I don't know what game he's playing, but his actions demand my interest.

My mind races while we cross the field. Walking behind Darith, I'm still tempted to attack, but how can I? I'm better than that. As we near the wall, my thoughts shift back to the man in white. *Who was that man and did he heal me?*

"I've never seen a rippling wall before. Have you?" He approaches the black jagged wall. His hand nears the coal textured surface then lands on it. My muscles tense up at the sight. Investigative fingers inch across its cracks as he attempts to pull at partially loose sections. Nothing happens.

"It's not working anymore?"

"Does it look like it's workin'?" His hands navigate across the area one more time to no avail. His eyes meet mine squarely.

"I've never seen something like that," I repeat, standing at a safe distance, ready to defend myself. "What do you think is on the other side?"

He shifts his weight from one leg to the other so I jerk my dagger up defensively.

"Whoa, now." He snickers. Obviously unconcerned with my weapon, Darith turns to start walking out into the field.

I stand awkwardly, my arm still extended into the air, holding the dagger.

"Ya comin'?" he calls back to me.

"I'm not going anywhere with you!"

"I'm gonna find out how to get through that wall, which means I'm gonna find the man or the guards that came through it. Ya got somethin' better to do?"

He has a point. I'm going to find out more about that man and it wouldn't hurt to have help. I follow cautiously. Hushed croaks babble behind me. Blue is on our heels.

"If I come with you, I want you to promise me one thing...you won't kill her." I motion my head in Blue's direction.

"I won't kill the damn bird," he utters in aggravation, but I think I sense a tone of honesty, if honesty exists in this world.

Taking in abundant tall trees, we walk silently through the landscape. Forming vertical zigzagged trails, different shades of brown bark coat their trunks. Tangled vines of a dark purple color elegantly hang from thick branches. We need to hurry, but food isn't a necessity to be passed up. Greed takes over. First one, then another, heavy, fuzzy red apple finds a home in my bag.

"Those could be poisonous," Darith points out upon catching my thievery.

"Not likely. Simul eats these during his announcements."

"Ya don't say." He smiles at me as he proceeds to pick an apple.

Despite our hurry, the fruit isn't the only distraction fighting for my attention. Sparkling petals of a little flower catch my interest. Nothing so elegant or bright exists in my world. The glittering object's fascinating beauty draws me closer. My fingers reach down to touch it. Darith strikes my hand, causing me to withdraw with a yelp.

Anger must be lit in my eyes because it bursts within me. Warmth burns in my cheeks.

"Really?" he lectures. "Gonna touch that flower? Not thinkin', are ya? Have ya learned nothin' in the labyrinth?"

A couple deep breaths begin to calm me. He's right. The only flowers in the labyrinth, Darktouch, are lethal. There's every chance this lovely sparkling flower would have killed me in some vicious manner. Despite the possibility that he may have saved my life, feeding his ego isn't on my agenda. "I wasn't going to touch it," I insist.

"Fine." He shrugs. "Use your brain, will ya?"

It's tempting to turn back, to run from Darith. Still, my footsteps follow his. Smug, murderous, he makes me extremely uncomfortable. He said he wasn't going to kill me, but it's difficult to rationalize that statement. I've watched him since my creation day. Like all the other Mahk, Darith kills to eat. *He's lying.* He even took that hit at my leg before the man in white showed up.

I'm a puppet and he's pulling my strings, like the Creators. At least I'm smart enough to have some idea what he's up to. Right now, he could prove very helpful in attaining the man in white, but after that we can go our separate ways.

"Why do you think those Creators were chasing that man?" Talking may have been a bad idea and yet I opened my mouth before considering better of it.

Darith shoots a frustrated glance at me "That's what we're tryin' to figure out...isn't it?" He shakes his head.

"I thought you might know something, since you decided to recruit back-up. It's not like you to have a sidekick."

"He must've done somethin' really sour, since generally we can get away with murder and the Creators don't care." His eyes shift to meet mine.

I glance at the ground, breaking the awkward tension. Darith of all people would know about getting away with murder. "I guess I'm curious about his offense as well."

He raises his eyebrow again, inquisitively.

"I mean, I'm very curious about him, but I also want to know what's on the other side of that wall. I want to know about the part of the labyrinth he came from. Or maybe he came from a place outside the labyrinth. And if he's also a Creator or if he's a Mahk."

Darith nods. I think about my knowledge of the labyrinth, how I leave no stone unturned. For the first time, it occurs to me that my curiosity sets me apart from the rest of the Mahk. My kind don't explore. They do what they're told: pay obsidian, fight, eat, sleep, and do it all again. Like Darith, most people keep to the castle area, or Sikla.

"That's just like ya, isn't it?" He shoots me a partial smile.

No response seems appropriate. It's hard to even process all the events of the day. He's acting like he knows me, which is agitating. My pace slows, allowing Blue to catch up. A smooth stroke on her soft head brightens her eyes.

He stops suddenly, almost causing me to trip over his slouched body. Darith's green eyes observe the dirt. He scratches at the olive-colored skin on his neck as he grabs shuffled grass from the ground. "Looks like they caught our mystery man." The focus is written across his face as he glances back up in the direction the tracks lead. "And it looks like they're taking him for a visit with Simul." He points his finger past the field to the castle.

The minarets of the giant dark building look down at us from on high. It's not as tall as the walls that reach out of sight, but it hovers far above us. Big enough to house all the Creators, the palace has to contain thousands of rooms. The Creators periodically added new wings on the sprawling structure, making room for more of their kind. Its exterior resembles the labyrinth walls, probably built of the same rough black material. For such a large structure, the main cylindrical building, central within the fortress, has few windows; likely for security reasons. Two particularly large pairs of towers, one set at the front and one toward the back, encase the structure. They feature tall minarets. Two giant watch walls, jagged across their tops, branch out from the towers. If the place wasn't the home of such evil residents, I would consider describing it as somewhat pretty.

The reality that at any moment Darith might bail on our truce, give up on this chase, and take Blue for dinner snaps me out of castle-daydreaming. "Do you think we can catch them?" I question as my muscles tense.

"We need to step it up a notch. Can that bird of yours run?" He takes off toward the castle, sending dirt into the air. I'm not entirely certain I've seen her run, but she can catch up. If nothing else, she can fly fast.

I'm passing him in a matter of seconds. He may be strong and muscular, but speed is one thing I've got that he doesn't. Running as if it's a race for survival, I slice through the air. My observations alternate between the guards' tracks and the field in front of me. Brief glances behind me ensure he hasn't taken off with Blue and I'm beginning to believe he does want to catch the man in white. This may not be a sick game of his after all. If he does have a heart beating beneath his murderous shell, more than curiosity is urging his interest in the unusual man. Hope is pulling us on this chase, hope of something better on the other side of that wall. My gut has always told me there's more to living than this place and now my gut tells me the man in white is the key. Despite my speed, there's no pain in my leg. Beneath the green material of my pants, the injury has completely healed. The man in white has got to be worth it, worth risking everything to find.

We're drawing fairly close to the castle. It must only be about two miles off. After I halt abruptly at the top of a hill, my body flattens against the ground. Hopefully no one has seen our approach. Darith catches up quickly and Blue… I whip my head in every direction, frantically searching for her.

"What did you do with her!" My dagger is in hand, held to Darith's throat. "Where is she?"

His smug eyes and head motion toward the outer edge of the field along the labyrinth wall. "I think she got hot and took to the shade. I didn't touch her!"

There she is, safe, like he claimed. My cheeks blush thanks to embarrassment. The dagger retreats back into my hair. To him, the gesture indicates trust, but my guard isn't dropped. He'd be surprised how quickly I can pull that dagger back out. "I'm sorry." My chin drops. "I just–"

"It's fine, but I'm not gonna complain if ya decide ya want to quit aimin' that thing at me constantly."

No response feels appropriate, so silence creeps between us. He should understand the lack of trust, but at the same time, I would be furious if he constantly pulled his sword on me.

We shift our eyes up in search of the Creators and the mystery man. "We must be too late," I tell him. They already made it to the castle.

"This is when we have to decide how badly we want to know more. How far ya willin' to take this?" His eyes meet mine again. Excitement shines on his face.

"You're really enjoying this, aren't you?"

"What's not to love? I made friends with a pretty girl and now we get to plan a castle break-in. This beats the day-to-day kill, eat, and survive."

All this time, Darith seemed so transparent. A selfish, deadly killer, programmed to survive and serve like everyone else. But every action since our first actual meeting today has begun to paint a different picture. It almost certainly isn't a pleasant picture, but a very different one. He does think for himself, even if he isn't particularly lovable. Based on his exploration of the wall from which the man in white came, he might be as hopeful as me that there's something important on the other side.

"What's your suggestion, Darith?"

"I'm thinkin' we go undercover." He points out two figures at the base of the castle, guarding a small entrance near the labyrinth wall.

"That's suicide. Are you serious? Have you ever heard of a Mahk inside the castle, disguised or not?"

"You need to relax, little Araina," he responds in a demeaning tone. "I think we have seen and done a lot of things today that aren't exactly normal. Unless you have a better idea…"

"Will you stop rambling?" His suggestion is the only idea we have so far. Sick of wasting time, I'm on my feet, headed toward the outer rim of the field, ready to meet up with Blue by the labyrinth wall.

Darith follows close behind. "Eventually, you should learn how to actually end a conversation. I assume you like my plan."

"That wasn't a plan," I counter, "it was a suggestion. This is a plan. Blue is going to get me in the air so we can distract the guards, giving you the opportunity to take them by surprise."

"I guess I have to hope you're really gonna stick this out. If you're not with me and I pick a fight with those guards, I'm dead."

My head shifts to face him. "Guess you're right. Good thing you seem to know me so well. You must know I'll follow through."

We reach the outer edge of the field where Blue is nestled into the grass, enjoying an afternoon nap. My fingers pat her head and wander through her long feathers. Petting the soft creature calms my nerves. "Come on, girl," I speak softly.

Blue starts to croak, but I close her beak gently, holding my finger over my mouth. She probably has no idea what I'm trying to indicate, but it works anyway. Quietly, she stands, and my hand runs beneath her wing. She knows that gesture well. Her wings spread as she waits for me to crawl on her back. My arms wrap around her neck, trying not to disturb her airways. In order to stay balanced, my legs cling tightly to her sides. As skinny as she is, it's a struggle not to slide right off of her.

"Ya flown on her before?" Darith inquires.

"We've done it a couple times, trying to reach the top of the labyrinth walls. She can't make it that high, though."

He nods. "Okay then. Let's get this over with."

He takes off down the hill, staying tucked in the shadows of the wall while Blue and I burst into the air. As we soar overhead, a slight breeze glides through my red hair and her feathers.

Given the distance from the hill to the castle, it doesn't take us long to get there. The guards haven't noticed our approach. Surprised by the shoe that drops between them, the guards' gazes shift up to find its owner. Blue and I hover yards above.

Their attention on us now, they're sufficiently distracted. Darith wastes no time before launching his attack.

He fares well for a few moments. A large rock launches at high velocity to the first guard's temple, taking him to the ground as Darith's curved sword challenges the second opponent.

We fly down toward them quickly, but the first guard has joined the fight before I dismount. My arrival is just in time. Darith is pinned to the wall at the hands of one, as the other guard prepares to dagger him. After pulling the dagger from my hair, I send it flying into the hand of the guard restraining Darith. He turns in agony to face me, dislodging the blade. The man tosses my dagger to the ground and our fight really begins. With one arm, he waves his large sword about in the air, swinging at me over and over. I dodge every time. His movements are slow, given the gaping hole my dagger left in his other hand. Rapidly, I sneak behind him and regain my dagger. Strength isn't my strongest attribute, but my agility makes up for it.

A forceful kick plows into my stomach causing me to lose my breath. The dagger falls from my grasp. It hurts so bad there might as well be a hole in my belly. I thrash about spastically on the ground, gasping for air. I don't make it to my dagger.

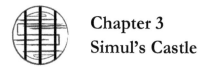

Chapter 3
Simul's Castle

I'm probably about to die by the guard's sword.

"Not today, scum!" Darith says and I hear a loud pop.

My shaky head lifts, vision blurred, to see Darith standing over the corpse of the Creator. He's snapped his neck. Both guards are dead. I'm holding my stomach, rocking on my back. It feels like a million heavy bricks were thrown at me. Darith drags my body toward the labyrinth wall, then props me up. He reaches to lift my shirt so he can observe the injury, but I smack him away. "It's not that bad," I spit out.

"Fine. Don't be so careless, Araina." Wasting no time, he pulls the guards into the shadows and strips them of their fancy outfits. He collects my dagger, running his thumb over the wooden handle.

"Ya etched the bird in it?" he asks, almost laughing.

He doesn't deserve a reply. Pain is still pulsing through me and we have got to hurry.

"Huh," he grunts, tossing the dagger beside me.

Yes, Blue has been etched into the wooden handle. She's always with me that way. But that's not his business.

"Can ya even walk?" He bends forward to help me up.

"Scrats, Darith! I can walk just fine." I grab a guard's clothing from his hands. It's true. It *is* possible to walk. It's going to hurt like needles to skin, but I can do it. I'm not going to let him see that it hurts. My condition has clearly grated on his mood. Despite his impatience or my pain, we have come too far to turn back now.

"Scrats?"

"Scrats. My two least favorite things: scars and rats." I walk behind Blue to change, using her body as shelter from Darith's prying eyes. This is the first time I've ever touched the smooth Creator clothing. They feel soft and new in my hands. The thin tan undershirt slides over my arms, followed by the thick maroon jacket. Even though the shining charcoal color pants were tight on the male guard, they fall a bit loose on me.

"What 'bout the bird?" he asks as he waits for me. He hides the lifeless bodies behind some bushes next to the castle.

"What about her?"

"I don't think she can go in with us. You gonna survive if we leave her out here a while?"

"Yes, I'll be fine, and she'll be fine." I appear from behind her.

"Look at that. Ya can pull off the Creator look fine," Darith laughs, his voice filled with sarcasm.

The guard's clothes hang on me, far too big. At least one of us gets a good chuckle out of it before we head into the castle.

I look back at Blue. Surviving this venture is no guarantee, so I memorize her face. Hopefully, we will be together again shortly.

My mind begins to overload with anticipation as we push the castle doors open, granting us entry into a narrow hallway. This is amazing. My mouth drops open. The inside of the castle is nothing like the rough dark exterior, or any place in the labyrinth.

Even Darith pauses with his eyes peeled. The walls seem to shine and complex designs fill them, top to bottom. A pale gold color comprises the background of the artwork, but there are also many blues and greens throughout. My fingers soak in the cool smooth of the marble. The intricate swirling shapes and beautiful colors draw me in like a bird to its nest. I trace a blue line with my finger before Darith yanks my arm, gesturing for me to snap out of my fixation.

We start down the hall, completely unsure of where we're headed or how long it will be before someone realizes there are intruders. The Creator boots make loud clicking sounds on the floor. Tall pointed marble archways line the corridor every few feet. They appear completely useless to the structure, serving only as added detail.

"This looks nothing like the room we were created in," I say. "It was dark and the walls were rough, like everywhere else in the labyrinth. I never could have imagined how beautiful this place actually is."

"It's almost like they didn't want us to know how fancy this place is. Joke's on them 'cause their gaudy clothes tipped me off."

"Right." I nod as we turn a corner to find another long stretching passageway. "They seem to think we can't deduce that kind of logic for ourselves."

We pace the halls quickly but not fast enough to induce attention from the other sporadic guards we pass. Spotting one guard's finger tapping the hilt of his giant sword causes my heart to beat a little faster, but it's imperative to stay calm. He passes by unsuspecting.

Stumbling upon a large dining hall, we encounter a banquet. Creators have been walking behind us for a couple minutes, so we go with the crowd into the big room. Fortunately, our guard clothing protects us from suspicion as we try to pass through the area without drawing negative speculation. So many feasting Creators sit on the floor, lining the table edges, it would be hard to count them. Scents of various herbs and seasonings like none I've ever known drift in the air and my stomach growls.

My eyes are drawn to Simul and his small crowd. They drink carelessly then devour chunks of meat and vegetable served on a stick. Sitting around a huge buffet of abundant food, while their creations starve—their selfishness makes me sick.

Those gathered around Simul appear privileged and proud, but they don't look like guards. A woman sits on a red cushion beside Simul. She looks older than me but younger than him with golden hair. Frowning is the only thing her lips care to do. The woman doesn't appear to be in tune with the conversation. She's clearly bored. Each cherry she snacks on steals my interest for a moment. Like the cracker the guard consumed earlier, I know these are cherries, though I've never seen one in my life. The stupid little cherries get me thinking again, asking questions. Why do the Creators take the time to build us with so much knowledge, with survival skills? Why do they give us weapons and put us in the labyrinth at all?

Darith lets out a nearly inaudible whistle under his breath, motioning toward the golden-haired woman.

"Ugh," I respond to his tasteless gesture.

Her cap-sleeve shirt is a glimmering bright purple color which covers only her chest, granting her midsection exposure. Clearly the bare skin has taken Darith's interest. The blouse is lined with the same dark blue of her pants. Lovely pale pink translucent pieces of floor-length material drape down around the blue pants. Though I'm unable to decipher exact details, elaborate beading is visible in her hair.

My face flashes across hers, a figment of my imagination. It's me wondering what her beautiful clothing would look like on someone like me: someone starved, skinny, and awkward. The embellishments would just weigh me down anyway. Attempting to picture myself dressed in something so ornate without a dirt-covered face is impossible.

We're close to exiting the over-populated room, but one more Creator catches my attention. His missing hand must be what subconsciously caught my eye. The man looks far more slender as well as a bit shorter than Simul. From my distant vantage point, his details aren't extremely evident, but stringy brown hair hangs over his face, which I find a bit unsettling.

Meats, fruits, vegetables, and bread of many varieties tease me. It might not hurt just to snatch a little. The risk would be high. Many of them are completely drunk anyway, but the guards around the edges of the room make me nervous. After exiting the gathering through a large archway lined with purple curtains and red tassels, I let out a sigh of relief, glad we put distance between us and Simul.

The clicking of our boots on the smooth floor resumes for a good thirty minutes before we locate a secluded bench at the edge of a courtyard.

The courtyard is the nicest part of the castle so far. It features the same pointed arches from the hallways, but these run all the way up several levels. Intricate balconies abound every twenty feet. Every single one is unique, with a different pattern designed in it. The patterns aren't drawn on, like I draw on walls. Each design is built that way with multicolored stones carved into different shapes. It's hard to fathom how long it took them to build this place, or more likely, how long it took the Mahk to build it for them.

Thinking about the creation of the Mahk piques my curiosity. It could be done in some of the rooms we've passed. I wish we could learn more about the process while we're inside the castle. After waking up to the world for the first time, the Creators simply sent me into the labyrinth with no further explanation. What my body consists of or how my brain is wired, how life sparked within me, I may never know. It's possible we could find where our bodies are produced or learn how they wire our brains, but realistically, we're already treading in dangerous territory without digging that deep. We really need to find the mystery man so we can get out of here, or we'll be killed.

Sweat crawls down my back and on my palms as my nerves threaten to expose my fear. Who knows what the Creators might do to us for sneaking into the castle. "This was a stupid idea... It's never going to work," I murmur. "Let's get out of here before they catch us. We don't even know where to find the man in white."

The expression on his face is more serious than it's been before. He looks down at his sooty boots. "Don't ya want to know how he came through that wall, where he came from?"

Sighing heavily, I shrug. "Lead the way."

"Let's get him and get out. It's time to rethink this game plan. We could spend days wanderin' this place lookin' for him and I bet, by then, he'll be dead."

He's right. My brain boils in search of a good solution.

"If you hadn't killed both the guards," I accuse him, "we could have forced information out of them."

"If ya think that's the best way, that's how we'll do it." He takes off away from the courtyard, motioning for me to follow.

It doesn't take long for me to recognize where he's headed. We passed a bath hall about twenty minutes ago.

"It'll be easiest to take someone that's off duty and unarmed," he announces.

My lips purse unintentionally, but he's right.

"Why don't you do the dirty work?" This seems like a good job for him. I'm not eager to see any naked people.

"I'm way ahead of ya." He motions for me to wait in the hallway as he slips inside.

As the mist flows out into the hall, warm slimy residue forms on my skin. I glance back and forth down the passageway. The wait for his return feels endless. A good fifteen minutes pass, but he still doesn't emerge with a guard.

I'm tapping my fingers nervously when the one-handed man in black from the banquet rounds the corner, then starts walking toward me. For a minute, I completely panic, thinking he knows I'm a Mahk. Then I remember I'm in guard attire. I stand stiff and upright at his approach; like I've seen other guards do for Simul.

Just when it seems he's going to walk right past me without a pause, he turns to face me.

Chapter 4
"Criminals"

His almost entirely black ensemble is actually fairly detailed upon close inspection. It's composed of a loose long-sleeved shirt tucked into pants which are not that different from Mahk pants. Ours are a little less baggy and certainly not as durable, but they also close at the ankles like his.

A slightly faded silk vest rests over his charcoal shirt and a particularly unique shining silver sash hangs from one shoulder. The designs on it feature two symbols, one that's stitched into all Creator clothing, including those that I'm wearing. Lines run parallel and adjacent, forming a maze, and it isn't hard for me to know this symbol has something to do with the labyrinth in which we live. What I'm not certain of is the meaning of the thick vertical lines slicing through the maze. Below that symbol is one which is also on Simul's clothing, a circle that has flames and ice in it.

The long brown hair hanging past his eyes is even more disconcerting close up, because it's hard to guess what he's thinking. I breathe heavily, attempting to maintain my salute.

He shoves me against the wall. "When did Simul start posting guards outside the bathhouse?"

"Oh, he didn't. I was waiting here for someone."

He leans in close to me. The man must be studying my face, but his eyes are elusive under all his hair. "Hmm," his raspy voice continues. "Simul's an idiot, but at least he's not posting guards at the bathhouse. You." He turns his attention back to me. "Report to authority and request a transfer." He runs his hand along my hip. "Pay me a visit sometime."

Gross, that was completely vile. Every muscle feels tense. He smirks and then turns away.

He's several feet down the corridor now.

"What a pig." He better be glad he stopped when he did. My dagger would have been up his stomach in a second.

The man continues down the hall only to stop about thirty feet away. After extracting a key from his vest, he unlocks a door then waits quietly for a moment. High-pitched creaking follows as he slowly pushes it open.

"You haven't mentioned if you're finding these accommodations pleasing?" he inquires hoarsely.

No response follows his question, so he pounds his fist against the doorway. "I assume they're to your liking. It's time to tell me the information I've been patiently waiting for."

A woman's gentle voice replies, "Why does it matter? We're minding our own business."

He grunts loudly, pulling her partially out of the room. She has long black hair, but her face can't be seen from my vantage.

"You've had enough time!" the man in black yells at her. "You tell me now, or you won't live for another opportunity."

"I'm not going to say anything, you animal," she retorts. He begins to push her inside the room. "Please don't…" she begs.

I start to glimpse part of her face when suddenly a woman wearing partially buttoned pants and an undershirt slams into the wall across from me.

Darith follows her, tossing the rest of her clothes at her feet. "Be quick," he threatens as he reaches for one of the trident spears strapped across his back.

"Quiet." My finger points down the hall. I lunge forward to muffle the scream our prisoner is about to let out.

A door slams heavily as I jerk my head back up. The one-handed man and the woman are no longer there.

"They're gone," Darith confirms. "Put those on now," he reemphasizes to our newly captured guard, motioning at the layered clothing piled next to her.

She narrows her brown eyes, grits her teeth, and spits in his face.

Extracting the dagger from my hair, I shoot her a heartless stare.

She somehow takes my unspoken threat more seriously. Dressed within a minute's time, the woman is shoved into the lead by Darith, and then we're off.

The woman's short hair is soaked. She doesn't stand quite as tall as me and is all muscle. She moves reluctantly at first down the passageway, trying to stall for time until my dagger nicks her shoulder, causing her to wince. She hastens her pace, leading us quietly through the halls.

Passing mostly bedrooms and the occasional closed door, I'm very dismayed to see the giant fluffy beds and satin pillows. Temptation begs me to go lie on one, just to experience the contrast from sleeping on solid ground.

"How'd you two get in here anyway? Didn't come through the front door I assume," our guide remarks.

"Doesn't matter how," Darith replies.

"A window?" She searches our expressions. "The field," she tries again. Her eyes meet mine. "It was the field." She smirks.

Darith scoffs at me.

"I didn't say anything," I defend.

"Not with your mouth. Just keep movin', lady," he tells the guard.

Scrats, she's clever; reading me like that. Wait, did I just see Blue? Squinting out into an open courtyard, for a moment, I think I spot Blue. But there are two, no three more of her. It's not her at all. This must be where she came from. Eleven other birds looking almost identical to her meander peacefully through the indoor pool and garden. They have the same tall skinny legs and blue bodies, but they don't have the same three random long dark green tail feathers as her. They wander tranquilly through the water within a confined small pool, looking almost like prisoners.

Darith smacks my arm, jolting me back to reality. "Come on."

We continue for what must be about fifteen minutes when finally the guard stops. She lets her eyes settle on a dark wooden door. "Here," the small framed, muscular woman motions, "this will take you downstairs."

My nerves suggest there's a trap behind the door. Darith also seems unsure. "Ya know, don't forget what I told ya back in the baths. Ya know what happens if ya try to pull somethin' funny, right?"

She shakes her head, taking in a deep breath. "Look, I'm not against you. I'm happy to help." She opens the door with a smile on her face.

I'm confused by her fake happiness to assist. That behavior makes me certain she's tricking us. The door swings open and she enters, motioning us to follow her. My fingers tap on my hip. As I glance at Darith, a puzzled look crosses my face. "Happy to help?"

He raises his already slightly higher eyebrow. Grinning without a care, he then follows her down the stairs. Another minute or so passes as I debate what her words meant before I then trail behind them.

We travel down the shadowy stair case until we reach another hallway. The surroundings are more familiar now, the same dark rough rock walls from the day I was created. Waking up in darkness among a crowd of people, they were one of my first sights.

There were Mahk of many ages all huddled together in a bunch. I still don't understand why they create us so uniquely, just to send us on our way into the dark labyrinth.

Even the musky air brings back my first memories of lingering moisture created by the collection of bodies in the room where I took my first breath. We were corralled into a line, then one by one taken through the door leading out of the space. Upon exiting the door, we discovered a stone table to our left lined with clothing. We were told to grab undergarments, a shirt, pants, shoes and to head to the next station. There we were given one canister of water as well as two loaves of bread. That bread will never escape my memory, because I have never had any since. Our last stop before being released into the world was the weapons table. The Creators allowed us to pick one weapon for self defense in the wild. That's when I obtained my handy little dagger. It has become like a physical extension of me; always either in my hair or my hand.

Preparing to make our exit, they gave us each a number. That was the one piece of helpful instruction given at the time of our creation. One guard lined us up in an obviously intentional order before announcing that when we communicate with the Creators in the future, we would need to tell them our number. "You must always give us your number to collect," the guard said. At the time, it wasn't clear what she meant by collect, but I was sure to remember my number when it was given to me: "P329111."

That was my first encounter with Simul. We didn't speak, but it was the first time my eyes absorbed his leathery face. He watched as we were shoved through the castle doors with our few belongings. "Live long and serve well," he would occasionally spout at us as we were released.

The Creators' statements that they care for us meant something then, before reality set in. When Simul would give his speeches of encouragement that we have done pleasingly on our obsidian offerings so we should expect to be greatly rewarded, I thought we would be. It seemed logical the Creators took pride in their creations, or at least desired us to find some joy in our lives. But there was no joy, only obsidian taxes and meager food and water enough to keep me searching for more obsidian.

The guard pauses and motions her head to the right. "That way."

"Ya sure that's where the man would be?" Darith asks with force in his voice.

"He'll be down this hall, I assure you."

"Ladies first." Darith motions for her to continue in the lead.

Moaning and occasional sobs leak from the walls as we work our way through the corridor. Curiosity overcomes me so I peek through the small barred windows of the doors. Men and women are in each cell, dressed similar to the man in white. They cling to the sides of their confinements in fear. All of them appear skinny and malnourished. The entire place stinks of human excrement. The disgusting waste piles in the corners suggest they're never brought out of the cells.

I raise my shirt up over my nose to help mask the stink and Darith does the same.

"Who are these people?" I ask our guide.

"They're Mahk criminals."

"Oh really?" Darith chimes in. "And what exactly earns one the title of a Mahk criminal?"

She pauses, as if carefully assessing the best response. "Anyone who refuses to pay their obsidian. This is what happens when you don't pay your obsidian."

"I thought you starve to death if you don't pay taxes!" I retort.

She's lying through her teeth. Still, I'm not really sure how to coax the truth out of her. It doesn't matter much anyway. We should find the mystery man soon. He'll likely be happy to answer our questions.

Trailing behind the two of them, I notice Darith has picked up an extra weapon or two in the baths. He now carries an additional axe along with a bow. That bow could come in handy.

The woman finally halts at a door. "This is where the prisoners are usually sent first."

"Get him out of there," Darith demands.

She scoffs. "You said take you to him, not get him out. I don't have a key!"

"Ya aren't really a bright one, eh?" he snorts. He shoves us both aside then forcefully kicks the door. It doesn't budge.

Commotion from down the hall draws my attention. "Someone's coming," I whisper under my breath.

The woman opens her mouth, but Darith knocks her out before she makes a peep. My arms swoop to catch her so she doesn't loudly crash to the floor. The wall and I keep her propped up.

"What now?" I ask anxiously.

"Follow me." He drags the woman with us two doors down and pushes it open. He must be extremely observant to have noticed a barely cracked door on our way through the halls. The cell serves as a perfect cover. We wait a moment until the guards pass.

Next we hear a door open down the hall, followed by some voices, then a struggle. Darith leans cautiously through the doorframe to inspect. He flies out into the hall before I'm through assessing the vexatious sounds. I timidly follow him. The guards have entered the mystery man's cell and one has him strapped to a stone table while another is forcibly pouring something into his mouth. One guard speaks to the other. Only a couple words are audible from my distance. They say something about the wall and Kathar. I've never heard that word before so it piques my interest. The other guard nods, but his response is interrupted by Darith.

Again, I've hardly taken in the scene; meanwhile, Darith is already in action. His towering body swoops across the room in an instant, attacking the guard who poured liquid into the prisoner's mouth. Darith's opponent is a fairly plump man that isn't particularly tall.

I'm close behind, kicking at the other guard, who stands barely above my height.

Knowing the muscles in my arms are pathetic, I rely on my lower body strength. Two good kicks at his chest followed by one to his groin send him to his knees. My dagger is out now, but I can't bring myself to stab him. Darith's already finished with his guard and he's freed the man in white from his restraints. The man in white massages his wrists where the prickly rope had been. I stash the rope in my bag; it's a potential tool I'd be foolish to leave behind.

"Quit wastin' time, will ya, Araina?" he lectures as he bops the guard on his shaved head with his fist, rendering him unconscious. Darith takes down anything in his path like they're little dandelions. Coordination combined with lack of fear clearly gives him an advantage in combat.

I huff at him a couple times, unable to invent a clever response.

The man in white is okay, but his system is full of whatever they were forcing on him. Two more bottles of liquid remain on the copper tray, so I assume they didn't finish their treatment. They might be useful in the future. I throw them into my tote. Hopefully they don't spill.

There's no time for more observations. Thunderous bells ring out around the castle. I take a deep breath. "I guess they figured out we're here."

My hand motions for the man in white to follow as we head back into the dark hall. Darith glances both ways and he propels back down the direction we came in. He launches a door open then disappears into a cell.

"Darith," I whisper. "What are you doing, come on!" I pause at the doorway to the cell and find him shaking the woman who led us here.

She opens her eyes, staring blankly in a daze before jumping up with surprise. Sharply tightened lips wordlessly convey her attitude as she remembers. Her eyes roll as Darith smugly says, "Okay, lady, I'm gonna make a sweet deal with ya. Get us out of this place and I'll let ya live. I'll even give ya back the bag I stole from ya."

"You're so kind," she replies with agitation.

When we head into the hall, she starts back the way we came.

"Think again. The guards will be looking for us that way. I bet you know a safer way out, right?" My dagger grazes her stomach.

She flinches as it almost pierces through her shirt to her tan skin.

"Fine." She takes off in the opposite direction.

The four of us swiftly glide through the halls until we come to a dead end. Despair burns in my stomach, my throat, and my lungs.

That's it, then. She cared more about our capture than saving her own life. Or never knew a good escape route in the first place. My shoulders jolt in response to the sound of Darith's fist pounding into the wall that denies our escape.

Chapter 5
Trapped

Sweat collects on my palms. My eyes shut for a moment, trying to picture Blue. Remembering our peaceful naps and her pretty big eyes, I escape for one second from the chaos I've gotten myself into. Accompanied by a deep breath, I open my eyes again.

Little balls of sweat accumulate above Darith's eyebrows as he shakes the guard violently. Knowing him, he could kill her at any moment.

The sound of running fills the halls. The guards will be here soon.

"Damn it, lady, I told ya what we'd do if ya decided to pull any tricks on us." Darith shakes her forcefully in frustration. He extracts a spear from the holder on his back.

"Wait," she insists.

Her hands flutter quickly to grab the torch on the wall. Standing on her tip toes, she pulls a metallic chain, one of several hanging from the ceiling. Gold, gray, copper, and maroon colors reflect across the space. They clang quietly as she pulls. Until she yanked at one, I assumed they were only decorative. The rest of them may not even have a use, but it would certainly be interesting to discover if they do. Each link in them is thick and formed into a unique shape: some circular, many triangular, and some rectangles.

Grating of stone rumbles as the wall to our left opens. It's barely cracked. The woman is already sliding through. We follow hastily. Light exudes from the torch revealing a skinny underground tunnel. Exposed roots protrude from the dirt walls.

She pulls another chain from within the dim passageway, causing the door to shut behind us. "That should buy you some time," she encourages.

Again, I'm unsure of her words. At times, she acts almost pleased to help us, but I don't know why. It's possible she wants to win our trust so she can deceive us. Hopefully she can get us out of here quickly so we can ditch her. Being a Creator automatically makes her unlikeable, but I'm rapidly approaching hating her. I'd actually trust her more if she admitted her disdain for us instead of pretending she's happy to help.

We stumble as quickly as we can on the uneven ground, making our way through the cramped space. Leg muscles tightened and throbbing, breathing staggered, my body is wearing down. We must've been in the castle a long time.

"Where is this gonna take us?" Darith inquires.

"Back to the field you came from," she answers quietly.

Eyes shifted to the ground and wavering in her voice convey her dishonesty. Still, I let every step carry me farther down the path. We can't very well turn back now. We follow her quietly through mostly straight passageways. Occasionally there's a turn in our path, but not often.

I utilize the travel time to talk with the man in white. He's been oddly quiet. The two of us bring up the rear behind Darith and the guard.

"I never got to introduce myself earlier today." I glance back at him.

A vacant expression occupies his face. The man's light brown eyes still haven't made contact with mine. He seems unsure of what I'm talking about. "Have we met before?" he asks.

"You remember? You came through the labyrinth wall. Then you healed me." I point at my leg, but the Creator guard pants I now wear conceal the undamaged skin. "It was amazing. I'd never seen anything like that before."

His eyes blink a couple times in such a way I can tell he's trying to figure something out. "Are you sure that was me? I don't remember. I don't really remember anything at all."

Darith and I shoot each other glances.

"Do you remember me?" Darith taps his black sword. "She and I were fighting when you found us."

"I'm telling you, I don't remember anything. I'm sorry, you must have the wrong guy," he insists with a tone of sincerity, as if he wishes he could tell us better news.

I replay the scene in my head and feel certain it was him. The dimple on his chin is hard to forget. The face of the man with the healing hands doesn't fade from memory easily. I recall a name the guards yelled out as they followed him through the field: "Korun."

"Korun, that's what the guards called you," I tell him.

He shakes his head as if the name is familiar to him, but he doesn't seem ready to own it.

I drop back behind him to join Darith. "That treatment they filled him with really screwed him up."

"Great. He won't be able to answer a single question." Darith sweeps deep brown hair from his eyes.

It's been hours and our bodies are beginning to tire. There's absolutely no way the woman is actually taking us to the field, it would have been a much quicker journey. Despite that obvious fact, we know what waits for us if we turn back, so we keep moving forward.

The tunnel comes to an end where we find an old ladder. The ladder extends so far above us I can't even guess how high it goes.

"That's it," I declare. Everyone looks at me. "I'm too tired. There's no way I can climb that right now."

Darith's in no shape to argue, leaning breathless against a rock wall. "Okay, let's take a break. I'll keep watch so the three of ya can try to get some sleep." He catches the woman's arm as she begins to sit. "And don't get any bright ideas. I've got my eye on ya."

Her expression is rebellious, but she nods with understanding.

"You better tie her arms for added security." I offer the thick rope from Korun's cell. Darith ties it around her wrists before attaching it to his own wrist. For added measure, he keeps a tight hold on it.

There's nothing comfortable about the rocky floor, but my back is accustomed to the discomfort. Our guide turns constantly in an effort to establish a pleasant position. Evidently, she has no success. Her obnoxious squirming sounds keep me up only a few minutes before my tired mind and body take over. Soon I am in my dream world.

Strange sights occupy my dreams: fresh water cascading down from one rock pool to the next and cozy homes built into giant skinny minaret rocks. Voices speak to me, maybe those who have gone hungry after not paying their obsidian taxes. Blue makes an appearance like always, but this time she's among her kind in the castle and she doesn't know me at all. After that, the man in white falls from the labyrinth wall again. This time he's confident, aware of himself, as he crosses the field toward me. For some unexplainable reason, I'm scared. It seems right to run, but my body remains frozen. His hand extends to land on my heart. Then I feel something so strong, so frightening within me, that I think I might die.

I jolt awake, drenched in perspiration. My fast-paced breathing and the heavy pounding of my heart make my head hurt. Everyone else is still asleep, except Darith, who stares at me with a smile on his face. "Bad dreams, little Araina?"

His tone is condescending as always. My lips purse tightly. Sluggishly, I lie back down. Everything goes blank this time as I make a conscious effort to fight away the dreams and nightmares.

Pounding footsteps wake me. My eyes jerk open to find Darith has drifted to sleep. Heavy eyelids and tight muscles tell me I've been asleep for a while. My mind takes a moment to verify the sound echoing down the hall before I'm on my feet, waking my companions. "Wake up. Hurry!"

Darith jumps with alarm. I shake the man in white. Korun wakes peacefully despite the chaos.

"Ladies first." Darith nudges our guide toward the ladder. She hesitates, so he pushes her. Forcing her up, Darith follows close behind. The guards are drawing near. As I make my way through the dark shaft, practically devoid of light, the thought of our capture becomes comical. It's not as if they could really do anything worse to us than the lives they force on us in the labyrinth.

The torch is withering and slowing down my escape. The others are now far ahead of me. Trying to hold the thing in one hand as I steady myself with the other isn't very practical. A jerk travels through the ladder from down below, almost causing me to lose my grip completely. Evidently they've reached its base. The guards are yelling obscenities, claiming I'll be dead in a minute.

I'm not a huge fan of the dark, but I'm running out of options. "Hope you three can feel your way up. The light is about to go out."

The object releases from my hand and dancing flames travel past my legs as it descends. Reflective orange light forms a ring outline of the tunnel. It soars down and then disappears.

Men scream in pain. Evidently, the guards received my gift. I'm moving much faster now, though I haven't quite caught up to the group. It's so strange to be traveling with a group at all. In fact, it's not just strange, it's uncomfortable. Mahk don't have friends. We don't rely on anyone but ourselves. Once they get me to the other side of the wall Korun came through, I'm headed my own way. For all I know, they can't be trusted to let me live.

Unfortunately, we exit the tunnel into yet another dark strange place. There must be some light, but its source isn't identifiable. The place is dank, drenched in the smell of rotting flesh. My boots make squishing sounds against whatever coats the ground.

"This is some lovely field ya brought us to." Darith still has a grip on our guide's arm.

"Sh," I insist. The room is quiet, almost silent, but some faint sound is repeating around us. At first I can't make it out.

Raspy breathing. There's someone in the room with us.

Korun seems to have heard it as well. "Is there someone there? Hello?"

Our guard's voice rings out, echoing in the space as she speaks, "If you take them and let me go, we'll deliver a group of additional Mahk to you in the morning."

Our company has formed a circle. Our weapons are in hand. Breathing quietly, I strive to discern what's moving all around us. Whatever is in here has us surrounded. This can't be good.

About ten Nabal emerge from the shadows into view. She has brought us into the Blood Caves.

As much day-to-day killing that goes on in the labyrinth, the Blood Caves still make me sickest. The Nabal inhabit the Blood Caves, murdering any Mahk who wander to the caverns and eating them. As if the average Mahk hadn't already caused me to hate my own kind enough, the cannibalistic Nabal only fan the flames.

"We don't make bargains with anyone, especially not a Creator," a raspy voice sprays his hateful words at our guide.

That serves her right. Being eaten to death will come as less of a trial if I get to watch a Creator die with me.

Barely visible in the dim light, the Nabals' motions are jerky and robotic. They wear dirty patchwork robes made from Mahk garb. The Nabal that spoke leads the attack. Like angry bulls, all of them charge toward us, clubs and maces in hand.

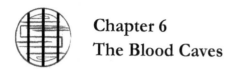

Chapter 6
The Blood Caves

We're fighting them off the best we can. They assail us wildly, using not only their weapons but biting with hungry mouths.

The leading Nabal's teeth latch onto Korun's wrist, causing him to let out a low shriek. He looks angry now. In retaliation, Korun quickly wrestles the cannibal to the ground. He snaps his neck.

It doesn't feel like it's been even five minutes since we exited the tunnel, but the guards are beginning to emerge at our backs. At the same time, more Nabal are joining the fight from other caves. There must be at least twenty Nabal and possibly even more guards.

The Nabal are ruthless with their attack. Launching at me with his club, one bashes at my arm. He punches twice before his frighteningly long, rigid fingernails drill into me. A swift kick to his knee tips his balance, allowing time for my dagger to make an appearance. I could slit his throat in a second, but I hesitate as he turns to face Korun, who throws a rock at him. I knock him unconscious from behind with the butt of my dagger.

Mercilessly, weapons submerge into opponents as the altercation rages on.

So many bodies fill the dark cave. It's nearly impossible to make out Darith or Korun among them all. Finally, I spot them. Slouched to the ground, I hope to be overlooked as I back toward them.

Korun must have found an axe. He handles himself fairly sufficiently with the deadly weapon. He doesn't appear to be a trained expert by any means, but he's still alive.

As the guards continue to flood the cave, I'm trying to determine how we can possibly survive this massacre. Even if all the Nabal kill the guards or vice versa, we still wouldn't be able to fight our way out of here.

Warm liquid flies across my face. I reach up to wipe it off my cheek, only to discover it's blood. A potential escape is about as likely as finding a blooming flower in these caves, but the blood triggers an idea.

Darith is still connected by a rope to the guard who led us here. Fighting my way into whispering range, I tell him the plan. Then I inform Korun. Korun's sweaty and blood-stained hand grabs my wrist briefly, a look of contest in his eyes. I shrug violently as my head gestures around at our situation, conveying our lack of alternatives. We don't have many options if we want to live. He doesn't seem very pleased, but he concedes.

Both of them continue warding off attacks. They keep an eye on my back. Attempting to be discrete, I steal three robes from the dead Nabal. Only a minute passes before I'm wearing my long dark patchwork robe. Darith and Korun swiftly wrap the bloodied robes I've provided around their bodies. Now we look like the enemy.

Nabal continue to fight the guards and die. New Nabal infiltrate the cave. It isn't long before we join in their fight, pretending to be part of their people. Despite lacking a weapon, our guide fares adequately between Darith's protection and her agility. Bashing savagely, we claw at the guards, hiding our weapons beneath our robes. Adrenaline overcomes me and in my fight for survival, madness takes me over. Wildly and without restraint, I'm tearing at the bodies around me. We have successfully executed the first part of the plan, but we aren't safe yet.

Darith's next action is the indication to move forward with our escape. He violently smacks the back of our guide's head, causing her to pass out in his arms. Korun and I push toward him, pretending to fight for her. Meanwhile we begin to gravitate toward an entrance to the cave. For a brief second, it looks like a Nabal will give away our cover as he stares at us, unconvinced. He needs confirmation. My teeth hastily sink into the guard's skin, ripping a small chunk from her arm. Wretched sour taste coats my tongue. My actions haven't swayed the Nabal, but my distraction has given a guard the chance to attack him.

The rest of our escape proves to be very simple. Darith carries the female guard as if she weighs nothing. Other Nabal don't question our authenticity when they see the blood and partial bit of flesh hanging from my mouth. The few that try to challenge us for the "meal" we're hauling are easily fought off between Korun and me. Bile chokes my throat before her skin is spit from my mouth.

The crunching of bones beneath our feet as well as screams and clashes of metal fill our ears. We flee, trying to find our way out of the giant interconnected caves. *Who knows how many dead Mahk have accumulated in this place through the years?* Jolting nausea resonates in my stomach when my mind processes not only the disgusting caves, but the bite out of the guard. It's fortunate I've never killed someone to survive because biting a person's arm alone makes me feel terrible. How the Nabal can stand to live off other human meat astounds me.

As we press forward, it's as if we'll never find our way. One dank and moist room after the next, we navigate in the dark. It can't be long before the Nabal will discover our charade.

Light shines ahead, luring us from the accursed home of the cannibals. My nose catches flurries of fresh air once we approach the exit out of the caves. The beating of my heart is still abnormally fast as we leave the abhorrent place behind. Even though I knew of the Blood Caves, I never truly understood the extreme grotesque nature of the Nabal. There is a loss of humanity in their wild eyes. Like rabid beasts, they live only to fill their own needs, no matter the expense.

As we slip away from the wretched place, I catch one last glimpse. We have to hurry, but my companions pause, observing miles of labyrinth entry points at the base of the incline. It is a sight to see, but we have no time.

"Hurry," I disrupt their observations.

We work our way down the jagged mountain rocks. Our approach to the dark labyrinth passageways abates the fear. I lead our small group to the closest corridor.

Nearing our entry, we spot a couple different Mahk battling over scraps of food. One man bites hastily into a juicy fish. His meal reminds me of my own hunger. He's oblivious to the uncomfortable black rocks he perches on or the gray smoke that chokes the air around him. Korun surely senses my initial instinct when he catches me eyeing the man—the instinct to steal anything he's got.

A spear buzzes through the air before striking and piercing both his unsuspecting hand and the fish in it. A Mahk drops down from a low branch in a tall black tree and wastes no time dislodging his winnings from the victim's hand. He consumes the fish.

The other man sobs in pain. Brutally injured, the victim holds what's left of his bloody hand as he rocks himself back and forth.

"That's what happens when you flaunt a meal," the man spouts. He licks the slimy fish residue mixed with human blood from his fingers.

We have managed to go unseen so far. I'm planning to reach the wall before he notices our presence. Despite the horror of the interaction, it's less disturbing having encountered the Nabal.

Korun's mouth hangs open, eyes narrow in response to the interaction. An ounce of gratification sweeps through me. He has witnessed firsthand the nature of my world. I've sensed he may consider me cold or callous. I can't blame him since I bit flesh from the guard's arm. But compared to the Mahk standard, I could be called a gentle butterfly.

The familiar rough-textured walls actually make me feel safe after the near-death experience in the Blood Caves. Was all this even worth the distress? It would be easy to slip away while Darith and Korun are so worn from the battle. I could abandon this strange group I've assembled. It would be so easy to go back to my daily activities in the labyrinth. My life hasn't been the simplest, but at least it's been consistent. In my determination to meet the man in white, to get answers, I haven't even considered what might happen to Blue if I don't make it back to her.

Despite the brief stillness and normalcy within the labyrinth, a longing to know where Korun comes from tugs at me. *Could there be something or someplace better on the other side of that rippling wall?* For a moment, my fingers dance across the portion of my leg which Korun healed. It's possible everyone where Korun comes from has the power to heal.

Too many questions and possibilities linger in my mind. I could live out my lonely life here in this labyrinth. An ounce of safety could be my haven in a brutal place I've learned to survive. Every day would be the same as the last two years: fingers burned by acid in the search for obsidian, hunger, fighting, and taking care of Blue.

Then again, have I really learned to survive? Plenty of Mahk have starved in this place. I've only managed to delay my fate. Abandoning this whole adventure isn't really an option. *How long can I survive at the Creator's hands? What about Blue?*

It's vital to learn answers to these questions. I need to know what and who is on the other side of the wall. Hope whispers in my soul that there must be something better, somewhere better.

After a couple turns and about an hour of walking, we reach a safe nook for a short break. Multiple exit points from this particular location make this stopping place ideal. Options are preferable in the event something or someone does attack.

My back slowly lies against a boulder near an exit as Darith hovers near a twisted tall tree. Dry bark is peeled in places and a long hole on its side reveals its interior.

"She needs a bandage on her arm." Korun points at the guard.

Darith shoots him a quizzical glance. "She's not gonna bleed to death. It's not like a lion bit her. You're new around here but I can tell ya: fend for yourself and don't worry about people like her."

Korun shrugs with disdain as he tears a strip of white cloth from his sleeve. He approaches the unconscious woman and wraps a bandage around her arm.

Darith shakes his head. "So, remember anythin', Korun? Anything comin' back to ya about who ya are? Where ya come from?"

"I still don't remember a thing."

Darith lunges at Korun, forcing him into a headlock. "I can help jog your memory," Darith threatens as he squeezes his arm tighter around Korun's neck.

"Darith, are you mad?" I exclaim.

"I'm not mad. In fact, I'm thinkin' clearly. What if he's lyin' to us?"

My dagger pulled from my red hair, I spring toward Darith. "Tone down your hissy fit and back off!" I demand. "I don't think he's lying, but he will if you treat him like that."

Darith spins Korun out of his arms, drops to a crouch, and points his sword at my rib cage.

"Really?" I back away as the beating of my heart thunders in my ears.

He doesn't follow, but his green eyes fix on mine. Now standing to his full height, his brows furrow, and his expression becomes stern. Even Creators would probably be scared by whatever madness is going through his mind.

Rushing air clashes against me as Korun comes to my side, axe in hand. He's also got a knife in the other hand, which he must've found in the caves.

"Damn it!" Darith shouts, pushing sweaty chestnut brown hair out of his face. "I should've left the girl, taken that bird for a meal, and forgotten all about that wall." He makes his way over to the twisted tree, slides down beside it, then closes his eyes.

Heat crawls through my cheeks. "We made it. We're alive, Darith!"

"Barely," he emphasizes, "made it." His head turns away, eyes still closed.

Moments of silence pass. My muscles are tense from the altercation. I briefly question how I got myself into this mess with that fool.

"Think he'll sleep it off?" Korun questions.

"I don't know, Korun. One of us needs to keep an eye on him. That's all I know."

"Do you have any water?" Korun questions as my green eyes dart back toward him and the guard.

"Just a little."

"I think she's going to need it." Sweat pours down his pitiable face. He must be miserable, knowing that a few hours ago, memories were stored in his head and the Creators took them all away from him.

"Why do you care so much? That woman helped take away your memories. She helped hold you captive and tried to get us killed in the Blood Caves."

"It doesn't seem right not to help her. At least she helped get us out of that place, even if it wasn't voluntary assistance," he finishes.

"Sure, helped serve us up to a bunch of cannibals."

Unconscious suits her well. Her face is calm, her muscles relaxed, and her short taupe hair loosely hangs into her eyes. To someone who doesn't know better, she might even look gentle. Thinking about her clever remarks and the Blood caves, I despise her. Still, we need her to get us through the wall.

"I don't have much water. You can give her one little swig when she wakes."

Korun pulls her toward a small twisted tree before propping her against it. He ties her rope to the trunk securely. His behavior is unusual, even uncomfortable. Like Darith, a small part of me does wonder why he helps the Creator guard. He seems to genuinely care.

What if he does remember something? No explanation would justify his pity on her. She's vile. Unlike me, he probably doesn't realize we need her alive to help get us through the wall. Then I think about Blue and her unconditional gentle and loving nature. Korun could be like Blue. My mind laughs that possibility away.

"You know, if you really want to help her, you could try to heal her," I suggest.

He looks at me questioningly. Then his stomach growls. An awkward minute passes. It's a struggle not to let a smile cross my face.

"Heal her?" he questions.

"Yes, like you healed my leg yesterday," I encourage. "Even though you don't remember, maybe if you just try…"

"I don't know how. How'd I do it before?"

"You grabbed my leg gently and within a few minutes, my cut healed. Try it." I want to know if he can still do it. Curiosity in me begs to see the process again. It is possible that wherever he comes from there's a science behind his ability. Then again, his powers might be beyond explanation. I'm not new to unexplainable phenomenon in the labyrinth, but his ability is particularly incredible.

He removes her tattered maroon jacket to get a better look at the bleeding flesh. The guard's eyes softly begin to blink open as she wakes. He reaches his hazel hands out timidly to set them on her arm.

At first, she flinches with fear, but then she appears to know what he's up to as he places his hands on her wound.

"I'm sure you must have a name?" he pries, making an effort to keep the patient calm.

"My name is Rase," she responds coldly. Despite her harsh tone, I sense a spark of gratefulness in her expression as her brown eyes watch him.

Korun focuses intently. For a moment, the tan skin at the edges of the bite on her arm starts regenerating. The process stops. Another minute goes by and nothing happens. Korun shrugs and gives the guard a small drink of water. The woman remains silent, looking away from the wound with a wince.

"That's a start," I offer.

His mysterious eyes trace every line on his palms, like he hopes they'll tell him the secret to his power. He doesn't say anything. The emotions on his face are difficult to read.

It's been a long day, so I let the others take watch and settle down to rest.

Pounding guard footsteps fill my ears as I run for my life in my dreams. Then I'm back in the castle trying to rescue the man in white, Korun. Next come memories of all the intricate details on the beautiful palace walls. My fingers trace the elaborate blue lines in circles along the smooth marble. Finally, I'm back to where I started: in my safe place with Blue. She's nestled beside me as I'm drawing on the walls in our secret place. I'm creating all kinds of landscapes. Strange things I've seen in previous dreams creep out of my mind through the rock in my hand as I apply lines on the rough texture. Everything is almost right with the world, but even in my secret place there isn't true safety.

"Araina, that's your name right? Araina, wake up."

My eyes blur as they blink open to see Korun.

He shakes my shoulder softly. "Araina, Darith is gone."

Chapter 7
A Predictable Departure

I jolt awake at the mention of Darith. "What? Where is he?"

"I don't know. He slipped away as I was tending the guard. Now I can't find him."

There's the guard, tied up like I would expect, and Korun stands beside me, but Darith is missing. Rolling my eyes before the escape of an unwelcomed yawn, I stand to my feet. "Scrats! Should have suspected. While you were tending the guard? Were you that oblivious?"

Of course Darith decided the "team expedition" wasn't his style. I, myself, had considered abandoning the group and staying put in the labyrinth. Keeping a closer watch on him should have been a priority. He hasn't earned my trust.

"I can't figure that man out," I declare "We're probably better off without him anyway." Then it occurs to me, the last thing he mentioned was Blue. She could keep him full for three weeks, or even a month.

The guard is awake but silent. My green eyes dart back to Korun. We don't have any time to waste. It's too dangerous to risk Darith going after her. She's my only friend in the world.

My breathing is heavy as the thoughts race through my head. Every minute I spend thinking of solutions, rather than taking action, might cost Blue her life.

"We have to get moving, now," I blurt out.

My two companions stare at me blankly.

"I think Darith is going after someone I care about."

"The bird?" Korun gleans.

"Yes. I have to go after him. I have to go now so I can save her. You heard what he said before he left. I hope you're well rested, because it's time to go."

The guard glances up at Korun. She must be desperately searching for an answer to her freedom.

Korun reaches down to unbind our prisoner's restraints, only to receive a kick to his leg. She struggles to dart away from him, but I catch her quickly.

"It's too bad we have to keep you safe" I mutter.

Korun's grabbing his sore leg as he eyes me inquisitively.

"We need her to get you back to your home on the other side of the wall."

He stares at me. "You want to help me find my home? Think that's even possible?"

"Of course, Korun, that's what all this is about. Why'd you think I went trumping into the Creator's castle?" This is a record selfish moment, telling him I'm trying to help him get home. Regardless of my true motives, pretending to help him will achieve the same results. "I don't have time to talk Korun. Let's get moving."

Korun nods.

Time seems to fly now that Blue's life is hanging in the mix. Everything is still. Ebony twisted trees and large boulders keep us company. Occasionally our path crosses with a Mahk statue. Cold and lifeless, they forever reside in the shadows. Even the Darktouch flowers are less active than usual. Despite the repetitive scenery boring my eyes, my brain feels overactive. Even though we ran for a good twenty minutes, my feet don't fail me. Long stretches of barren passages mirror the unending dread rising inside me. Darith can't possibly have mastered the labyrinth as thoroughly as I have, but there's still a possibility he could get to Blue first. He might have a sizable head start. My only hope is to have courage and move swiftly.

Generally, it takes about three days to get to Blue from where I left Korun. If I only sleep one of those nights, it should shorten the time it takes to reach her.

We pace ourselves, walking through certain areas, avoiding pocket eruptions. Having seen so many others blown to bits, I keep my distance from the red dirt that indicates an explosive area.

"Watch out for those red dirt patches" I warn Korun. "The rock wall fumes should be avoided as well. For that matter, it's better if you just follow my lead in general."

The heat is starting to weaken me. Using my dagger, I pin my red hair back up in a side knot. Korun healing my leg and beginning to heal the guard's arm replays in my head. I've never seen anything like it. My mind isn't wrapped around the rippling wall he magically fell through. *Magically.* I shake my head. There must be rational explanations on the other side of the wall.

Though his entry through the wall and his healing abilities are astounding, unexplainable things aren't completely foreign in the labyrinth. The Darktouch flowers twirl through my mind. They move like they're alive. They grow from the walls as if from soil. Their tiny size enables their stealth. Coming in contact with one is lethal. Most things in the world are explainable, but Darktouch flowers elude me.

Fortunately, the first time I saw one, someone else ventured up to it first. She was a Mahk probably aged to about twenty, at that time only a few years older than me. The woman pranced right up to the thing, her expression glowing with amazement to find something so lovely in our dark world. Her eyes took in its dark purple center, adoring its pale gradient dancing petals. I was as transfixed as she by the liveliness of the flower. She reached out to touch the twirling floret. The ashen-tipped petals wrapped around her finger. She began screaming as her finger then her hand turned to stone. Within a couple minutes, she was transformed into a stiff statue.

My mind envisions her tearful face, sending shivers through me. Like so many other Mahk deaths, I desperately wish I could erase the memory from my thoughts.

Abruptly, a piercing sound fills the air. Our hands swarm to cover our ears and muffle it. Paralyzed and dizzy, I drop to the ground fearfully. The ringing is coming from the direction of the castle. The sound diminishes as quickly as it came.

The ground shakes, causing the walls to seem as if they waver. Grinding and hissing noises unexplainably overcome the labyrinth. I shrink cowardly to the wall, bracing myself defensively against it for support.

As I turn to check on Korun and Rase who were a few feet behind me, the sounds subside. Before my eyes settle on them, sudden pain engulfs me. Horrible anguish consumes me. It feels like a thousand swords submerge into my back and under my legs all at once. That's the last thing I remember or feel.

Chapter 8
Am I Still Alive?

A weightless sense of existence carries me. Time has no meaning and everything is dark. I can't feel my body, can't hear or see anything at all. Is this death?

"Araina? Stay with us," someone pleads.

The stabbing pain in my back and legs comes back. I want to scream, but I still can't see anything or move. I focus on trying to make sense of my body. I tell it to breathe.

"That's it!" the voice encourages. "Keep fighting."

Crippling pain is still shooting through me. I'm drenched in some kind of liquid. As I gasp for breath, my eyes pry themselves open. The slimy substance is my own blood.

My chest is tight and every breath is painful. The entire back side of my body feels like one giant open wound. For a moment, I wish I was dead. Despite my pain, I tell myself to keep breathing and not to worry about all the blood.

Korun is kneeling beside me. "Let's see, you're going to be okay," he assures. His hand moves down my back then across the underside of my legs. The pain is subsiding. Once again, I witness his remarkable gift. Unfortunately, his effort is draining his own strength rapidly. He continues helping me until he starts to turn pale. Everything still hurts, but not like it had before. My body is no longer on the brink of extinction, so I motion for him to take a rest. It would be ideal to thank him, but not even my mouth will move.

Long breaths draw air deep into my lungs. As I stare at him for a moment, warmth sweeps through me. Not only has he healed me, but now he has saved my life. My eyes trace the soft curves of his face and take in his dark features, but then they shut tight with shame. *He must have some selfish motive for what he does.* After allowing my body a few more moments of rest, aggravation fills me that I ever trusted Darith and that I venture to think Korun is any better than the rest of us.

You offer obsidian, you eat, you kill and you survive. It's time to quit hoping for a new reality.

"He should have let you die," a venomous female voice whispers. Rase is standing a few feet away, tied to a tall black tree.

"If he let the blades do their work on you, we would have been minus one more Mahk. You're all heartless and savage creatures." Her tone screams remorse for my survival.

I want to tell her how much I hate her and all the Creators. Her words are so ironic. The Creators make us the way we are. I'm still too weak to vocalize anything, but my eyes shoot daggers at her.

"Think you can breathe now?" Korun inquires as he adjusts himself against the wall near me.

Unable to verbally respond, I nod.

"You're really lucky to be alive. You were at the brink of death."

He's able to read the confusion in my eyes. I still don't even know what happened.

"When the piercing sound started, Rase charged toward the nearby boulders. Swords and blades sprang out of the ground and walls around us just as we climbed the rocks. I'm sorry you were injured so badly. Had I known what was happening" he eyes Rase accusatively, "I would have warned you to do the same as us." He softly touches my back. "You were pierced through the shoulder with a sword and several blades sliced into your back and legs. You lost a lot of blood."

"I still don't understand." The words barely fall from my dry mouth. "Where did it all...come from? How?"

Rase rolls her eyes as Korun shifts his gaze up to her. "You want to tell her what you told me?" he presses.

"Look, you aren't going to make it to the other side of that wall. It isn't going to be possible. Mahk don't belong on the other side. I promise, Simul isn't going to let it happen. He must be on to you. This labyrinth is rigged, Araina. The minute he decided you were a threat, he unleashed precautionary measures to kill you and all the Mahk. He doesn't need you." She pauses, as if carefully calculating her next words. "He can create more Mahk that comply with his wishes. This labyrinth has changed. Not one shred of hope is left that we're going to survive this place now. Good job."

Glancing around our surroundings, I become aware of the metallic and dangerous blade jungle. Everything does look different. The walls themselves may have even shifted.

An even sharper pain than that of my back and legs swells inside my chest. A small and manipulated puppet, I despise that my strings are in the Creators' hands again. I hate Simul so much. I want to scream at Rase, telling her I deserve to live, to be free. No evidence supports that argument though. I think of the Mahk killing each other. For a minute, I consider how different we are from Blue. Maybe the Creators treat us this way because we don't deserve better. What if they have shown pity by not outright killing us before? Every day they're probably trying to create something better than the time before, something better than themselves or us.

Something else she mentioned bothers me. Rase said that Mahk can't be on the other side of the wall. Then does that make Korun a Creator? Or is he something else from the other side of the wall? And does she mean I'll die if I make it there?

My breathing has hastened in my frustration which only causes my body more pain. It's important to slow down, to take deep breaths. I need food, water, and more rest. My body is so weak from all the fighting in the last couple days. Food and water, my eyes roll at the thought of them. Both are items essential for survival and the Creators would have kept providing for me, if it weren't for this venture. *Then again, is an existence of dependence and following demands really living?* Either way, now I'm a dead woman. Everything is falling apart.

Korun avoids eye contact. "Are you still going to help me get home?" he inquires.

"I'm more determined than ever." I shoot Rase a stare. It might be a long shot, but despite Rase's claims about the other side of the wall, she clearly can't be trusted. "We're going to get through that wall. We'll find answers. As badly as she wants to prevent us getting there, it's worth doing just to tick her off."

He smirks. My sense of humor isn't completely lost on him.

"Hey, focus on regaining your energy" he lectures.

I ignore him. "What other surprises can we expect, Rase? You knew about the blades, so if you cooperate and get us to the wall, then we'll let you live."

Her usual sarcastically helpful demeanor again overcomes our guide as she smiles at me. "Miss Araina, let me show you right to that wall through every obstacle." She squints at me "For Grol's sake! I don't know! I didn't know about the blades."

"Grol's sake?"

"Don't worry about it. I'm not explaining," she replies.

"Fine. And you supposedly didn't know anything about the blades?"

"I knew that sound most likely meant danger, given the disturbance you've caused. The boulders seemed like the safest place to be, but I had no idea what to expect and I still don't. As a standard guard, I'm not really privy to details. I just know this labyrinth is now one giant death trap. Every move could be our last."

"Well, thanks for being so helpful," I retort. "Could you both give me a minute?" I motion for Rase and Korun to close their eyes. For extra measure, I step behind a tree.

Withdrawing my Mahk clothes from my tote makes me surprisingly happy. My fingers peel the blood-drenched guard garb from my body. Being so low on supplies, it's clearly smart to reserve the water rather than cleaning up. At least my body is finally in my own Mahk clothing again. I never thought I was so attached to my outfit, but somehow it does offer me comfort. The guard clothing could be useful in the future, but unfortunately, they're far too tattered and bloody, so they get ditched.

"Let's keep moving forward. No reason to sit around here, waiting to die," I tell them.

As we walk, I'm certain Rase knows more about the labyrinth traps than she lets on. More importantly, she could tell me about the other side of that wall, if she wasn't so nasty. She could probably tell us who Korun is and she might even know something about his healing ability. At some point, drastic measures may be necessary to pry that information from her. For now, my goal is to get us all to Blue and that wall.

The completely lethal labyrinth ground around me is anything but comforting. How did they even pull this off? Such intricate defenses seem like the work of magic. Rase's comments about the power of the Creators hits me harder as I process what's around me. Her words play through my mind again, "He unleashed precautionary measures to kill you and all the Mahk." There haven't been any Mahk bodies yet, but we're also far off from the most populated area of the labyrinth.

Suddenly it occurs to me that almost everyone is likely dead because of me. Despite the lengths I've gone not to kill anyone, I managed to take out almost all of the Mahk as a result of my curiosity, my rebellion. I might not be particularly proud to be a Mahk, but I hadn't wished them all dead, at least not at my own hands.

Chapter 9
The Rotting Pass

Blue could even be dead by now. Sickness writhes in my core, like parasites eating away at my perseverance. My body moves through the maze of hazardous objects, but my spirit is trapped.

Rase struts beside me, knowing we won't hurt her. It's tempting to leave her strapped around a tree to die. She's so irritating, she and every other Creator.

Commotion sounds behind us in the distance. Korun seems to pick up on the noises as well. We both whirl around in sync to observe their origin.

Fifteen Creator guards are advancing on foot in our direction. By this time, they've seen us for certain.

"Let's see…" Korun looks at me inquisitively. "Now what?"

"Now we run!"

Korun takes Rase, his strength making it easier to force her along.

I bolt swiftly but find myself hanging back for Korun and Rase. She refuses to make this simple for us.

I'm problem solving intensely as the guards gain on us. They're probably a quarter of a mile away.

Korun finally catches up to me. "We aren't going…to make it," he says hoarsely, trying to catch his breath.

"No, I agree. We can't outrun them like this." My finger points a different direction from our initial route. "We need to head for the Rotting Pass!"

"Rotting Pass?" he repeats nervously. "Doesn't sound good."

"You're mad!" Rase's lip curls. "The Creators don't even venture there."

"Exactly," I respond, "it's our only chance to lose them. Come on." I motion again down the newly selected passageway.

The guards are drawing nearer. Their arrows speed through the air.

Grabbing Rase's other arm, I help Korun drag her as we run for our lives.

I've never actually gone through the pass before. Rase is right to be scared of the place. Still, we stand a better chance of survival there than in the hands of the Creators. Fortunately, we make a couple turns so the walls provide cover from the guards' deadly arrows.

"We're almost there," I tell Korun. The foggy path beneath towering canopy trees comes into view. "There!" I point.

He nods. He must have a million questions, but he refrains.

We converge with the dark overgrown valley of decay. "Stay behind me," I tell him. "There are things to look out for in this place. Be careful."

"That was my plan. Think you've got this figured out better than me."

We all take in the maze of giant tree roots along the ground entering the Rotting Pass. Attempting to maintain our speed, I navigate the roots smoothly, sometimes having to leap across them. Korun doesn't stray from the path my footprints create. Upon our entry, even Rase is cooperating. That's in her best interest. Now that we have dragged her into this death trap, she'll have to work with us to survive.

The guards have let up on the shooting now, probably due to the large trees protecting us from their view. They laugh as we work our way deeper in this place.

"We'll keep guard here, but they aren't going to make it out anyway."

"Can you believe how stupid the Mahk are?" another chimes in. "Intentionally running into the Rotting Pass. They'll never make it out."

They're all so smug and proud. *At least our impending deaths can be of entertainment to someone.*

"Looks like they're not coming in after us," I tell Korun and Rase. "For that matter, I think we're far enough they can't shoot at us."

"It does look that way," Korun agrees.

My root skipping comes to a stop as musty air settles on my skin. Despite the chilling atmosphere, the trees are breathtaking. They're far wider than others in the labyrinth and much taller. The branches tend to grow away from the parallel walls, forming a canopy roof over the pass. Black and silver moss hangs hauntingly still above us. The entire area is shaded, enabling it to be cooler than most of the labyrinth.

"Rotting Pass?" Korun interrupts my thoughts. "Why such a daunting name?"

"Because no one ever survives this place and we assume their corpses all rot in here," Rase answers bluntly.

"Thanks, Rase, for putting that so delicately," I respond sharply. "That *is* where the name comes from, but that doesn't mean we can't make it through. Other people might die in here, but they don't have a miracle worker with them." I bat my eyes cleverly and smile at him.

Despite the dismay in his slouched body language, a small grin cracks across his face.

"At least we have some idea what to look out for," I encourage him.

"And what's that?" he replies.

"Based on my previous observations from the edge of the pass, it's filled heavily with fumes. Those are common in the labyrinth. Not a problem. They're small steaming volcanoes attached to the walls. Small, as in tiny," I emphasize, "and easy to avoid. As long as we don't set one off, we'll be fine. There's one now." I point.

"What happens if we set one off?"

"It releases poisonous gas."

"The fumes aren't exactly comforting, but they can be avoided. That can't be all there is to this place," he pushes.

"There's more, be patient," I scold him "Some reports suggest the ground consumes people."

He doesn't look pleased as he warily eyes the terrain.

"That's not going to happen to us. Stay away from the softer looking patches of ground. Basically, near the trees is best."

"That doesn't sound too bad," he admits. "That all I need to know?"

"No," Rase jumps in. "She hasn't even told you the worst part. Go ahead, Araina." She nudges my arm.

"The saber tooth mutts are supposed to be a bit problematic," I confess. "I don't know much about them, or even if they really exist. Rumors say they devour anything that enters this place."

"You know any secrets to dealing with those?"

"Climb the trees?" I offer.

"I guess we'll deal with that if and when the time comes," Korun replies. "For now, let's try to get through here as quickly as we can manage."

I don't argue with that statement. This creepy place makes me shiver.

"Now that I know all about it, let me lead," Korun insists.

"I'm fine. I've dealt with the rock wall fumes for two years, so let me." I push past him and Rase.

We make our way, step by step, through the obnoxious tall roots on the ground. Staying near those makes the soft ground easy to sidestep. Unfortunately, the roots bring us in close proximity to the jagged labyrinth walls, but working around the fumes doesn't pose much of a problem either. We cover a decent amount of distance in about an hour, which increases my confidence we can make it to the other side if no other problems arise.

Every couple minutes, I glance behind me. Korun and Rase are making sound progress.

"I guess you over-estimated the pass," I tell Rase.

She rolls her eyes. "We're not through yet," she retorts.

I look over my shoulder preparing to spout a smart comeback, but my foot catches on a tall root. As I fall forward, my body threatens to sway toward the soft ground. In a panic, I dart back toward the wall, but my hand braces my fall only a couple feet from one of the miniature steam volcanoes.

Korun grabs my arm, yanking both me and Rase past the danger. Then we hear a loud pop. Gas starts spewing into the air.

We're running again, this time from the gas instead of the Creators.

"Cover your mouth!" Korun's muffled voice instructs.

I've already done that and so has Rase, but he didn't notice. Our shirts are pulled up over our noses, but I know that isn't going to do much good.

As we push forward, I'm getting dizzy.

"Don't stop!" Korun demands, but it's obvious he's being affected too. He's stumbling and his speech is slurred.

I'm fighting to keep my focus, despite the fumes. Things are getting hazy.

"Korun?" I call out when I lose sight of him in the mist.

I vaguely make out a response, but I'm not sure which direction it came from. The sound was so muffled, I'm not even positive it was Korun.

Growling rumbles around us and I'd guess it didn't come from the gas. I try desperately to keep my eyes peeled, but they sting. It's difficult to distinguish each root on the ground from under my barely open eyelids.

Animalistic growling still fills my ears, but I can't see anything around me. I'm moving laggard now, from one tree to the next, pausing to prop myself on each one.

The roars are getting louder. They might be a figment of my imagination, brought on by the poisonous gas. My arms and legs feel heavier than usual. It's hard to think clearly, as if I'm drifting in and out of awareness.

"Korun?" I say again quietly.

This time I don't hear anything but rumbling.

Two dogs appear in front of me. Mist mostly conceals their details, but they growl ferociously. The bloodthirsty canines must be thrilled to have found me in my disoriented state.

One barks loudly, causing me to jump with fright.

They're waiting for me to make the first move, probably excited for the chase.

The effects of the gas are so strong, stifling. There's no way to outrun them. I waver for a moment before reaching for the branches above; applying all my strength I pull myself up.

The mutts charge ferociously, some yipping while others howl. Evidently the rumors of the saber tooth mutts were true, or else the poisonous gas has brought on some very serious hallucinations.

My arms barely hoist me onto a large branch in time. The sharp tip of a claw scratches my foot before I pull it up.

Energy is draining from me rapidly. Just a little higher, I need to get a little higher in the tree. Out of reach from the mutts, but I still need more distance from the gas.

My eyes are failing badly now. Only blurry objects are around me. I grasp for a branch within my reach.

Snap!

Now I'm falling. Don't even have the ability to scream. Like a wilted flower tumbling from a tree, I'm helplessly writhing through the air. My weight collides violently with the ground, my back making first impact. There must be pain, but I'm too shaken up to know. Any second, I'll be dog food.

Drool drips in my eyes. It's pointless to open them. *Why keep trying?* My body refuses to respond to anything I ask of it. Korun and Rase are likely in no better shape. It's the end of my road. I close my eyes and greet the unconscious abyss brought by the poisonous gas.

Chapter 10
House of Mutts

Everything before my loss of consciousness is unclear. The guards chased us into the Rotting Pass. Korun, Rase, and I were making our way through the tall roots of the huge trees. Attempting to avoid the soft ground, we pushed forward, dodging the rock wall fumes. We were doing well. The Rotting Pass didn't seem so bad after all. At some point, cockiness got the best of me. Rubbing Rase's face in how well we were doing led to me tripping and setting off the fumes. It's extremely difficult to recall anything that happened after that. I can't discern in my memory what was real or what was dreamt.

A dank smell makes me sick to my stomach. The patter of animals running around, along with other various noises, invades my ears. I'm fully conscious now, but I'm too afraid to open my eyes. My pinky wiggles, so I guess my body is responsive. My eyes open.

My vision has recovered. Everything is clear around me, but it's not a pleasant scene. Two saber tooth mutts sit directly across from me, watching me intently. They're fairly sizable creatures, about four feet tall in their seated position. Drool drips from their mouths as they pant heavily. Little drops of blood fall from their giant fangs every few seconds. It's not my blood, but whatever the blood came from must have fared poorly against them. They're a deep ashen color with short-haired shiny coats. All the skin on their faces is scrunched, giving it a wrinkled appearance. Ears pointed straight up in the air, they refuse to look away from me. I hate their beady little eyes.

Rope binds my arms and legs to a chair. There's more going on than I've been able to discern. I can't imagine what or who would have tied me up in the Rotting Pass. For a second, I think Simul and the Creators are behind this, but this isn't their style.

Wiggling in an effort to dislodge myself from the rope proves useless. Its coarse texture scrapes my skin. I try standing, attempting to bring the chair with me, but it's a permanent fixture, attached to the ground.

Whining sounds to my left. My eyes look up past the terrifying mutts. I would have guessed the sounds came from animals, but they came from people. They're crouched over or lying on their sides, whimpering pathetically as if they were animals. Collars around their necks connect to the wall via chains.

"Help me." I try to get their attention.

No one responds. They won't even look at me.

"Hello," I keep trying. "What is this place? Can you help me?"

They're horrified to communicate at all, or they don't even know how. Realistically, they should probably be the ones asking for help. Some of them are wearing Mahk clothing and others Creator clothing. The round labyrinth symbol has been torn from their garb. Obviously, not everyone who enters the Rotting Pass dies, though this seems a worse fate. Some end up here. I still don't know where here is.

I force myself to focus. My gaze travels the space around me. If I'm quick enough, maybe I can get out of here before whoever bound me to this chair comes back. With the poisonous fumes out of my system, it may be possible to outrun the mutts.

The walls are comprised of dark wooden boards. I follow the lines between the boards up to the arched ceiling. Really, the place isn't that big. My chair is facing two large windows in the back of the house. The same huge trees from the rest of the Rotting Pass can be seen through their dirty glass panes. Shelves line the twelve-foot tall walls. Carved wooden dogs in various poses live on the shelves.

Some are playing and others taking a nap. All are carved with delicate care. Whoever created them spent a lot of time going into elaborate detail.

A single door positioned behind me is the only exit. Oddly, there's no flooring at all on the ground. It's just dirt. A large comfortable-looking bed sits in the corner. Six feet from the bed, a small fire burns. Over near the front window sits a table with a couple benches. A third mutt is sprawled across the surface, chewing on what looks like a human bone, then lapping water out of a cup. Of all the strange things about this place that makes me the most uncomfortable.

A good fifteen minutes go by. Attempts to pry out of the binds yield no result. I start jerking the chair up in an effort to rip it from the ground. When that doesn't work, hope of escape begins to fade. Neither the rope nor the chair will give. Discouraged and wondering what happened to Korun and Rase, I sit in silence. *What's going to happen to me?*

I try again to communicate with the Mahk and Creators tied to the wall. "Help," I plead.

They don't speak at all. A couple even look my way and whimper, like they know what I'm saying but can't respond. Bones protruding from her cheeks, one fixes her eyes on me, licking her lips like she's hungry.

Shivers shoot through my back, but I speak anyway. "What is this place? Who did this to you?"

One of the mutts yaps angrily at me, followed by a deep grunt.

Now the people go back to ignoring me. Uncomfortably strapped to the chair, I become restless after an hour or so passes. My gaze won't tear away from the people tied to the wall. Terrible things must have been done to them that they would become so complacent.

A couple sleep on their sides, curled up in fetal positions. Others cling to the wall and whimper. One crawls to lap his tongue into a water bowl, barely in his reach. He doesn't lift it in his hands to drink, the man laps at it like a dog.

The door swings open behind me. I'm tempted to whip my head and observe who enters, but I restrain myself. My eyes close as if I'm still asleep.

Discerning the many sounds that follow is difficult. For certain, more mutts trot inside. All of them get excited, yapping at each other almost as if in conversation. I strain to hear any human footsteps or the thumping of boots, but I never do.

My eyes stay shut tight, even though I only heard the mutts. My gut tells me there's something else in the room with us. The people by the wall all stopped whimpering and got extremely quiet when the door opened. That could strictly be due to the dogs, but I doubt it.

My muscles have got to stay relaxed. Eyes need to stay closed. Resisting from tapping my feet is nearly impossible, but I manage.

Rattling comes from the direction of the table. I would guess that sound is a bag of bones. All the mutts start barking again as they run around the house. Bones hit the floor and the dogs fight over them.

I still don't hear anyone cross the floor, but a couple minutes later, water sloshes in the corner. I presume the sound is the filling of water bowls, but I can't be sure.

The sound of the water ceases. All that can be heard for the next ten minutes is dogs gnawing on bones and prisoners lapping up water.

That's when hot breath suddenly coats the back of my neck followed by a low growl.

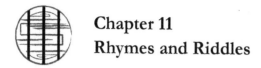

Chapter 11
Rhymes and Riddles

The breath intensifies on my neck. Hands grip my shoulders and my eyes jerk open in horror. I'm too terrified to look at whatever is behind me.

Hello, my pretty pet,
I knew you were awake.
You should never try to trick me.
I know what's real and what's fake.

A raspy voice whispers in my ear. The last word tapers off into a louder growl. I can feel my body shaking now.

Still I haven't seen a face, but I'm able to observe the strange hands on my shoulders. They look almost like human hands, but they have coarse hair at the knuckles and animal claws instead of fingernails.

Shudders shoot through me when something wet drips on my collar bone.

Abruptly, he releases my shoulders and swings around me, placing a hand on my upper leg. His face is close to mine and I'm staring into giant round dark eyes. His breath smells like that of an animal as he pants in my face.

He has normal human skin but instead of hair, the top of his head is covered in coarse fur. His abnormally round dark brown eyes make me cringe. Goop is accumulated at the crease of his eyelids. The creature's ears are small and point up. The sides of his lower lips sag a little. Saliva hangs loosely, waiting to drop. Awkwardly he stares at my face, blinking a couple times.

Silence goes on for so long I can't take it. "What do you want from me? Who are you?"

The left side of his upper lip rises when he talks. Giant sharp teeth like those of a lion are revealed as he opens his mouth to speak. His words are accompanied by a rumbling undertone.

> *My pretty pet, I've been so rude,*
> *of course my name you'd like to know.*
> *It is Sir Riddles, if you will.*
> *Think of me as neither friend nor foe.*
> *Instead call me master,*
> *you'll be glad when you do.*
> *I will teach you tricks,*
> *and possibly even feed you.*

His words come out slowly and sometimes aren't even spoken but instead growled. He lets go of my leg before backing away toward the people chained at the wall. The monster walks with a bit of unsteadiness, but he wears long robes, preventing me from seeing what's wrong with his legs.

> *See, these are my pets.*
> *These are good and those bad.*

He points at the people chained to the wall, indicating they're his good pets. His gesture suggests the bad pets are outside the back windows, but I can't see anyone. Straining to set my eyes on what he's referring to, I finally make out dead bodies and bones scattered about on the ground outside.

> *They reap their fate.*

Pets do better when they don't make me mad.

He pauses in front of the prisoners then snaps his fingers. The Mahk and Creators instantly sit up, their legs tucked under their bodies, leaning on their front hands. They stare at Sir Riddles without flinching.

Sir Riddles cackles heartlessly. He smiles at me, like I should be impressed.

Next he extends his arm straight out horizontally in front of him. All the people chained to the wall lay down, stretched out on the floor. He motions his arm around in a circle and the people roll in response.

Good little pets,
now it's time for a treat.
You all do so well,
and that's why you get to eat.

My stomach writhes in sickness from watching the display. They're all miserable, but they don't have a choice except to obey.

Sir Riddles walks behind the table to pull out some food then sluggishly moves back over to the prisoners. Green and black mold coats parts of the food. He throws it to the ground in front of his "pets," and they hastily swallow it down. Their skinny malnourished bodies are bruised all over. I wonder if they're beaten when they misbehave or if they fight each other for scraps.

I think you're going to be good, pretty pet,
and behave all the time.

He turns his attention back to me and inches in my direction.

I can punish you if you're not,

83

that's not a crime.

"I'd rather die than live like that!" I retort.

The prisoners whimper.

"I'm not scared of you." I *am* afraid, but I'm more terrified of living like the people chained to the wall. I'd rather stand up to him than be degraded.

He snarls back at me with a wince.

> *I am patient and I will wait.*
> *I can play fair.*
> *Until you're ready to be good,*
> *you can sit in that chair.*

Yet again I find my strings are being pulled, this time by a different puppet master. *I refuse to be the puppet again.*

He continues to go about his own business. After retracing his steps back behind the table, he extracts food from a bag. His hairy hand pulls a meaty bone from the pan he has now placed in the center of the table. With no sense of dignity, he shoves giant portions of food in his mouth and clumps of it miss, smearing to his face. A couple of the dogs lay on the large table, also eating meat from the pan.

So disgusting, it's offensive to watch. I close my eyes, trying to flee from it all, but chewing noises and raspy panting still haunt my escape.

> *It's dangerous in the labyrinth anyway.*
> *There's nothing good outside.*
> *Good pets are safe with Sir Riddles.*
> *I help them hide.*

"Hide from what? You're the most terrible thing I've seen in the labyrinth. They don't want to be here." I look at him. Crumbs have collected on his robes.

Oh no, my pets tell me differently,
I know about the real dangers.
There's lava, snakes,
and all kinds of evil scavengers.

His eyes narrow at me.

Many things about the labyrinth,
are kept secret from you.
So many dangers creeping about,
hidden from view.

"How could you know anything about the labyrinth since you hide in the Rotting Pass torturing people? I know almost every inch of this labyrinth. I've managed to survive on my own for two years. There's nothing that can surprise me in it."

Oh, but there is still something big,
about which I am certain you don't know.
Its brothers are a snack,
and it's double a foe.
A difficult thing to kill,
but from its grave, a gift it will bestow.

"You're just making things up to scare me. Is that what you did to them?" I motion my head in the direction of the people tied to the wall. "Did you make up lies and beat them until they submitted?"

He continues shoveling food into his mouth. The dogs are off the table now and piled around the bottom of the bed, all twenty-two of them sleeping.

Abruptly he stands up from the table and moves over to the bed.

Good night, my pets,
and think of sweet things.
Fight the nightmares away,
and we'll see what tomorrow brings.

He throws off one heavy floor-length robe, revealing another underneath. I still haven't seen what's wrong with his legs. Instead of crawling into the bed, he leaps across the dogs into it. The iniquitous monster walks in a circle a couple times before curling his body like a canine on top of the blankets.

I can't help but wonder what exactly is wrong with him. Perhaps he's a Mahk the Creators didn't get quite right. He's not only physically abnormal. There's something very wrong in his mind.

Lying in the bed, he repeats a riddle while he drifts to sleep.

Which little pets,
live in the penitentiary,
eat dead rats,
and have selective memory?

He cackles every few minutes after he says his riddle. This goes on for a good thirty minutes before finally fading to loud snorting and snoring.

I sit perplexed, wondering how I'll ever get out of this dog house. My only hope is Korun, but he may not even be alive.

Flames dance above the burning logs, casting dark shadows across the room. Snoring, panting, and whimpering fill the space. Fearful of what I'll wake to face, I struggle to stay awake, but eventually, my eyelids insist on shutting and my surroundings fade away.

Sir Riddles doesn't leave me alone in my sleep. The hot breath is on my neck again as drool falls from his mouth. He forces me to be a good pet, making me do tricks and drink like an animal. His words dance through my head. In my nightmares, he feeds me to his mutts.

I have no idea how long I've slept after I come to. As I open my eyes, I hope somehow I was rescued in the night and won't find myself in the chair. Unfortunately, my wish doesn't come true. I'm still in the wooden house of mutts. Sir Riddles, the mutts, and the prisoners are all real. A part of me had hoped I was still knocked out from the gas, imagining Sir Riddles in my head.

Across the room, Sir Riddles pets his saber tooth mutts, cuddling them.

Such sweet friends I have,
always watching out for me,
spending all our time together,
so happy are we.

He is mad. It would feel so good to slap the rhymes right out of him.

He stands up to stretch then walks over to the table. His mutts are eager for a meal, but he tells them it's time to work, rushing all but three out the door. Repeating the same riddle from the night before, he picks up bones and cleans.

Which little pets,
live in the penitentiary,
eat dead rats,
and have selective memory?

Sir Riddles works his way over to the food and eats a meal.

I'm conflicted as he does so. My stomach is starting to hurt, but I'm also sickened by his way of consumption. He looks up in the middle of a bite to see my cringing face.

Offended are we, my pretty pet,
to see me eat.
But I'm tired, you see,
after I made this whole place neat.

My head drops as I close my eyes. Darkness and decay are nothing new in this world, which is why there's always a better place to go in my imagination. I go to the beautiful land with cascading water and take Blue with me. We enjoy a picnic together, eating cooked fish, bread, and strawberries for dinner. Elaborate pictures spring from my mind onto big boulders and songs burst from my mouth. Blue dances in the water to her heart's content. Nothing can harm us there.

Reality demands my return with more of Sir Riddles' obnoxious growling speech.

There are so many things,
we can't explain.
Yet it is so true,
if we open our eyes, they are so very plain.

What's he going on about now? I have to question if he, himself, knows what he's saying. Done with his meal, he goes back over to his bed and slides on the extra robe he took off the night before. Now he works his way across the room and stands in front of his "pets."

He pauses and looks over at me.

No chance you've decided to be good,
I would venture to guess.

So I'll give you more time to observe your options,
and let your mind really assess.

He turns his attention back to the prisoners. Again, he makes hand gestures, and they all seem to know what they mean. One arm stretches up, next straight forward. He rotates his palm up and wiggles his fingers. Following the demands closely, the people sit, lay, roll, and even beg. After he's content with their cooperation, he feeds them all.

My stomach growls at me, angrily begging for food. I'd rather starve than give in. I fight the pain in my body and sit up straight. Hunger is an enemy I'm far too acquainted with so I know how to push it away.

My good little pets,
I hate to leave you.
I'd love to stay and play,
but I've got things to attend to.

Right, things to attend to. He's out looking for more people to kidnap, I'm sure.

He leaves three mutts watching me and the other prisoners. Today, only one sits directly across from me. Another takes a nap in the bed and the third makes his rounds, drinking out of the prisoners' water bowls.

Another ten minutes pass and my bottom is getting sore from sitting in the chair. If Korun survived, he would have come by now. If I want to live, I need to get myself out of this.

Getting out of this chair isn't possible. If I don't escape before I end up chained to the wall, it will never happen. It's painful, but the answer is to agree to his terms. He'll have to release me from the chair before moving me to the wall. That will be my only chance.

The chair is nailed down, so it won't be useful for defense. There's a junk pile in the back left corner where my bag has been tossed. If my bag is there, chances are my dagger is too.

Once he unties me, my best bet is to get a forceful kick at his head, hopefully knocking him out. After that, I run for the tote. I'll jump through the window and be rid of him. That's the best I've got. Realistically, I'm going to end up dog food during my feeble attempt at freedom, but it's better than living out my life in these conditions.

Now all that's left to do is wait until I can play along with Sir Riddles' game.

Chapter 12
Attempting an Escape

I must have faded off again. I awaken to the loud bang of the door swinging open. The prisoners cling to the wall and whimper loudly. He must be home.

I inhale deeply. "Sir Riddles, I'm ready to be good."

The saber tooth mutts start growling. Their eyes narrow as they begin to charge toward the door. A knife flies into one of their skulls before blood splatters across the dirt. The dog drops dead at my feet. The others disappear from my sight, attacking someone behind me. I hear a struggle and a grunt followed by a chopping sound and a whimper. A thump on the ground causes me to jump. I whip my head around to observe. A saber tooth mutt lies on the floor with a gaping hole in its head. The other mutt is running away.

"That's too bad," a familiar voice answers my previous statement. "Let's see, I don't think Mr. Riddles is going to get to hear that." Korun appears in front of me.

I exhale with relief. "It's Sir Riddles."

"Haven't lost your spunk, have you?" He laughs as he dislodges the knife from the dog's head. He cuts off my restraints.

I can't help but to swing my arms around his neck with gratitude. "Did you kill him?"

"That ghoulish thing? No. I've been waiting for him to leave. Think he'll be mad I killed his dogs?"

"We've got to get out of here. He's absolutely crazy and has twenty-two saber tooth mutts at his command."

"Twenty, now." Korun points with his bloody axe at the two dead mutts.

He starts to lead me out the door when I remember my bag.

"Wait." Frantically I run toward the back of the house to find my bag, but my dagger's missing. "Damn it." I turn around to face Korun.

He's left my side, distracted by Sir Riddles' "pets." Horror screams in his eyes as he looks them over. Having seen the skinny bruised bodies multiple times already, I'm still shaken. I can't even imagine what he's thinking. He pulls his knife back out.

"There's no time. He could be back any second."

He glances at me shamefully. "We can't leave them like this."

When he reaches to cut off a woman's collar, she snarls and bites his hand. He jerks back and we move away from the wall as they all start growling. We almost reach the bed before we stop. "What did he do to them?" he questions.

"I told you, he's completely crazy."

At that moment, I hear Sir Riddles' low growl.

It's not very nice,
to talk bad about your owner.
And do my eyes play tricks,
or are you running off with a stranger?

Korun and I both whirl around to face him.

He stands at the doorway. Drool drips from his sagging lips. His eyes get big at the sight of his dead mutts. He begins to howl.

Korun and I look at each other with frightened eyes. Tree branches shuffle outside and loud pattering clamors in our ears.

"The other mutts!" I exclaim.

Three are already emerging from the tree line outside, swiftly approaching the open door.

Sir Riddles snarls at us, revealing nasty canine teeth, then leaps high into the air, headed our direction.

In a panic, I jerk Korun over toward the fireplace. My fingers get slightly burned extracting a lit log from the fire and launching it toward our attacker.

His robes light up instantly, causing him to whimper. He drops midair, letting out his awful loud cackle. A sharp cracking noise cuts the air as he hits the ground. Rolling around in his attempt to put out the flames, he manages to set his bed on fire.

Korun takes his axe to the only mutt that's made it inside so far. In two strikes, he kills the thing. The flames and mutts have us backed into the house. Fire is spreading to the walls. We're across the house from the door, the exit.

Another reaches me. It's jumping at me, ears back and mouth struggling to tear at my skin. The mutt takes a full bite out of my baggy pants but only barely scrapes my skin with its teeth.

Korun spins around, swinging the axe up into its midsection, flinging it across the room.

"Come on." I grab his arm and charge for the back of the cabin.

He catches up with me. At the same time, we launch our bodies through the air at the huge window. Glass sprays on our impact. I close my eyes, afraid of being blinded.

We hit the ground hard, descending on the rotten flesh of dead bodies. Our rough landing isn't great, but as I notice the many sharp pointed rib cage bones a few feet away, I count us lucky. The smell is atrocious.

Korun's on his feet first, pulling me up beside him. "Go, go!" he yells.

My dagger's in a pile of weapons behind the house. "Wait!" I insist.

I backtrack a couple feet. Just as I reach the pile, a mutt jumps through the window at me, knocking me to the ground again.

"I'm coming," I hear Korun yell.

"I've got this," I assure him as I grasp the dagger in my hand, slamming it into the angry dog's eye. It whimpers as it runs off, tail between its legs.

Once again, Korun helps me to my feet. We take off running. I situate the dagger in my hair like it should be.

"Think we could move faster?" Korun urges. Faster would be ideal, but we're headed uphill and my empty body needs food. "Don't look back. Just keep going."

What if Sir Riddles is behind us? And those mutts, how many are on our trail? We reach the top of the small hill behind the cabin and I can't resist any longer. Briefly, my gaze travels behind us to see the condition of the fire. The whole house is in flames now. There can't be any way Sir Riddles or his prisoners escaped. His prisoners—I'm torn between guilt of their deaths and frustration at their refusal to accept our help.

Despite the smoke brought on by the fire, some of the mutts picked up on our scent. They chase us a good ten minutes before Korun pushes me at a tree. He gives me a quick boost before pulling himself up about the time the dogs catch us. They bark ferociously from the ground and scratch at the trunk.

"We could have outrun them," I state as he points for me to continue crawling upward.

"We could have, but we need to get Rase."

Somehow, she slipped my mind during all the chaos. It's amazing she didn't escape or die between the gas and the mutts.

"Smart choice to leave her tied up in a tree."

"Didn't have much of an option. You know how she likes to make everything difficult. I didn't think it was worth bringing her along just to cause problems. Couldn't take that kind of risk." His hand brushes mine as we grab for the same branch.

"I'm sorry I got us into all this," I offer as we advance upwards.

"It's not like you had a choice. If you hadn't brought us here, the guards would have killed us."

94

"I meant I'm sorry for setting off the gas and nearly killing us all... then going and letting myself get captured."

He pauses for a minute and indicates for me to do the same. After placing his hand on my cheek, his thumb brushes away dirt from under my eye. "Don't be sorry for anything, Araina. I'm sorry that happened to you. Did he hurt you?"

"No. I don't think he really intended to injure me. I can't be sure, but he would have let me starve to death if I didn't obey him."

Korun shakes his head.

It's actually helpful to vent. Saying things out loud rather than only in my head feels freeing. "He had them trained, Korun, like animals. I really thought I was going to die in that house."

"Were you really going to give in?" His tone isn't condescending but instead one of concern. Sadness manages to speak not through his voice but the look in his eyes.

"No, I had decided I would try to make a run for it after I pretended to cooperate. I thought he would have to unbind me at some point. Then maybe I could find my dagger in my bag. I knew it probably wasn't going to work." I shiver and shake out my hands, like I'm shooing away Sir Riddles and his mutts.

"Let's see, she's right there." Korun points up at Rase, who is sleeping through my hysterics and the barking dogs. That makes me smile a bit.

We finish our climb and Korun jostles her awake.

"You took long enough," she scolds. "I figured I was going to starve up here."

"Quit being dramatic," I reply. "If you weren't such a pain, he could have brought you with him."

Korun releases her from the tree. Once again, I take her rope.

"Sounds like trouble," Rase remarks, when she finally hears the barking dogs.

"She's right," I tell Korun, "and I doubt they'll let up."

"I've already considered that. This canopy is pretty thick, don't you think?"

"Sure" I answer, unsure of what he's thinking.

He looks both directions. "We climb the rest of the way. Probably just as fast, but a lot safer."

"Safer as long as we don't fall," I point out. His idea has merit though. "Really there isn't any other option aside from trying to wait the mutts out, but there's probably around twelve of them, so they'll be keeping an eye on the tree for a while. I think it could work."

He nods.

"I'm desperate for food though. I've got to eat something." Nothing edible remains in my bag. Sir Riddles swipes food from his victims. I huff at the realization that I've got no food or water left on me.

Korun graciously offers me a potato. My angry stomach would be glad to consume the whole thing, but self-control equals survival. This is going to be an issue though. The three of us are going to have difficulty finding enough food the next few days or, more importantly, water. We could swipe those items from other Mahk, but we have to find some first. My eyes catch Korun watching me, maybe even admiring me. Scrats... He won't have us stealing even if it would save our lives.

"We're really going to have to move as fast as possible," I tell him. "That food isn't going to last the three of us long. If we can make it to my hiding spot, we'll have access to some fresh water as well as vegetation." Our hiding location makes me think of Blue. Who knows if Darith's on his way to kill her as we speak?

"Sounds like you've got a pretty nice setup at your spot," he observes.

"I didn't even realize that until a couple days ago. Most water around the labyrinth is acidic, so when I found the water pool at the bottom of the wall, I thought it was too. Blue showed me I was wrong, and it's all thanks to her I found the food. All because of her I found the wall."

"You miss Blue? And she's the bird, right?" he presses.

"My pet." It shouldn't be uncomfortable talking about her, but it is. I guess it's my protective nature.

"I kind of got the impression it would be hard to have a pet around here."

"It's complicated." My lips scrunch together.

Rase scoffs as she makes a point to absently stare into the entangled branches. Clearly our conversation is of no interest.

"I hope I get to meet her," he comments. "I can tell she's special to you."

I allow his words to hang, and it feels reasonable not to respond. He can see I'm starving. Focusing on the food going into my mouth is all I can do. It's slowly working its way into my system. Trying not to further delay our exit from the wretched pass, I finish quickly.

We climb even higher into the tree, about fifty feet up. The mutts are probably still howling below but can't be heard from this distance.

Then we start working through the branches, limb to limb. At first, my fingers are sore from the rough bark, but eventually they become numb as their coloring changes to a deep red. Continuing forward, I realize Korun was right about this going faster. Having to look for the fumes and avoid the soft ground had really slowed us down. This canopy is so thick we move tree to tree in a matter of minutes.

"Not a bad idea to travel the canopy," I compliment Korun as we continue on.

Reaching from one giant branch to the next, I inquire what happened to him and Rase when I set off the poisonous gas.

"I remember trying to pull you two through the gas and losing hold on you," he says. "Then I searched around but couldn't find you anywhere. Of course at that point, things were getting very hazy.

Then those dogs showed up and tried to attack. We couldn't run fast, so we ended up in a tree. That's when I had the idea to climb the rest of the way out of this place."

I nod. My memory of the time between the fumes and Sir Riddles had been foggy until now, but it's coming back to me. "That's right. I tried to climb, but a branch snapped and I fell. I thought for sure those mutts were going to eat me. Then I lost consciousness. Next thing I knew, I was in that awful house. So you made it to a tree?"

"Obviously we were pretty disoriented, but we just kept climbing up as far as we could. We got about as high as we are now before the gas disappeared. It took a good hour for the effects to wear off. After that, we waited a long time for the gas to clear below. Occasionally, we would work our way back down a little, hoping the gas was gone. It must have been a few hours before we finally made it back to the ground."

"How did you find me after that?" I inquire.

"Didn't know what happened to you," Korun answers, "but we found some strange tracks and drag marks. I hoped it would lead us to you and it did."

"Thanks, Korun. I'd be dead by now if you hadn't gotten me out of there. I don't think I'll ever be able to block that monster out my head. He really messed with me."

Korun nods.

Time passes as we move on. Fatigue setting in, we need to stop for a rest, but we avoid snacking. We have got to make the food last as long as possible. With Rase secured to the tree and our position in the branches, we decide no one has to keep watch.

The dreams aren't pleasant, so I'm happy when Korun wakes me. "We need to keep moving," he says.

My arms stretch as my awakening mind reaches for full awareness. The three of us climb on for another couple hours. We venture through the tangled trees, stringy moss, and near silence.

Finally, the moisture in the air is lessening. "I think we're getting close," I announce excitedly.

"Don't get too excited and trip again." Rase shoots me one of her snotty expressions.

I ignore her, too happy at the sight of our potential survival.

"Look, I can see more light up ahead." Korun points.

Another hour brings us to the edge of the pass. We exit the trees carefully, keeping an eye out for mutts within and guards on the outside. We get about twenty feet away before I look back at the Rotting Pass. I'm relieved to have survived and hopeful that Sir Riddles died in the fire we started.

"This is the last time I ever plan to come close to this place," I announce. "Now let's get going."

Chapter 13
Navigating the Blades

We have been inching through the metallic jungle for hours. So far, the structural layout of the labyrinth seems unchanged. I worry as we make new turns that we'll come to an entirely new set of paths, but it hasn't happened yet.

Despite how little time I spent with Sir Riddles in the Rotting Pass, I'm haunted by the experience. I try to imagine what the Creators intended for him to be, or if they even know of his existence. Recalling his breath on the back of my neck and his hand on my leg makes me shake. It reminds me of the one-handed man's advances toward me in the castle. The only thing that brings comfort to me concerning the Rotting Pass is that I watched Sir Riddles and his house burn down.

I wish the prisoners would have let us help them. Creator or Mahk, I don't care which they were. I can't stand the thought of them living or dying like that. I find myself hoping they did die in that fire along with Sir Riddles, so they wouldn't have to be haunted by memories of him.

As I try to shove his rhymes from my brain, the journey before me taunts my psyche. If things go okay, we could reach Blue in about two and a half days. Feeling guilty when I glance over at Korun, I find myself willing nothing else to go wrong.

We've already eluded the guards, survived the Nabal, and navigated the Rotting Pass. It's fair to hold out hope that we'll make it back without another hitch. Aside from the possibility of more "Labyrinth attacks," like the blades, there shouldn't be any more fatal threats on our way.

The minutes fly by as we work around the sharp objects through wide then narrow passages. My senses would get bored looking at random boulders and scattered trees, but the added blades keep my mind busy. Like a thread, my body weaves through them. Occasionally, Sikla makes a little volcanic rumble but aside from that, quietness fills the air.

Korun breaks the boring silence. "So, tell me more about yourselves." He runs the handle of his axe through his fingers. His brown eyes trace over the patterns carved into it.

Flinging her short brown hair away from her face, Rase rolls her eyes then looks away.

"What do you want to know?" I respond. It isn't really in Mahk nature to socialize. I'm not very good at talking about anything, much less myself.

His attention lands on a lovely Darktouch flower dancing on the wall. Clearly trying to be sneaky, he slows down as if preparing to pluck it.

"Don't!" I smack his rising hand.

His eyes are wide as he stares at me, dumbfounded. "Why?" He shrugs. "I thought you might like it." He smiles at me.

I'm not comfortable at all with his attempted gesture. I shoot him a scolding stare. "Those things will turn you to stone with one touch."

"Sorry." His vacant expression and fidgeting thumbs give away his embarrassment. He attempts to push our conversation along, "What do you do in the labyrinth?"

I'm still put off by the flower incident. He could have been dead in an instant.

"How is it you know every corner of the labyrinth?" he tries again. "I know you live here, but you're obviously exceptionally savvy with the place and its pitfalls."

"Exceptionally savvy implies others aren't as clever in the labyrinth. How would you know that?"

102

I'm giving him a hard time, but his prying is grating on my patience. I'm supposed to be the one asking questions. Yet, I've got nothing to hide. Around here, people don't make polite conversation, but I decide to play along. If nothing else, it'll make the walk go by faster. Maybe the conversation will help him remember something about himself.

"I don't really do much, I suppose. The Creators made me two years ago. They don't tell us anything about life or survival." I shoot Rase an angry look. "So I figured it out. I learned that I need to take care of myself if I want to live. If I weren't on this insane journey with you, I would be collecting obsidian right now from around Sikla."

A look of confusion lands on his face.

"Sikla is the volcano in the labyrinth."

"Why would you be collecting obsidian?"

"For the Creators. Obsidian and kimberlite are the taxes we pay, and that's the only way we eat. As you can see, there aren't exactly any other sources of food around here." I'm getting bored with the discussion. "So that's it really. I collect obsidian and that's how I survive."

"What do you need all that obsidian for?" Korun looks at Rase, trying again to engage her in the discussion.

"We make obsidian stew." She laughs at him. The condescending tone is just right for her.

All this time, I've been thinking Korun is innocent like Blue, but his strong efforts to connect with us make me think he's extremely sly. He might be feeling us out, learning what he can for some ends of his own. It's not working though. Rase would never give up information about the Creators. They're ancient people with the ability to create life. Just because Mahk are made in Creator image doesn't mean they think much of us. It's juvenile to think we could get anything out of them. They're too proud for that.

Korun turns his face back to me. "So why do you know your way around this place so well?"

Unintentionally, I inhale deeply before I respond, "I like to explore... That's all."

He stares at me, like he thinks there's more to it. He got me away from Sir Riddles and he healed me, which makes me grateful, but I'm still not comfortable being social. In the labyrinth, no one cares about anyone else. In fact, I've already talked to him far more than I'd ever interacted with anyone other than Darith. Korun's knowledge of me from our conversations and experiences already makes me feel vulnerable. Vulnerability isn't something I wear comfortably. Interaction isn't my forte and that won't change for one person.

It feels like a good time to stop sharing for today. My gaze settles on the route we travel. Maybe he'll think that's cold, but he doesn't have to like me. He doesn't need to know anything about me anyway. What does it matter? When we get to the other side of that wall, I'm on my own again. Trusting Darith proved to be a mistake. He already abandoned me. That taught me a lesson about trusting people. There's no desire in me to go down that path again. It's safer to keep to my own agenda. Mine and Blue's survival is the goal. Whatever else happens, happens. Korun doesn't play into the long term picture of my priorities.

"I guess exploring might be something you can do a lot of when we get to the other side of the wa—" he starts.

"Shhh!" Rase insists.

We pause still in our places to listen.

Voices come from somewhere in front of us.

"Think those are guards?" Korun whispers.

"I don't think so," I respond. "Listen closely."

The voices say things like, "Keep going." Smothered sobs and crying accompany scattered words.

I shake my head with surprise. "Not sure who that is, but I don't think they're guards. Stay quiet no matter what." I threaten Rase with my dagger. If I'm wrong and they're Creators, we don't need her giving us away.

We sneak along beside the labyrinth wall quietly, making our way to the voices. Snooping, my head barely pokes into a side passage, allowing me a quick glimpse of the strangers.

Reality suspends for a moment. There's a group of Mahk walking together and it seems like they're helping each other. Among them is a very strange looking man. He's unusually tall, towering about a foot over the rest of the group. He's very muscular and his dark green hair distinguishes him from the others. Mahk typically have brown, red, blonde, or black hair. The strange man looks very different from anyone I've seen before. Creators and Mahk don't ever have hair like his or even such muscular bodies. Certainly I've never seen anyone his height before. Instinctively, I glance to see if Rase reacts to the unusual man, but she doesn't appear to be surprised by his existence.

One Mahk is crying as she walks. Another consoles her by patting her arm gently with reassurance. Withdrawing tasty-looking crackers from a pouch, one Mahk offers food to someone beside him. They all walk in close proximity, clearly as a group.

"Something isn't right about this picture. I don't even know what the thing with the green hair is and the Mahk are far too friendly with each other," I whisper to Korun.

He smiles at me. "What if all Mahk aren't what you thought of them, Araina? They might help us get to the wall. They may even want to go with us to the other side."

His words raise conflict in my mind. The suggestion makes me nervous. Never in my two years have I seen friendly Mahk. Even when they aren't killing each other, they're temperamental, violent, and selfish. Mahk don't help each other, ever. On the other hand, they obviously have a fair supply of food and water, which are things we need desperately at the moment.

His comment about them coming with us to the other side makes me a bit uneasy too. Still, if they're willing to come with us, we could use the manpower. Chances are the wall is heavily guarded now. My hopes are high of a new life on the other side of the wall and bringing the Mahk with us poses a problem for that plan. In all fairness, their predicament does merit pity now that Simul is igniting the labyrinth attacks. The truth is that bringing them through the wall could offer a fresh start for our kind.

"Fine, but don't let your guard down. I'm telling you. No one can be trusted."

"Not even you?" he retorts cleverly.

A faked smile evades his question. In all honestly, yes. I can't be trusted. When we get to the other side of the wall, it will be time to bail.

My arm motions to indicate it's time to make our presence known. We step out from our hiding spot, revealing ourselves to the small Mahk group.

They whip their weapons out defensively. We do the same. A silent standoff takes place for a few moments as we all assess each other. They're sufficiently armed with an array of swords, axes, maces, daggers, and even a club. It looks like they raided a Creator's store or something. Most of them carry more than one defensive object in hand plus additional spears and arrows on their backs.

My gaze takes in all the sharp objects pointed at us, causing me to question for a moment if we made a mistake. It's too late to go back now. They haven't massacred us yet and silence isn't doing anyone any good.

"My name is Araina. Who are you?"

The group looks at each other then back at us. The strange man steps hesitantly forward. "I'm Soll. Before I tell you anything more... Why don't you tell me why you have a guard with you?"

I haven't seen Soll before in the labyrinth. He has probably been elusive through the years. Or maybe he's a survivor from the recent awakening day. Judging by his muscular shape and strong tone, it isn't surprising that he survived the metal blades. An uncertainty speaks through his narrowed brows. The skin lining his eyes is a dark green similar to his hair, but each iris is a very brilliant lime color.

He stares at me steadily without blinking. "The guard," he reiterates, "why is she with you?"

"Soll, this guard is named Rase." I jerk the rope in my hand, which pulls at her wrists. "You don't need much more explanation aside from the fact that she's our prisoner."

At first he looks as if he's impressed, but then he exhales with frustration. "Are you the reason Simul brought the metal blades on us? And the Creators are massacring the Mahk?"

Shaking my head defensively, I say, "Of course not—"

"Yes, yes, it's their fault!" Rase interrupts. "Turn them in and return me to Simul if you want to live."

"No!" I retort. "This is a long story, but that isn't going to help you. Do you think the Creators care about you, Soll? About any of the Mahk?" My gaze surveys the group in front of me. "The Creators made us the way we are: hateful, savage, and selfish. They never care when our kind starve to death or when the Nabal eat us in the caves. They want us to believe this is all life is! But there's got to be more to life, a better way of existence. What if there was no murder and betrayal? What if there could be solitude without disruption? We could all live independently, in peace." My gaze shifts over to Korun. "He's my proof." I point. "This man came from a better place. He came from a safer place. I watched him come through a wall into this land. Isn't that right, Korun?" I encourage.

Korun nods uneasily. He's seeing me for what I am, a liar. We could walk through that wall into a confined brick room. But what's on our side of the wall makes the risk worth taking. It can't possibly be worse than this side. So I'm promising them a utopia. Delusional or not, maybe if I believe in a better world with enough conviction, and convince others to believe it as well, then it will be real. Korun doesn't argue with my claim, so at least for now, he's willing to play along.

Looking back at Soll, I continue, "This mess…" I motion around to the swords and blades. "This is the result of this revelation. The Creators are killing us because they don't want us to rise up and overcome them. You can turn us in, but I'm telling you they will either kill you anyway, or you will keep living like wild animals."

Pulling Korun along with me, we step closer to Soll. The other five Mahk back away, but Soll stands fearless towering over me. My sweaty fingers wrap around his, lifting his hand from his side. It's covered in blood, neatly wrapped in thin fabric. My gentle removal of the bandages from his hand reveals a deep gash across his palm. Korun knows what to do. He wraps his hands around Soll's while the Mahk group watches us timidly.

Their eyes widen, even Soll's, as Korun retreats his hands, leaving no trace of the gash on the stranger's palm.

"Fate be," Soll gasps, impressed.

"There's a better world, a better life out there. There has to be." My arms fold across my chest. "Come with us and we'll help you out of this labyrinth prison."

Soll nods. The others stand in silence, as if frozen with awe in the moment that already passed them by.

"I've never seen anything like it. You seem to be people worth trusting. Thank you," he tells Korun.

"And may I ask where you all were headed?" I inquire.

If the slight smile and lit up eyes on Soll's face are any indication, it would appear we have won his trust.

"We were looking for a way out of here," he responds.

"And I guess we found it," a small voice pipes up from behind him.

The voice comes from the girl who had been in tears. It's shocking to see how young the Creators made her. In fact, she might be the youngest aged Mahk to have been spawned since me, but she looks even less physically mature than I was. My body is probably close now to exiting teen years, but she must be barely fourteen.

"My name is Keelie," she says softly as she reaches out her hand to shake mine. It seemed like she simply appeared by my side, she moves so fast.

Hesitantly, my arm rises. Their overly friendly nature is overwhelming.

Korun shakes her hand sweetly though and smiles kindly at her.

"Yes, this is Keelie." Soll shuffles her blonde hair. He goes on to introduce the other four people in the group: Rifan, Saige, Olum, and Laon. I'll never remember all of that but still nod graciously through the introductions.

"We don't have any time to waste. These blades may not be the only attack Simul has planned for us. I don't want to wait around to find out." I try to get the group moving.

"We can't leave without the rest," Keelie pleads, twirling her hair.

"The rest of what?" I question.

"More like who," Soll replies. "We left our people back in the den."

I tap my fingers impatiently on my hip, waiting for more explanation.

"There's a…colony, I guess you could say. We didn't want the Creators to find out, so it's fairly small, about two hundred of us. Only around half of us survived the blade attack. We all share our earnings and protect each other. We were content living that way until the recent labyrinth attacks. After so many of our friends were killed, a small group of us set out to search for a way out of here. Seemed impossible until now."

A shred of hope dances in my heart. I'm overwhelmed at the notion that these people take care of each other; that they care about one another. For a moment, that sounds appealing to me. His description of the colony reminds me of Blue. But it's hard for me to comprehend a true functioning community of Mahk. It's bothersome as well that he claims they've remained in hiding. That seems impossible for the Mahk because we have to report to the Creators for food and water. Surely my explorations would have led me to them at some point. The questions bubble in my brain until finally they burst, "Why did I never hear of this colony?"

"Like I said, the colony was small and we didn't want to be discovered. We feared the Creators would kill us all for banding together," Soll replies. "Araina, if all you said is true; then there's hope to save the colony." He's able to read the defiant expression on my face. "We won't leave without them."

"Stronger in numbers!" I announce.

Agreeing to help a colony of Mahk doesn't seem wise to me. The whole story about their supposed concern for each other causes me to question if this is a trap. These people could be Creators dressed as Mahk, leading us to our deaths. But that's probably irrational. The Creators are too prideful for that. They don't think highly enough of the Mahk to go through any efforts to trick us. The pain from the blades in my back replays in my mind at the sight of them all around us. Who knows what other disasters could come next? If they're telling the truth, we might stand a better chance of finding Blue and getting to the other side of the wall with their help.

My hand gestures for them to lead the way. "We need to get moving."

Pulling Rase beside me, we resume our travels. It immediately becomes difficult to tune out the talkative young teenager walking in front of us. Scrats, she's a chatter box. Despite being only a little older than her, it feels like a big difference. Chatting with Korun about the labyrinth, the colony, and her hairstyle, Keelie strokes her blonde hair that ends below her elbows. Her flirtation isn't subtle at all. Korun's desperation to avoid looking at her green eyes gives away his awkward predicament. The girl is a skinny little thing with no muscle to speak of. It's amazing she has survived the living conditions in the labyrinth. I've never heard anyone talk so much.

Her high-pitched chatter doesn't quit for the next hour as we make our way around the blades and through the dark passages.

In an effort to ignore the interactions around me, I let myself take in the unusual amount of glow shining down from the sun. The walls stretch so high, typically there's very minimal light in the labyrinth. Smoke from Sikla drowns out most of what does shine in. Rare days when the luminosity is particularly defiant of the walls are days to treasure. The heat is intensified, but I've developed a tolerance for that. My eyes have trouble adjusting to the pale pink and yellow hues, but the discomfort is worth the beautiful scene. Eventually, I'm able to actually let my eyes wander upward. The sun rays are marvelous, landing against the jagged rocks' textures.

The beauty only relieves my eyes, but my ears still can't escape the girl's prattle. Unable to stand the endless sound of her high-pitched little voice, I push my way to the front of the group to walk next to Soll. Only a couple minutes of peace go by before Soll feels the need to start a discussion.

"You know, we have been watching you, Araina."

"Who?"

"The colony. You've always seemed to be unique from most Mahk."

The tall man's statement makes me very uncomfortable. What does he mean the colony has been watching me? He could be insinuating something very disturbing. His words also make me think of Darith, who professed to know me because he had been watching me. Suddenly, it feels like I've never had a moment to myself. Hiding in shadows and observing has been my way of life. But apparently the shadows were in plain sight.

"Then why did you pretend not to know me at first?" I ask.

"We weren't sure about your companions, if they could be trusted. We have watched you for a long time though."

My lips purse shut. Heat of anger pulses in my cheeks "Okay...so you and your colony sat by the last two years while I almost starved and died over and over." My head drops. "I don't know why you're telling me this or what you are trying to say."

"More like, I'm trying to say that you are special, Araina." He looks into my eyes for a brief moment. "Your lifestyle is inspiring and exceptional among the Mahk. You've never killed anyone, even though it would have saved your own life. The violence that plagues our people has never seemed to really touch you. You've always been different than anyone else in this wretched place."

My feet stop moving forward now. It is strange feeling frustrated and somehow betrayed by people I don't even know. "So you let me fend for myself all this time even though I was inspiring."

Conflict battles inside me. Fast, or smart possibly, but inspiring? That is not a word for me.

A look of guilt and shame crosses his face. "It's not like we didn't try. You were always one step ahead of us."

I shake my head, running my fingers over the edge of my ear with irritation. Pressure gathers at the corners of my eyes. Tears threaten to explode. Composure and strength aren't coming easily right now. *You offer obsidian, you eat, you kill, and you survive.* Yet, those words don't provide me the comfort they once did.

"Nothing is different, but everything is changing," I whisper to myself. My need for survival and the means that must be utilized in that effort haven't changed, but my world has become a very confusing place.

Soll shakes his head. He seems unsure what I muttered under my breath.

Keelie migrates to the front of the group. She chips in, "Right, he's telling the truth, Araina. We did try to bring you into the colony. We couldn't say anything about it in public. Then you would disappear as soon as you went back into the labyrinth passages. You know?"

Most of my time has been spent hiding with Blue. Our friendship has been my only haven in this smothering life.

"Even when someone would track you down, you'd run."

"Of course I ran. You've seen what Mahk do to each other."
Sure, I can think of a Mahk or two that didn't immediately try to kill me. There have been many Mahk who tried to speak to me. Sticking around for a conversation was asking for a fight to the death. There's never been a reason to trust anyone but Blue. I'm not convinced Soll and his group are trustworthy for that matter. A few isolated encounters with potentially tolerable Mahk doesn't discount two years of being savagely attacked and watching others fight to the death.

A soft stare from Korun seems to convey pity.

"You never trusted anyone. None of us knew how to help you because you were so distant."

Small vibrations stretch across my tongue in reaction to my grinding teeth "I don't want to hear any more. Let's just get to the colony and get to the other side of that wall."

I've heard enough of their explanations. My speed picks up. I'm more than ready to get to our destination. I didn't need them before. I don't need them now.

# Chapter 14
The Surge

This is my existence, walking down the paths of a deadly world with people who can't be trusted. No one else can be blamed though. This mess is my own doing. Maybe I could blame Darith. He did help get me into all this, but it's not likely I'll ever see him again.

Wearily, one foot and then the other treads beneath me. Attempting to focus on something, anything, proves useless. Emotions refuse to let my brain find clarity. The rippling wall and Korun's abilities come to mind followed by being certain Darith meant only to kill me, but he hasn't, at least not yet. Now seeing that some Mahk aren't what they seemed to be has me analyzing everything. I'm really starting to question my perception of the world.

Then Sir Riddles creeps back into my thoughts with his rhymes:

> *There are so many things,*
> *we can't explain.*
> *Yet it is so true,*
> *if we open our eyes, they are so very plain.*

I chew on that for a few minutes and then question my sanity for repeating that crazy monster's words in my head.

My mind won't let me find solace until Blue enters my thoughts. Her innocence and sweet demeanor are so unique in this world of saturated killing...or so it seemed.

She's my friend. Being without her is like being lost in a desert. Letting us get separated was a huge mistake. It's not too late to abandon this group to go find her, but to what end? This group may be the only way to survive the labyrinth attacks. Without Rase to get us through the wall, Blue and I would wind up stuck in this death trap with no hope anyway.

A few days ago, it was me and Blue. Now I'm surrounded by a guard, Mahk, and the man in white. Sometimes, it's like this is all a dream. How did everything get out of control so quickly?

Bodies surround me as we move forward. Speech tries to infiltrate my ears, but the words are easy to ignore. Even the peeking sun rays that had cheered my soul are now gone, leaving behind only dark walls and deadly blades. The world is a haze, seeming to laugh at my troubles.

Suddenly, Sikla grumbles ferociously, louder than ever before. Her growls are followed by what sounds like thunder claps. The ground shakes again like it did before the blades and swords sprang up.

Everyone knows something terrible is about to happen, but it's anyone's guess what to expect. We run at full speed to the closest boulders and trees. We're all able to fit on the boulders nearest to us, but for some reason, Soll chooses to climb a tree. In the blink of an eye, he's several branches up.

Fearfully, we all stare out at the labyrinth floor, waiting for disaster to strike. Sounds resembling that of a tormented prisoner yell out from Sikla, interspersed with threatening hisses.

Yet only sounds come for us. No blades or swords emerge. Everything is the same. We wait for ten, twenty, then thirty minutes.

"All right, we're very close to the den," Soll finally yells to us "It seems to be safe to move forward."

As the words leave his mouth, we see something in the distance coming toward us.

Advancing fiercely, orange goopy substance approaches, covering every bit of the ground and working its way around the sharp blades. Like a cloak of boiling death, it threatens to wrap around us.

"Lava!" Keelie's hand rushes up to muffle the shriek that bursts out of her mouth.

She's right. The red hot lava flows toward us at a steady pace. The force and height of the surge is alarming. Instinctively, we all start to run in the opposite direction. Charging our fastest, we make our way farther from the den. As we feared, Sikla's screams were a warning of danger.

My mind tries to plan out a wise escape; however concentration is difficult amidst Keelie's screams. Climbing the walls the rest of the way to the den could work, but that's risky. I've tried climbing them before, only to discover how brittle and unsteady the material is.

So focused on my own survival, I only notice now that the rest of our companions have fallen behind.

Korun is at the back of the group, helping those who trip and refusing to leave anyone. I'm not surprised to see Keelie is the closest on my heels. Her lightning speed comes as no shock. Rifan is near to Keelie, but Soll, Saige, Olum, and Laon are pretty far behind. Every second the lava gains on us.

"We aren't going to outrun this!" Korun exclaims.

"Just keep going," I respond, "It has to end at some point."

"Some point might be too late," Soll interjects, "I have an idea."

What could he possibly be thinking? This situation seems insurmountable. Still, my pace slows, my ears eager to hear a reasonable solution. Despite Rase's efforts to push forward alone, we lessen our pace to wait for the group.

"This may seem to be a long shot but try to trust me. Everyone start climbing the closest and tallest boulders you find."

My fingers tap at my side.

"If you're planning to sit out the lava until the flow is done, we could starve to death," Korun says. Sweat pours down his brown face. It's gratifying to finally see him break a sweat. "For that matter, these boulders might not be tall enough to keep us above the lava."

He took the words right out of my mouth. Making a run back to the Blood Caves seems smarter than waiting out the lava. We have no idea how long it might last, or how deep it could get. Personally, I'd rather run back to the Rotting Pass and climb the trees.

"We have backtracked a little, but we still aren't far from the den. All right? Trust me," Soll insists, "I can get us to the den. Run for those boulders near that tree. Now!"

Soll, Korun, Saige, Keelie, and Olum have already started climbing some boulders next to a tall twisted tree. Just as their feet vacate the labyrinth floor, lava rushes over to erase their footprints.

Time for debate has diminished. Soll's right. There's no chance to outrun the lethal scorching liquid on our heels. Rase fights, making me drag her toward the nearest boulders. She insists we should run the other way. We're starting to make our way up when Soll yells at us again, reiterating to run for the boulders near the tree, even though they're across the passage from him. He gestures frantically, signaling us to hurry.

"Are you crazy?" I protest.

"More like too smart for other people to get. Do it… quickly before the lava reaches you," he insists.

"Ugh, his pride is nauseating" Rase comments.

Rifan and Laon have already climbed the boulders Soll directs me toward.

Twinges of pain race through me at the mere thought the lava might get the best of me. "Come on," I yell at Rase, jerking her rope.

We sprint back in the direction of the lava and regret builds within me with every step. Keelie's making noise again, like usual. She's trying to cheer us on, but she lets out the occasional fearful scream.

Within minutes, Rase and I manage to join Rifan and Laon atop the fifteen-foot stack of boulders.

"And why exactly was it so important to run for these boulders, instead of those?" Rase demands, as she points to the other boulders.

"You almost got us both killed." She yanks her maroon guard jacket off to utilize as a fan.

Soll doesn't even glance at Rase but looks instead at me. His actions are certainly reasonable. I'm not Rase's biggest fan either. "You should be able to reach that tree," he says to Rifan, Laon, and me.

There's a tree over to our left, but what's it got to do with anything? This might have been a big mistake.

"For Grol's sake, we're all going to die!" Rase exclaims. "You Mahk are such useless excuses for human existence." She rolls her eyes before she plops down on her side as if she plans to take a nap in the middle of the crisis.

"Why do we need the tree?" I inquire as calmly as I can manage.

"We grab the branches and vault boulder to boulder. We have got to move fast, but we can still make it to the den."

"Without you, we'd all be dead." Saige smiles at Soll. I'm a little peeved to pick up on her flirtatious tone in the middle of our peril.

He nods with gratitude at the compliment. "We need to move quickly. After we get our poles ready, we need to vault off of the shorter boulders scattered between the tall stacks. If we don't move quickly enough to utilize those small boulders, I'm not sure how long our wooden poles will last in this lava."

It's irrational not to admit that Saige is right, despite my irritation with her. Soll is brilliant and the only one of us smart enough to think of an escape out of this mess. A small twinge of jealousy hits me. He's had the opportunity to earn respect from the colony. He wasn't left alone in this forsaken place. Saige, Keelie, Rifan... all of them care about him. Again, I feel deprived of something non-existent in my life: companionship.

Guilt beats heavily in my chest. That's not true. I've had Blue. She's shown me unconditional love.

"Help them!" Rase demands, snapping me out of my wandering thoughts. She looks over to Rifan and Laon who are strategizing. They need to reach the tall tree.

She has some nerve, but there's no time to deal with her right now. There wouldn't be anywhere she could run to and she doesn't have a weapon, so I tuck her ropes into her belt. Rifan and Laon are trying to reach the nearby tree. It isn't quite close enough.

"Someone is going to have to jump," my wavering voice responds. Every breath brings tighter restriction of my throat.

They nod, unable to provide a better solution.

"I could try, but my dagger isn't going to cut through those limbs so I'll need to use something else." I look for a different weapon.

"No, you stay here," Rifan insists as the large-boned man pulls a small axe from a satchel across his back. "This should do the trick." Judging by his hairline, I'd say he's likely older than the rest of the group, perhaps in his thirties. He tucks the tool back in the bag before working his way to the farthest end of the boulder. Laon, Rase, and I clear a path. Rifan runs past us before launching his weight through the air toward the tree.

"Okay," I call after him quietly.

Only fragments of what's happening are visible through smoke and ash. He grabs onto the tree a bit lower than he intended to, causing him to let out a grunt. After he gets settled in the tree, he immediately lifts his axe to hack at the bark ferociously. Pressure clearly increases his strength and he works at a fairly impressive speed. The rest of us wait helplessly, hoping for the best. My dagger isn't going to be useful for chopping wood. Laon only carries double daggers and a club, so he can't offer assistance either.

Across the lava, Soll uses a sword on his own branches. Korun helps as well. His axe is turning out to be extremely useful.

Smoke thickens in the air as the men work. The lava taunts us. It remains about a foot deep for a while, but at any moment another surge could come through, deepening the deadly substance.

"If we don't get to the den fast enough, the smoke might kill us before the lava does," I say calmly.

They're working quickly but probably not fast enough. A strip of cloth from my Nabal bag now covers my nose and mouth. I tear off a couple more strips, tossing them to my companions. Across the lava, Korun tears more fabric from his white clothing. Then they follow our actions. It seems to help a little. My throat no longer feels as tight. Deep breathing offers little relief. The threat of death looms just feet away. Finally, we each receive our branches. About half an hour after the lava first covered the ground, we're finally all equipped for Soll's plan.

"Only a couple hops over some lava and we're home," Rifan states sarcastically.

"Right, that's all," I respond.

Chapter 15
Boulder to Boulder

Another surge of lava rushes toward us, doubling the height of the original flow. There's no time to waste. Every minute brings us closer to our potential demise in Sikla's boiling outpour.

Soll takes the lead, insisting he be the person to test his own plan. "Here goes."

The group watches breathlessly as the tall muscular pale man runs across the boulder, positions his branch against the large rock below, and vaults toward his destination. Fingers tapping again, my own tick annoys me. My mind tells them to stop. Korun has allowed Keelie to tightly grasp his arm as Soll flies into the air. Large body thudding onto the rough rock surface, he makes it across the steamy orange liquid.

"All right, come on." He turns, motioning his hand for us to follow.

Laon is the first to vault off of our boulder safely. Meanwhile, across the way, Keelie's next to vault after Soll. Her small body struggles to maneuver the branch in her arms. Determined, she runs across the boulder as quickly as she can before extending the pole to the rock between her and her destination.

Keelie attempts to launch her little body off the boulder but lacks the strength to get all the way through the air. Violently, she falls back to the huge rock from which she came. I flinch as she crashes to the boulder. She lies still for a minute. Saige squats by her side.

From my vantage point, it's difficult to make out her condition. She appears to have gotten the breath knocked out of her and takes a moment to recover. Then she stands to her feet, lifting the branch as she argues with Saige.

"I can do it, you know," Keelie insists, her hands on her hips.

"You can do it," Saige encourages, "I'm just going to help you launch." Something about Saige's gentle voice is familiar to me. The interaction between them also strikes me as particularly unique.

"I think I can do it alone," Keelie pleads.

"Make a deal with me?"

Keelie cocks her head, as if waiting for details.

"You try one more time and then hear me out?"

"Right, but you'll see I can do it," Keelie compromises.

Her small body runs across the boulder once again. This time, she extends the branch to the small rock but abruptly stops before taking off. It is hard to tell from my angle, but it looks like her eyes are watering.

"Okay," she chokes out. "I'm slowing us down. Please help me, Saige."

Saige smiles at her kindly. "Okay, run as fast as you can and make certain you get that branch in a sound position. I'll make sure you get through the air."

Korun stands near Saige, looking as if he might dive into the lava if necessary to save Keelie in the event of an accident.

Keelie nods, walking for the third time to the other end of the boulder. "I'm ready," she announces nervously. She darts across the boulder with her branch in hand.

As she positions her pole preparing to launch, Saige sweeps beneath her with remarkable speed and utilizes her entire body to help launch the small girl into the air.

Keelie flies across the lava with a shriek, landing safely in Soll's arms on the other side.

A sigh of relief slips from my mouth.

"You seemed distracted, so we went ahead and got Laon and Rase to the other side," Rifan demands my attention. "You're next." He clears the path for me to run.

"Oh, you can go," I offer.

"No, I think it would be better if you go ahead. I'll hang behind the group."

There really isn't time to argue. "If you insist."

The opposite side of the boulder would be the best place to start. A deep breath sucks heat into my throat. My eyes can't help but survey the tall swords and blades scattered across the ground and, of course, the lethal lava that fills the gaps. I stab my branch at the boulder beneath me a couple times testing its strength. It feels solid. As I turn the pole in my hands, my fingers identify a good place to secure a grip. The bark isn't pleasant against the skin on my palm. Given the choice though, rough bark on the skin seems better than lava consuming me.

One more time, I glance across the lava to assess the progress of the other group. Everyone but Olum has made it across. In fact, he also appears to be preparing for his leap.

Wasting time won't get me to my destination. It's time to focus. This is it. My eyes firmly fix on the other boulder. Hastily, my legs propel me forward. Nearing the edge of the giant rock, I glance down long enough to position my pole before setting my sights back to my intended landing spot. My weight leaves the boulder and I glide through the smoke-filled air. My mind is aware this activity is purely to escape death, but the freedom of the air rushing through my hair creates momentary enjoyment.

A sudden scream startles me, bringing my heart to a stop. My eyes dart to survey the area around myself fearfully. My feet land securely on the boulder, but Keelie's screams continue. Olum is the recipient of her frightened stare. He leaped about the same time as me, but it looks like his branch was not as solid as mine. I can only conclude that his branch snapped. His body is impaled through the stomach with a sword from the ground.

He must have just fallen because he still attempts to move for another moment. Despite the lava engulfing his lower legs, he tries once to push himself up off the sword. Failure wins over his efforts as his arms fall limp.

Keelie's screaming comes to an abrupt end. She buries her face in Soll's chest. Despite how many times I've watched Mahk die, somehow this moment strikes me differently. We spoke only one time, but that's more interaction than the other Mahk I've seen die. Something touches me too about the response of the group. As an awkward spectator, I watch them all bow their heads quietly then grasp their hands to their foreheads.

"We will remember," they say quietly in unison.

Their united expression of sadness captures my attention and stirs my heart. Pressure builds in my chest and time seems to stop. It's like the world paused when his life drained away.

It's hard to rush them, but we're flirting with our own deaths. The lava is going to get higher and we need to get moving.

Thankfully, Rase interrupts them. She waits until Keelie happens to make eye contact with her before she offers words from across the expanse of lava, "May his spirit be at peace, but he would want all of you to keep going."

I'm surprised she doesn't come across harsh, judgmental, or even happy.

"We really do need to keep moving." She looks to the ground as the last word leaves her mouth.

She can't possibly care, but sometimes, she's convincing at pretending she does.

"She's right." My hand sweeps a strand of curly red hair from my face. "I'm sorry for your loss, but we don't have much time."

Soll nods, regains his composure, and continues onto the next boulder. Laon and Rase make it to our next boulder pretty quickly.

Korun has now placed himself at the back of the group, demanding he be the last to vault. He carries himself with a slight hunch now and a saddened expression across his face. Korun doesn't really know any of them, but it seems like Olum's death hit him almost as hard as it hit the others. Again, he reminds me of Blue. His compassion for strangers when he himself is far from home and seeking answers in his own life is surprising.

We all continue on, trying to pretend we're immortal. Time soars by as we fly from boulder to boulder. For the next hour, survival is the prize as both groups vault forward. Two more surges of lava have come through in that time so the surface now stands about four feet off the ground. The swords and blades have disappeared under the orange liquid substance. Short rocks which have enabled us to leap to the larger boulders are dangerously close to being covered up.

"How close are we getting to the den?" I finally yell across to Soll.

"We're almost there, Araina. It's going to be all right," he insists.

Keelie backs him up. "Right, we can get there, I know we can. It's around that next turn."

Hopeless dread flies away with my sigh. At the rate the lava has been coming through, we should reach that turn before another surge. The smoke that has been thickening in the air is an equal threat, but if we move fast enough we could survive.

"Okay, let's power through this last bit." I smile at Keelie. Her little squeaky voice and crying can be very obnoxious, but her determination is admirable. "Wait, which side is the den on?" I blurt out.

Everyone pauses for a moment to take in the question. No one considered how the adjacent group was going to cross the lava river to join the other group.

Soll's face turns even paler than its natural shade. Despair barks viciously at my spirit. Realistically, I'm not the kind to give up easily though. If I'm going to end up in the lava, it won't be without a good effort to avoid it.

Then Keelie's expression lights up. "Keep moving. There's something at the den to get you across."

She then stretches upward, signaling Soll to stoop over as she whispers something in his ear.

"Fate be, you're right!" he exclaims. Soll turns to Korun with a stern look. "I'm going to have to move ahead of the group. I can get your friend across, if you can get my friends to the den safely."

"Please hurry." Korun nods.

Soll takes off, moving with impressive speed from boulder to boulder as the two groups continue at the same pace as before. We have only moved forward two boulders and Soll has already disappeared around the corner.

The rest of us keep pressing forward, jumping from one large boulder to the next. My arms are becoming incredibly tired. It's amazing Keelie is still going. She looks even weaker than me.

We make it to the turn in the labyrinth passages, but there's still no sight of Soll.

"He should be almost ready," Keelie comments. "He'll need our help. We'll be back as quickly as we can."

Keelie, Korun, and Saige work their way across three more boulders before coming to a towering mountain slope. I've seen that part of the mountain many times before. We've come back around to a different side of the same mountains the Blood Caves are in. I've seen this mountain area several times and never spotted a cave. Where is the den?

It's hard to make out anything they say, but Keelie, Korun, and Saige are discussing something. Keelie points toward the mid-section of the mountain. Then Saige and Korun help boost her to a small rock shelf. Keelie hikes up the mountain a few feet. A dust trail rises behind her as she moves. Every few feet, she kicks a rock loose that tumbles downward.

Still, there's no visible door or opening in the jagged mountain. She decreases her pace and shimmies out of view, disappearing into the slate-colored rocks. She vanishes into what I assume is a small entrance. Korun, who had lifted himself up on the shelf behind her, follows. Clearly there's some small tunnel entrance to their den on the mountain. The entry is completely out of view. It now makes sense that they've been able to sneak in and out unseen by outsiders.

Saige waits on the boulder at the base of the mountain, her icy blue eyes fixed on the den entrance. She's a pretty woman and appears to have been created only a couple years more aged than me. Like the rest of us, she scratches at her bone-dry skin, which is a couple shades darker than Rase's but not the same color as Korun's. As she scoops a couple of loose black hairs back into the tight bun on her head, her compliment to Soll surfaces in my memory. It seems ludicrous for any Mahk to hope for affection from another, but as a woman, I sense that's what she desires from Soll. I've seen that kind of attraction between Creators before, but never imagined Mahk would act like that. In a world of kill or be killed, how could a relationship involving that much trust exist? Those dreaming of passion are likelier to find themselves dead in the arms of affection than happy in love.

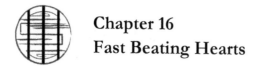

Chapter 16
Fast Beating Hearts

Lava continues to flow. Hopelessness continues to grow. The air is getting so thin it's hard to take in deep breaths. As I monitor the entrance of the cave, my eyes burn from the intense smoke. Time drags on, leading me to thoughts about my two years of life, and how different they could have been had I known about and joined the colony. Aside from Blue, would there be friends in my life? *Would my heart be in Saige's shoes, falling for some Mahk man?* Or maybe the colony would have granted me some respectable role. It all sounds so picturesque yet so unreal. It would be an illusion. The relationships and the security could never last in this labyrinth. The Creators would have eventually caught on.

Aside from the risk of losing all that, I imagine having lived without Blue all that time. She sparked a change in my heart that I'm not sure anything or anyone else could have brought on. The gentleness she radiates softened me, yet her dependence on me taught me responsibility. Without her, I don't know who I'd be, but I don't think Soll would be calling me "exceptional."

The minutes drag on and still they've not emerged from the mountain.

"A trap in the den?" Rifan whispers.

The question was rhetorical. How would I know? But I have to admit, I've had the same thought. I prepare for the worst. Anticipation lingers that this boulder may become my grave. My chances of a potential future diminishing rapidly, I'm suddenly saddened never to have discovered Korun's origin or learned more about his abilities.

As I think about his healing hands and the strange dream about him before our encounter with the Nabal, Korun emerges from the small entrance of the cave. He maneuvers backward carrying something. The entrance is so tight he has to set down the object in his hands and wiggle out before grabbing it again.

Finally he starts making his way a couple feet down the mountain. The unknown item is still emerging from the entrance behind him. After a couple seconds, I identify it as a ladder. Soll eventually comes out of the cave holding the other end, but Keelie doesn't follow them. The ladder looks fairly lengthy. Valiant as their efforts have been, it doesn't look long enough to save us.

Korun losses his footing as they inch their way down. Falling to his knees, he jerks the ladder from Soll's hands. For a moment, it looks like Korun and the ladder might fall into the lava. Small rocks tumble down the incline as his feet swing around to steady his weight. Defiant to the setback, he regains his composure. With one hand grabbing at nearby rocks to balance his body and the other holding onto the ladder, he's barely able to swing it in the direction of the boulder before he loses his grip. The ladder slides down the slope a few feet. Saige catches it. She props it up on the mountainside as the two men work their way down to join her.

They talk for a couple minutes, pointing at the lava then at us. Soll vaults twice, landing on the boulder directly across from us, about thirty feet away. Korun vaults only once, placing him on the boulder between Soll and Saige. It takes the men a few minutes to maneuver the ladder.

The men lift the ladder in our direction, across the deep lava. Their arms strain as they attempt not to let it touch the orange substance. On our end, Laon and Rifan work together to extend a branch, which they're able to hook into the ladder, alleviating the weight for Soll and Korun. Finally, they pull the ladder toward us, and it forms a bridge between our boulders.

My heart beats fast as Rifan insists he be the one to cross first and ensure its stability. I'm tired of everyone else putting themselves on the line, leaving me to sit around and watch.

"No, let me do this," I insist. I push past him.

Korun yells at me from across the lava, "Let him go first, Araina."

Despite his request, my hands grip the sides of the ladder. It feels pretty sturdy. The colony probably built it using wood from the twisted trees throughout the labyrinth. Crawling across this thing seems like the smartest approach for me. Not only is it easier to maintain balance, but the weight distribution is less likely to strain the wood. Minimizing the chances of it breaking is worth crossing it a little slower.

With every inch forward, the steam's intense heat engulfs me. Telling myself not to look at the threatening lava below, I focus on the ladder. It feels like every inch consumes minutes of time, but surely my progress is quicker than that. Sweat has become thick on my palms. It's becoming difficult to grip the wood. Of course, my boots are no help in this situation either. It's hard to say if I'm getting close and my eyes won't leave my path to see how far to my destination. No matter what, I certainly don't try to look behind me. Progressing slowly, putting weight on the rims of the ladder, I finally see stone in my grasp. As my hand is about to descend on it, my focus wavers, causing me to wobble. Yanking me up effortlessly, Korun pulls me into him, his hand stroking my back.

My heart is beating so fast I can hear it in my ears. He's holding me in his arms. Like the rhythm of drums, his heart beats at the same pace as mine. "You okay?" he asks with concern.

Suddenly aware that my jaw is hanging open, I jerk away from him "Good. I'm fine." My fingers straighten out my scrunched shirt. "Thank you." *Thank you?* This man continuously saves my life and treats everyone in a way I've never seen before. Yet, "thank you" is all he gets. I'm pathetic company.

He nods then lifts a branch at me. Mine is still on the boulder I came from across the ladder. "I want you to go ahead and get to the cave." He hands me the pole.

"What about all of you?" I ask. "I want to try and help."

He smiles warmly at me. "You're so tired and weak from lack of food. And I can tell you are having serious trouble breathing." His light brown eyes seem to stare right into my core. Then he points to the others. "And there really isn't much you can do, so use this and go on. We'll be right behind you."

I take the branch in my hand and prepare to vault. The small boulders are partially covered now, but a portion of the surface is usable. As quickly as is manageable, I work my way to the boulder where Saige is waiting.

Rase has just made it across the ladder and Korun has handed her the other branch. She prepares to vault toward us as Rifan is crossing the ladder.

Weak and exhausted, my body props against the slope, waiting for the others to join us. Rase reaches our boulder long before Rifan makes it across the ladder. Crossing the ladder is no short process. He reaches Korun and Soll, so finally, Laon starts his journey across the ladder. Rifan waits with Korun and Soll on the boulder. Now that Rase and I have taken the vaulting poles, the rest of them will have to use the ladder to get here.

After Laon reaches the boulder, once again, Korun and Soll work together to lift the heavy ladder and this time Laon and Rifan also assist. They bring the ladder in and extend it toward the middle boulder. They need to move faster. The lava has gotten so high that the shorter boulders are now completely covered.

Nervous tapping overtakes my fingers. I hate waiting helplessly. For a moment, I become concerned about Keelie, wondering where she is, until it occurs to me she already made it to the den. Evidently exhaustion truly has its grip on me. My eyelids feel so heavy. I'm vaguely aware of what's happening around me, but I'm partially losing consciousness for moments of time.

It takes only a second and the men have all made it to the middle boulder. Rifan has already joined Rase, Saige, and I on our boulder. Saige is yanking my arm. "Keep breathing, Araina, we're almost inside. Come on."

Everything is so blurry from the smoke. It's ten times harder to breathe.

"Okay." The single word chokes from my mouth.

She isn't in much better shape than me, but she assists me to my feet. Rifan helps boost me up to the rock shelf and Saige next. Rase is holding up in the smoke better than the rest of us but offers no help. Time won't allow for dealing with her attitude. I put all my attention on forcing my body to make each necessary move. As Saige and I near the entrance to the cave, I glance back to survey the others.

I must be moving pretty lethargically, because now everyone but Korun has made it to the final boulder. Though Saige tries to get me to enter the cave, my gaze won't disengage from the others. She enters, but I wait to make sure everyone is okay. Korun finishes crossing and they help each other onto the rock shelf. Lava is now covering a good portion of the large boulders, but everyone makes it onto the rock shelf quickly. At last, we can enter the den.

Without an ounce of grace, I wiggle into the entrance then let myself slide through the twenty-foot tunnel into the cave.

My landing hurts a little, but I'm so weak and tired I barely notice. My body moves only a few feet from the den entrance. Fresh air soothes my throat and lungs. It's dark in the cave, but no one has screamed or indicated any trouble, so it seems we're safe. I'm too tired to care if we're not. Every muscle aches, my lungs burn. Rest is what I need, what we all need. As a yawn escapes me, my head nuzzles on top of my bag and I greet sleep happily.

135

Chapter 17
Fresh Air

In my dream world, sparkling water cascades down layered shelves of ground. It's so cool and fresh to the touch. No labyrinth walls confine me and a pale blue sky stretches as far as the eye can see. Breeze flows through my hair. Gentle sounds of nature whisper peace into my soul. Blue is there with me, enjoying the beauty as if she had never known the darkness of the labyrinth. All of it feels so real and then it all goes away.

A couple times, my mind tries to escape the suspension of consciousness. My eyes bat open, but my body refuses. Reality drifts off again.

It's hard to say how much time has passed when slumber finally relinquishes its hold on me. My waking thought is a pleasant one as I wonder if a place like the one in my dreams exists on the other side of the wall.

I'm no longer close to the entrance of the den. It appears someone moved me to a fairly comfortable, soft bed. For a moment, I become disoriented and wonder if I'm still in the den at all.

Confused, I sit up fearfully and reach for my dagger in my hair. Keelie is only a few feet away from me, sitting on another bed. Our beds aren't really beds at all though. Beneath us are piles of clothing.

The den itself is fairly large, which makes sense given that the colony at its max included about two hundred people. Keelie and I are sitting on a natural rock shelf lining the circular cave. Our shelf isn't the only one. There are actually several at different heights. Two dozen ladders like the one we used to cross the lava stand against walls, used to get up to the shelves. Some of the ladders are much taller than the one we used. Some probably stand about sixty feet. Only a couple ladders go all the way to the top.

Blue and purple stalactites hang across the roof of the place. Some protrude straight down in long cone shapes, while others form unique swirls. Sparkles glisten from the moisture on their surface.

Given the limited resources accessible to the Mahk, it's hard to believe the elaborate decor of the den. Circles of carved wooden and stone shapes are mounted above the rock shelves. The carvings mimic everything from stars to human forms. The shapes of the swirling stalactites fill the gaps between the carved images.

The most striking part of it all is the fire feature in the middle of the floor. Staggered layers of circular stone form the structure stacked one on the other. Fire burns in every other layer while metallic flower statues reside in the others. It resembles a fountain in shape. Around it sits Saige, Soll, and Korun. Laon and Rifan are probably sleeping somewhere on the shelves. Rase isn't on the shelves. Where is she? Scrats! After reaching the cave, who knows where she ended up.

Wait. There she is, tied up near the back of the cavern.

Having been so focused on the details of the cave, it just now occurs to me that there aren't any other people here besides our group. My gaze drifts back to Keelie. This time, her mood captures my attention. Knots intensify in my stomach. Something is terribly wrong. She's been crying, so I work my way over and sit down beside her. It isn't easy not to ask a million questions, but that doesn't seem like the right thing to do in the moment. I'm not good with social interaction. It's time to wait.

A few more quiet minutes pass. Then tears burst from her eyes. She practically falls into me. My arms wrap around her tensely. I still haven't said a word to the girl, but I have no idea what words to use.

After many tears and a few deep breaths, she starts talking to me. Pointing around the cave, she talks about how the colony should have been here when we arrived.

"Where would they have gone without us?" she tearfully questions. "They didn't abandon us. Simul must have found them!"

"I know, Keelie. I know."

My hand moves up and down her back occasionally, trying to offer some comfort. I'm amazed by her confidence in the colony. She's so positive they wouldn't have abandoned the den. I don't know how she can trust them so effortlessly.

"It must have been the Creators, you know?" she reiterates. "They did something to them. I don't know how they could have found the den though. It's so well hidden. Only colony members know about it."

"That's for sure," I confirm. "Even climbing up the mountain, it wasn't visible until reaching the entrance."

"Right... exactly. Something is very wrong! Where are they?"

"You're right. The Creators must have done something." I pat her back again "I'm sorry they aren't here, Keelie, I really am."

This is what comes from trusting other people: they abandon you. My finger strokes a random blonde hair out of her face. The colony abandoned Soll and his group, just like Darith abandoned me. In our world, it's unfathomable that Keelie hasn't been exposed to more darkness, or maybe she has and doesn't realize. I see no point in mouthing my opinion to the girl in tears, but I wish she understood the world like I do.

Words seem to be frightened away as we sit together. She's given up on wiping away the wet liquid from her eyes. A few more minutes pass. Her skinny fingers untangle her long blonde hair.

"You should try to get some rest," I suggest.

After the last remnants of salty water dry from her eyes, she refuses to attempt sleep. Splotchy cheeked and congested, she grabs my hand. "Thank you for listening, Araina, it means a lot."

"Oh. Sure, it's no problem." Despite how immune I've become to the suffering of others in my life, seeing her devastation wells up a knot in my throat. For her sake, I hope her faith in the Mahk isn't misplaced. On one hand, it would be good if she is right, because that may mean the colony does have a sense of love and takes care of its own. In contrast though, if the Creators do have them, they're likely dead.

"I feel a little better. Can I have a few more minutes by myself?"

"Of course."

As I exit the shelf, my heart hurts for Keelie, but it's also warmed after comforting her. I haven't felt this rested in a long time. Sleep must have kept me for quite a while. Making my way down the ladder isn't the daunting task it would have been when I first entered the den. The astounding stone and wooden carvings along the walls again hold my fascination.

I cross half the room to join the group by the fire. After our encounter with the lava, the cool air in the cave is refreshing. Deeper and smoother breaths flow through me here in this place than anywhere else in the labyrinth. Regardless of the burning fire, there's enough of a chill that some goosebumps raise on my neck. The fire feature lights the cave surprisingly effectively. Then I notice small fire pits lit along the edge of the room.

My closer perspective of the strange lit fountain structure makes it even more intriguing to me. The sheer number of metallic flowers is overwhelming. It's curious that the colony came to possess enough metal they felt some could be spared for such a decorative display. Various round rocks, small boulders, and long benches are placed around the large fire for seating. Despite being distracted by the details of my surroundings, hunger forces itself on me. My stomach feels swollen, but somehow empty, as I plop down on a boulder near Korun. By the time I sit, Soll has left the pit and disappeared toward the back of the cave.

"Where'd he go?" I inquire.

"He thought you might be hungry." Korun shoots me a cheerful glance.

"You look like you're feeling better." Saige pokes at the stone base of the fire fountain with her long spear.

"I am. It feels like I could have been sleeping for years. How long was I out?"

"Almost twelve hours," Korun answers.

In this place, that's more than a fair amount of rest to hope for. Usually naps only last a few hours before disruption.

"Thanks for the soft bed," I offer to Saige.

"Not a problem." She smiles, but like Keelie, sadness resonates from her. A twinge of melancholy dances on Saige's face. She's the most mysterious of the group. Sensing the unknown in her is what I'm used to among the Mahk. That quality makes her the most relatable. She's probably consumed with the same worries as the rest of us, but it seems other issues are tugging at her.

"They aren't here," she answers my body language.

Faint traces of sweat reside on her forehead as she reiterates her point. How in the world is she sweating in the cool cave?

She goes on to repeat the same information Keelie already conveyed. Saige points out personal possessions the colony left behind. "Why would they have gone without any extra supplies, or their personal items? They didn't leave us. Simul must have done something to them."

"Right, killed them all." That may have been in my mind, but I didn't intend for it to come out so bluntly. Soll is approaching to offer me food as the words finish falling out of my mouth.

Her face looks like stone as her eyebrows tighten. Korun looks at me shamefully.

"I'm sorry. I just hope you're wrong. I think we know their fate in Simul's hands would not be promising. There could be some answer we haven't thought of yet. They could have found a safer place," I say, trying to redeem myself.

"It seems to be best if we don't dwell on that subject," Soll announces as he passes me some crackers. Despite his efforts to push the conversation along, he's clearly disheartened by the situation.

My eyes must be huge when he hands me an entire baked potato.

"We have stores in the back. You can eat it all and more." He smiles at me.

The cooked potato is warm in my hands, soothing my spirit. Every flavor awakens in my mouth and my stomach growls. They've managed to season it somehow. It's so good.

Reacting to the enthusiasm in my expression as my mouth absorbs the flavor, Saige mentions the colony has been experimenting with extracting and cooking leaves from Thorn Patches Valley.

"More like mastering not experimenting," I compliment. "Surprising to hear of anything good coming from the valley."

Soll hands me some water. "Now there isn't much of this to go around, so this is all I can offer you for now," he cautions.

It's a full flask. I drink it like an animal, appreciative of its healing touch on my scorched throat. The conversation goes on in a new direction, but I'm too preoccupied with my meal to join in.

"All right, the point is," Soll speaks, "they aren't here. That's the fact of the situation and we need to decide what's next with this change of events."

Everyone is quiet for a second.

"I may be speaking out of line," Korun says, "but we still need to get to the other side of the wall near the castle." He glances over toward Rase. "That plan hinges on her being able to get us to the other side, but we don't have much of an option."

"You're right," Soll agrees. "This labyrinth is determined to destroy anything within its walls. Our best chance is to head for that wall and hope we can get through it."

I've managed to inhale the entire potato in a few minutes. Now I'm ready to chime in. "What about the lava?"

"That's right," Korun responds. "You've been in dream land. We've been keeping an eye outside. The surges let up about five hours ago. We think it's done, at least for a while." The smoky air has transformed his garb from white to an ashen color. The man is such a conundrum. His abilities and origin make him so mysterious, yet his friendly and caring demeanor make his personality so transparent.

"For a while?" I question skeptically.

"Hopefully for good," Saige jumps in, "but either way, it's not like we can hang around here. If Simul did find the den, the guards are likely to sweep back through to check for survivors."

"I didn't say we shouldn't keep moving. Trust me, I want to get back to that wall as much or more than the rest of you," I say.

"Good. You're going to want to visit our back room first though." Soll motions for me to follow his lead.

Soll, Korun, and I walk farther back into the cave. Just as I'm observing the layer of boulders lining the edge of the circular cave, we stop in front of one that's been moved slightly out of place, revealing a small tunnel.

"It's a bit long," Soll warns. "We found crawling all the way through to be a waste of time." He maneuvers onto a long canoe-shaped wooden object with wheels. Korun and I join him. He pulls at a rope and hands us each a portion to tug on. We pull our way through the long tunnel until it finally opens to a small room.

I'm so impressed by the collection a sigh seeps from my lips.

"In a colony, we all help each other out." Soll points a finger around the room. "And when our members pass on, they always leave their supplies to us." He continues speaking, but I'm busy being overwhelmed so I briefly tune him out.

Weapons rest along one wall. Swords, daggers, axes, spears, and even crossbows hang from hooks and are lined neatly across a couple tables. Unable to resist the urge, my pale fingers explore several of them curiously. Shields fill another table. Shields are something the Creators don't even supply the Mahk.

143

"These were all handmade by the colony?" I inquire.

"Every last one," Soll replies proudly.

Piles of rope are at the end of one table. Beyond that rest a couple crates of clothing. In another corner is a tall stack of fire wood.

On the other side of the space are shelves of food. Even some bread sits on a tall shelf next to a collection of cheese.

"For special occasions," Soll says when he sees my gaze wander up to that shelf. "Although I guess we aren't going to be around here much longer, so take all you want." He smiles at me.

Near the shelves of food stand two barrels of water. Even as a group, it amazes me the colony was able to collect so much fresh water.

"All right," Soll interrupts my aimless wandering and observations. "Here's what I want you to see." He points toward a table in the back.

On the table are a couple clean shirts and pairs of pants, along with a few small bags and canisters.

"For you," he offers. "Both of you go ahead. Pick what you like. I tried to pull out some clothing that looked like your size. Fill those bags and canisters up."

It's thrilling to be offered a new, practically unused outfit. The bright color of the pants is a noticeable contrast from my dirty green bottoms. The Creators only allow Mahk a new set of clothes once a year. My favorite thing about unworn clothes is pausing to take in their clean smell. Usually I don't get all that excited about what I'm wearing, but having spent time with Keelie, I'm inspired. She creatively reworked her Mahk outfit. My boring attire could definitely benefit from her artistic touch.

This doesn't compare at all, but it occurs to me that access to so much food and clean clothes is daily life for a Creator. This is the closest experience to their existence I've ever had. Where does one even begin with such a buffet of food or clothing options?

"Take as much of anything as you think you can carry," Soll reminds us. "Don't know when you'll have options like this again."

"Speaking of that topic," I say as I start to load one of my bags. "We still don't have a plan."

"I thought the plan was to head for the wall," Korun responds.

"Yes, but I'm guessing it's going to be heavily guarded."

"That's true," Soll responds.

"And we also need to make sure we can force Rase to cooperate when we get through the guards," I explain further.

"Also true," Soll replies again.

I hoard supplies into one of my bags. "So what's the plan?"

They look at each other blankly then back at me in silence.

"That's what I thought." I pause. "Before we actually head out of this place, I think there needs to be a plan: an intelligent route to the wall, supplies for anything we know we're going to encounter, and a promising way of forcing Rase to get us through the wall. Now you two turn around." I motion with the twirl of my hand, reaching with the other for a clean shirt on the table.

"She always this authoritative?" Soll quietly questions Korun, as if turning away made them inaudible.

I whirl around to face the wall and change my clothes.

"Think that and a couple times worse." Korun chuckles.

"I resent that," I chime in, causing them to jump.

Chapter 18
To the Wall or Nothing

Another half an hour passes. Soll, Korun and I brainstorm in the weapons room. The rest of the group must be wondering what's keeping us, but no one comes looking.

The labyrinth is as engrained in my mind as my own name, so my brain travels the best possible routes to the wall from our current location. "We have really gotten ourselves into a bit of a bind backtracking toward the mountains. Now that Simul initiated the labyrinth attacks, there isn't any way to know what other obstacles may pop up whichever direction we go."

Korun nibbles on cheese.

"However," I continue, "we can make some smart decisions based on the normal labyrinth conditions. A fairly fast way to Blue's spot exists, if we swing around toward the castle in an open space. But we'd be facing a lot of guards through there. It won't be wise to take a route with such high visibility."

Before running into Soll and the group, I was headed down the easiest route. From here, going back that way will add at least a day to our trip. Wasting time could be to our detriment. Given that our other options aren't very practical, the snake pit route may be the best option. It sounds terrible to them at first.

"The snakes are easily avoidable since a bridge leads over them. The snake pit route is fairly quick and offers the most boulders and trees, which will come in handy if there are more lava surges," I explain. "What of the guards that are likely to be posted by the wall?"

"I'm confident that challenge is manageable. With all of the guards focused on killing the Mahk, it might not be that heavily guarded. Even if it is, I've got a good plan. Let's be clear... strategy and wit are my strengths," Soll says.

"You mean aside from your muscles?" I laugh. It was really meant to be a joke but probably came off flirtatious. How embarrassing. "That's all you've got?" I rush past the awkward moment.

He stares at me as if I've just bared his insecurities to the world.

"Think that's enough for me," Korun interjects, breaking the silence.

"Me too," I concede. Who knew the man had so much pride in battle tactics? Forcing details out of him would make me feel better, but he clearly doesn't want to divulge more.

"Okay, that leaves Rase," Korun points out.

"I've had that figured out for days." A smirk hangs on my face. "I enjoyed keeping you on your toes about her."

Both men scowl at me with their arms crossed. Milking the advantage of knowing something others don't gives me gratification.

"Yep, I've been saving something for her," I reiterate. My revealing of the two stolen tubes in my bags is accompanied by a dash of pride. These things are handy. I dangle them at eye level as the liquid within them sloshes.

"What are those?" Soll inquires.

"I'm not really sure what's in them, but it's the liquid the Creators gave you, Korun, so they can't be good. Rase will know what these are and I'm pretty certain she would rather help us get through that wall than have to chug whatever is in these." Carefully, I insert the bottles back into my bag.

"Clever girl," Korun admits.

"All right, that's it," Soll announces. "Let's get moving."

As we pull the rope working our way back down the tunnel toward the main room, I run through a checklist in my mind. All the food that can be carried, two big full canisters of water plus my own smaller one, and, of course, fresh clothing on and in my bag is enough to meet my needs for a while. The same old dagger is still in my hair, but I also have a crossbow on my back. A single shield was so nice that it made a home in one of my totes for now, since it's small and compact.

I've never felt so prepared and yet so scared. There was a time when my existence was predictable. When turning the labyrinth corners, I knew what to expect, but now it's anyone's guess what Simul might have waiting for us. Any horror the mind can conjure could step into my path. Despite my high hopes, there's no guarantee what we might find on the other side of that wall either. Dread sinks down my throat into my core as we near the main room. It's about time to lead the group toward the wall.

Soll circles the large cave, calling a meeting around the fire feature. "By now, everyone should be sufficiently rested. I know most of you have collected all the supplies you plan to take, but check it all over one more time. Take another short nap if you need to, because we're leaving the den for good at dawn."

Seated near Korun and me, Laon picks at the wooden bench beneath him. Saige has an arm around Keelie and an expression that's difficult to read. She clicks her fingernails together. Maybe she wants to abandon the group, but surely her relationships with Soll and Keelie are too important to her. My shoulders shrug away her nervous behavior. We all have our reservations and fears. Her way of showing that is just particularly odd.

"What's the plan anyway?" Rifan inquires. He stands a few feet away from the group and his chiseled face wears disappointment. "What chance does our small group stand against the Creators?"

Soll pauses as a look of frustration crosses his pale face. "If we work together and stick to the plan, we'll be fine. Hopefully we won't even run into many Creators."

"Right, where are we going from here?" Keelie asks innocently.

Soll smiles at her. "We're starting over. Korun and Araina are going to get us to the wall, and Rase is going to get us to the other side. Korun is going to show us where he came from."

As he finishes his words, a look of guilt flashes on Korun's face, like he might confess his lack of knowledge concerning the other side of the wall. Giving Korun an opportunity to rethink our little fib isn't an option, so I move the discussion along. "Everything is going to be better there," I reinforce.

"So we're going to act like there never was a colony?" Rifan huffs.

"It's not like we have much of a choice," Saige interrupts. "We're never going to be free here. I don't know what happened to the colony, but we can't afford to waste time trying to figure it out. In my experience, the Creators get what they want. If they want us dead, then our chance of survival is comparable to that of a rat in a snake pit. What would you have us do?" Her icy blue eyes are set sternly on Rifan.

"I don't know." The color of his cheeks grows red. "But I don't understand why we're putting so much faith in people we don't know and abandoning the colony. They could be in need of our help."

Keelie shakes her head before letting it drop into her hands.

Soll pats her on the back. "Rifan, you don't have to come with us. We aren't going to force you. There just doesn't seem to be a better option. Until we have another lead on the colony, we need to try and get out of here. Simul could have a million other death traps waiting for us and if we survive that, eventually his guards will kill us. We can't sit here."

Rifan tightens his fists then marches off to the weapons room.

"All right," Soll yells after him. "Everyone joining us needs to be ready at dawn."

Soll turns, walks away from the fire, and climbs a ladder to a bed shelf.

Everyone else besides Korun and me disperses from the meeting. We sit awkwardly a couple minutes in silence. Conflict is burning in his eyes. He stands up to walk toward the entrance of the cave then enters the small tunnel.

I'm fast on my feet to follow him, unsure if he's fed up with all of us and leaving. Reaching the entrance, I wiggle part way through it to find him perching near its rim. He sits quietly, staring out at the smoky atmosphere.

"I thought you were leaving us," I finally admit to him.

"Us? Do you actually admit to being associated with a group of people?"

I shake my head. "I might not be completely incapable of social interaction after all. But don't get used to it."

"Humph," he grunts. "I guess you're right. You're extremely capable of interaction." He looks at me. "And manipulation."

"It's for the best," I defend myself. "If they stay here, they're certainly going to die. I may not know for sure where you came from, but I feel positive it has to be better than this place."

"I guess. I'm sorry. Sometimes you're hard to follow. It's difficult to pretend I know things I don't. At the same time, there's nothing I'm completely sure I do know. I don't want to let them all down."

That kind of thinking makes us so different from one another. He thinks first of what's best for the group and I think first of what I want.

"Sometimes, I really wish you and Darith had gotten me out of that prison a few minutes sooner, before they had time to mess with my mind."

Observing my hands in my lap, I'm unsure what to say next.

Out of nowhere, his stomach growls like it did when he healed Rase's arm.

A giggle bubbles from me as if in conversation with his stomach gurgle. After all we have been through, I choose not to fight the sliver of lightness in the air.

"You still hungry? I thought you ate already?" I smile at him.

"Nope." He laughs. "Not even a little. I think that's a nervous reaction I have."

"Nervous?" I purse my lips anxiously.

Sweat begins to collect on my palms as we sit quietly a few seconds.

"Do you remember anything from before we found you?" I ask. "Anything coming back to you?"

"Still nothing." His seated position is odd and his shoulders tense up.

"I'm sorry for what they did to you."

"I wish I knew why. I wish I remembered more than the past couple days." His mouth forms a grin as he chuckles almost inaudibly. "Knowing you makes whatever I lost seem less important though."

My mind starts racing. Are there feelings between us? But a few days ago, aside from Blue, everyone and everything in this world was a threat. I don't know anything about him. He doesn't even know what kind of a person he actually is.

Panic overcomes me as he stares hopefully into my eyes. A million thoughts and questions run through my brain. I want to throw caution to the wind and seek comfort in his attention. What would it be like to be held? To be cared for?

As I fight through the haze of thoughts clouding my judgment, it becomes impossible to ignore the irony. Clearly he thinks I'm manipulative, yet he's acting like he cares about me. And the man doesn't even remember who he is. At any moment, his memories could all come flooding back and who knows what doors might open.

"I've got some business with Rase. Then I might try to get in another nap." My words cut between us as I break away from his gaze. I turn to make my way back inside.

"I'll let everyone know when the sun starts to rise," he calls after me.

Making my way to the back of the cave, I could hit myself. My heart's winning the inner battle as my brain cowers. Wiping the tears from Keelie's face reminded me how unreliable people are, yet

152

emotions keep getting the best of me—emotions that shouldn't exist in the first place. Survival was doable without any of these people for two years. My head stayed on straight navigating life on my own. These developing dependencies are going to end the minute I get through that wall.

The cave darkens farther back. There's Rase, tied to the wall. Her aggravated stare is so normal to me that I'm not even fazed.

"This is how it's going to be." I toss a pair of Mahk clothes snagged from the weapons room at her. "You're going to wear this and you're going to do everything I tell you."

She begins to roll her eyes, per usual.

"If you don't," I continue, "then I'm going to give you a healthy dose of these." I hold up the bottles in front of her.

She tries to hide her concern, but a slight wince crosses her face.

"That's what I thought," I finish with a confident grin.

"Don't look so proud. What happens when I get you through that wall?" she whines.

"You can do what you want when we get to other side."

"Do what I want?" she mimics annoyingly, like I've mimicked her before.

"I need you to get us to the other side of the wall. After that, we're bolting and you're free."

"We're as in Korun?" she guesses.

"That's not your concern," I answer.

She shakes her head. "I thought so."

"I thought so," I echo. "What does that mean?"

"Nothing," she scoffs.

Attempting to pry further explanation yields no results. She isn't worth it. It's best to walk away. Between leading a group to Blue and anticipation of the other side of the wall, Rase is the least of my concerns.

Chapter 19
Walking on Lava

We emerge from the den a few minutes after dawn. Instantly, I miss the cool fresh air in the cave as the smoke welcomes me back. Everyone is loaded with supplies. Surprisingly, it appears that Rifan has decided to join us.

The entire group is refreshed, dressed in clean baggy green pants, patterned sashes around our waists, form-fitted shirts, and sleeveless orange shrugs. The nice knee-high black Creator boots gives my Mahk garb some variation. The others are dressed almost identical except Keelie. Keelie's pants have somehow been adjusted to fit tighter to her legs. She's managed to turn her pale orange shrug into a short bra top. It's layered over flowing material I would venture to guess she swiped from a spare pair of pants. The green portion of the shirt flows loosely. Her white shirt, like the ones the rest of us wear, has been cut down the middle to be worn as a shrug and has some decorative pattern designed into it.

Catching my observations of her detailed clothing, Keelie comments "I find the creativity therapeutic, you know?"

"You're really good at it." I can't even figure how she did most of the designs, but her statement is familiar to me. My rock drawings aren't so different.

Rifan stands tall, with his sword in the holder at his side. His axe is likely still tucked into the tote on his back. Saige carries a spiked mace and two long spears on her back. A heavy club hangs at Laon's side and two daggers are tucked in his belt.

Keelie has strapped a small bow to her back, but I don't know how practiced she is with it. She still has the same whip attached to her sash that she was already carrying. She was sporting a knife before, but it must be tucked out of view now.

Soll appears to have grabbed an additional sword in the weapon room. He now has one strapped to each hip. I've never seen someone fight with two swords, so one is likely for back up. A lasso rope is also coiled on his back.

Korun carries his same axe but also strapped a crossbow to his back. I've still got my dagger and now the crossbow on my back as well.

Lined up on the mountain slope outside the den, we survey the altered scenery. The lava never started up again and has cooled, leaving a textural coal surface.

"That's safe to walk on?" Keelie questions.

"The usual lava trickles that Sikla puts out cool pretty quickly and this lava should be the same, so I'm sure it's fine," I console her.

For added measure, Soll helps me dislodge and chuck a large rock, which lands with a crunch on the cracked coal surface.

"Okay," I signal for the group to follow, "we're going this way." Finally my curiosity concerning every detail of the labyrinth is paying off. The place looks so different though. The layout of the pathways has remained unchanged, but the dark swirled pattern coating the labyrinth floor now covers most of the tall boulders. My mind experiences some disorientation now that I'm walking at least ten feet higher within the walls. My theory about using the boulders to dodge anymore lava is disproven, but thankfully it seems like the lava might be done. Nonetheless, this is the smartest route.

To have people following me creates a strange feeling. Typically, if someone is tracing my footsteps, my response is to elude them. Guiding a collection of people isn't a natural task for me. At times, my old habits resurface, and for a moment, I have an urge to run off. Then my brain processes that they aren't a threat.

We try to move at a fast pace while still remaining cautious. As the crusted black lava occasionally crunches under my feet, it occurs to me how many dead Mahk we might be walking across. I wince and my stomach tightens. It's like we're stomping across a giant fresh graveyard.

"How long do you think this route is going to take?" Keelie interrupts my thoughts.

"Oh, probably about two days. Now that we're all rested, we could possibly do it in a day and a half."

"And what about the snake pit I heard someone mention? Why are we taking a route that involves snakes?"

Her inquisitive nature is a bit entertaining. "Don't worry. It's a pit, so they can't get to us as long as we cross the bridge over them."

"Assuming that bridge is still there," Soll points out.

I shrug. "Even if it's not, we have tools. We can utilize a nearby tree and make our own bridge."

"I never knew about a snake pit," Keelie pipes up. "Did you know about that Soll?"

"Yes, I knew." He chuckles.

"Couldn't we have been hunting the snakes for food?" she questions.

"Um, trust me," I answer, "be glad you didn't try that."

She glances at me, perplexed. Long eyelashes cast shadows over her questioning eyes.

"I've seen people get desperate enough to try and eat those snakes, and it killed them. They must be poisonous to us."

"Why are they even there if there's a bridge over them anyway?" Keelie continues.

"I honestly have no idea. Why don't you go ask Rase some of these questions," I suggest sarcastically, "seeing as how she's a Creator."

To my surprise, she nods, halts, and swings to the middle of the group to strike up a conversation with Rase.

"Now look what you did," Soll huffs at me.

"Sorry," I defend, "I didn't think she would take me seriously and actually try to be friendly with a Creator guard."

"You don't know Keelie very well," he responds harshly, like I did something wrong.

"I don't need your scrutiny." I set my focus back on our journey.

Occasionally, I glance over my shoulder, expecting to see Keelie in tears after Rase has said something harsh to her, but instead they're carrying on a friendly conversation.

There she goes again. That girl needs serious protection. Even living in the colony, it's astounding she could be so sheltered and naïve in this world. Fortunately, her stupidity isn't my problem, but I have to admit she reminds me a little of Blue and I have a soft spot for anyone like Blue.

Recent events haunt me. Darith's last words play in my head: his threats about Blue. Between him, the blades, and the lava, what's become of her? She may not still be alive. She must be okay though. Any bird that's survived years in this wretched place could survive anything. When we're reunited, we'll make for the other side of the wall. All this mess will be forgotten. We may even find the cascading water from my dream world on the other side.

Every now and then, a conversation strikes up among the group or between a couple people, but for the most part, our traveling is fairly quiet. Quiet is probably best, given that guards could be around any turn. Surely it is imagined, but sometimes the others seem to have the same insecurity and fears. For the first time, I try to perceive things from other perspectives. Korun must barely be sane, having lost his memory and been thrown into this mess. Everyone else lost their entire community and watched a friend die painfully in the lava. I've never been part of a community, so I have no idea what they're feeling, but I suspect it isn't pleasant. Getting everyone to the wall is the best I can offer them.

Most of the day passes quickly. We take a few water breaks to rest our feet. For the most part, we're making good time. As anticipated, it's looking like we're coming up on the snake pit in the mid afternoon. It occurs to me as we draw closer that the lava probably killed the snakes.

As we approach the pit, everyone is getting tired.

"Once we're past the snakes, we can rest a few hours," I announce.

That plan pleases all of them.

The bridge comes into sight, which makes me anxious to find Blue and reach freedom. The next several hours can't go by fast enough.

"We should be careful," Soll warns. "There could be a trap here… I have a bad feeling."

I nod, but he's probably overreacting. I don't see anything suspicious.

Upon closer proximity, it is clear the stone bridge itself is covered in the cooled lava and walls are now standing on either side of its entrance. Strangely, the usual strong sour scent of the pit is gone.

"Simul protected the snakes." I can't tell if Soll is commenting or asking.

"I guess," I respond.

We inch cautiously toward the bridge, wondering why such efforts would have been made to protect the small snakes. As Keelie already questioned, why were they ever there in the first place?

Toes only inches from the bridge, I prepare to shift forward. Korun reaches out, his strong grip pulling me back. He and Soll step in front of me, insisting they go first.

This is so typical of them both. It's fine this time, but they don't need to treat me like I'm helpless.

"Here, take some rope, in the event it collapses. We'll keep a hold on you," I suggest before they begin crossing. All of us grab onto the other end of the rope as they proceed.

They walk into the middle of the bridge and nothing happens. Suspiciously, each of them glares over the edges, probably checking the condition of the snakes. Unsettling silence lingers around us.

Korun looks at us densely. "The snakes aren't even there."

Rase shifts her nervous eyes.

"Do you know why that is?" I press accusingly.

"I don't know," she insists.

My fingers tap my hip impatiently. "Really? Because you looked like you knew something important."

"I swear," she pleads, and then looks at Keelie. "I really have no idea why that would be."

Now that Keelie has been friendly with her, she thinks she has an advocate.

Eyes wide, we all stare accusingly. Troubling quietness extracts more of her diversions, "It doesn't make sense that they put up walls to divert the lava from the pit, especially if the snakes aren't even there."

"Fine." I don't believe her at all, but she obviously isn't going to tell us anything useful.

Korun and Soll have now safely made it to the opposite side of the pit.

"I don't know," Soll calls out across the stretch of space. "No sight of the snakes, but no sign of trouble either. I suggest you come over two at a time while we keep holding onto the rope for extra security." The two men grasp the rope tightly in their hands.

"All right, Keelie, let's get you across and Saige." I tug at their arms.

The duo begins to cross slowly. Soll's thundering yells bring them to a halt. Both girls scream frantically as he jiggles the rope.

Their shrieks are followed by Soll's loud laughter. "Sorry, I couldn't resist." He smirks.

Holding tight to one another in terror, they break away from each other.

"Ugh, you're a rat, you know?" Keelie grunts as she darts the rest of the way across and punches at his muscular arm.

Saige is more amused with his actions than Keelie. Quietly, she joins them on the other side, a scarcely noticeable frown on her face.

Rase and I follow. Laon and Rifan cross last.

"Looks like you really did pick a good route," Laon comments.

"I was nervous for a minute when I saw those walls, but I guess this worked out fine," I tell him.

"Right, time for a rest?" Keelie inquires anxiously.

"Not quite," I answer. "Even though I said we'd rest right after the bridge, this place makes me nervous. I'd feel better if we continue a little while then make camp."

No one argues with my plan. The empty snake pit is probably as unsettling to them as it is to me.

Charred smells linger in our noses as we continue. Closer proximity to Sikla grants us some higher ground on the dried lava. Who ever knew we'd be walking on blades? What else could be deeper in the ground that we have never known we stomp across? A question only a Creator is likely to know.

Only a few Darktouch flowers have made an appearance since the lava. My eyes shift upward. It's possible they fled up the walls. They may be deadly little things, but their purplish hues are a refreshing contrast to these black surroundings.

Half an hour later, my feet start dragging. We need to stop. We settle down into our own little groups and Laon offers to keep watch for three hours then switch off with Rifan. I've definitely worked off the potato from before we left the den as well as the few crackers since then. Diving into one of my tightly packed food bags, I extract some bread and raisins. They'll do the trick. The taste of something remotely sweet is rare to me. My tongue wrestles with their tacky texture and graininess.

Saige and Keelie chat for a few minutes. Soll is deep in his own thoughts. His playful stunt on the bridge really surprised me. It was freeing to see Keelie actually smile for a moment when she punched his arm after the fact. Again, I'm jealous of his ability to do and say the right things at the right time.

Korun must be pretty tired because he falls asleep almost instantly. The dwindling light brings a nice cool air with it. I settle down, using my clothing bag as a pillow, then force myself to relax. Sleep will make the next six hours fly by. Then I'm off to find Blue. Thinking of Blue brings nostalgic dreams as I drift out of consciousness.

A gentle tap from Keelie on my shoulder wakes me from my peaceful escape. My body almost feels like it's getting spoiled by the long hours of sleep it's been claiming. My arms stretch. I glance around. Everyone is accounted for. The trip to the wall is proving to be much less eventful than I had feared. It's possible the Creators assume the blades and lava killed all the Mahk.

Darkness still prevails around us, but evidently someone lit a torch at some point, so we have a decent range of vision around us. We take a couple moments to eat and strap on our gear. Everyone knows each step brings us closer to danger, but also closer to our potential freedom.

Chapter 20
Fangs and Fire

A year ago, I never could have predicted the massive turn of events I've recently experienced. One unexplainable phenomenon after the other has shaken reality. Korun walking through walls and being capable of healing wounds still seems surreal. Realizing there's more to existence than what I've known ignites hope inside. Happiness feels like it's finally in my grasp. Or this is what it feels like before all is lost.

Averting conversations that come my way proves simple. Pretty soon, everyone traveling beside me is going to go their own way and I'm going to be with Blue. But sporadic conversations do grab my attention. Rifan doesn't open his mouth much, but when he does, he usually shares some pessimistic view of the past or future. Keelie now has Korun caught in her question web. She asks him how he heals people and what the other side of the wall is like. He plays off his lack of knowledge, telling her that he would hate to ruin the surprise.

Since she can't extract any information about the other side of the wall, she keeps to small talk.

"You know, I'm a really good cook," she brags.

"Really?" Korun responds.

"Yes, I am. I'm really creative with it, you know. I like to make raisin paste bread and cheesy potato soup."

"I guess that's good," he compliments awkwardly.

"Don't worry. Sometime I'll make it for you." She laughs and points at his stomach.

It's difficult not to be amused by her display. What's funnier than her flirtation is his awkward attempt at aversion.

"I don't really cook much," he tells her.

Her bubbly eyes glare slyly at him through her long eyelashes. A teasing smile sits on her face.

"So I don't know much about cooking," he reiterates, a crack in his voice.

She pauses and looks at him, then giggles. "You'll really like my food then. I've spent a lot of time creating worthwhile recipes, which isn't easy to do around here."

Everyone is quiet but the two of them. The others also seem to be enjoying their conversation, but a strange background noise I've never heard before diverts my attention from them. It isn't loud, but it's certainly distinct. It sounds like a hushed hiss.

A nervous glance over my shoulder reveals nothing alarming.

"You hear that too?" Soll whispers.

I nod and rotate my neck to see if the others have reacted. No one else has picked up on it, or if they have, they aren't showing it.

Rase discreetly leans in toward me and whispers, "All right, I'm ready to tell you what I was thinking when we saw there were no snakes left in the pit."

Stress jumps down my throat at her sudden need to confess and my fingers graze my neck nervously.

"Look, I didn't tell you before because I've only heard rumors."

I shake my head but remain quiet so as not to upset the group. "Rumors?"

"It's almost more of a legend than a rumor. There are stories about twin Buyus."

"Buyus?"

"Dragons, snakes, serpents, or whatever you want to call them."

"Okay... And?"

"It's just the legend says that they can hibernate for indefinite amounts of time, these creatures can sleep for a thousand years if needed, and they can only be roused by the scent of Makta." She pauses like I should know what she's hinting at.

"Makta?"

She rolls her eyes. "The snakes that were in that pit," her voice rises slightly.

"Shhh," I warn her, "the last thing we need is to start a panic."

She nods. "Right, sorry."

"Why is it that this legend is vaguely familiar to me, Rase?"

"What?"

"Why is it that I feel like somehow I've heard this legend before?"

Her eyebrows tighten. "This isn't the time, Araina. I've been hearing a noise, and I think it could be the Buyu. Those fowl creatures are supposed to be merciless, especially if they're near each other. Supposedly, they're very competitive with their killing. We should try to move a little faster."

"You said yourself the Buyu are just a legend," I argue.

"Your stubborn attitude is going to get us all kill—"

Her words are interrupted by the sudden heightened volume of the hissing. Now it's obvious the sound is coming from behind us, so we all whip around instantly.

My breathing halts for a moment as my eyes take in the wild creature. A huge serpent hastens toward us. It must be at least thirty feet long and at its widest area about five foot in diameter. The giant thing looks like it could devour our whole caravan in two or three bites. Spiral horns protrude from its forehead and its face is a dark red color.

"Run," I tell Keelie as I push her away from the group. There's no way we can all outrun the massive reptile, but we can at least give her a chance to escape.

Everyone equips their weapons.

"Araina, take to that tree," Soll motions. "This is when that new bow of yours can come in handy."

He has a point, so I dash toward the tree, dragging Rase with me. I scurry up fairly quickly but not without some resistance from Rase. After Keelie's made some good progress ahead of us, I set my focus on my arrows.

Everyone else runs toward the creature in a staggered line, Soll taking up the lead.

"For Grol's sake, we're not going to survive this," Rase insists.

"Shut up!" I tell her.

My arms shake as I attempt to remove the arrows from the quiver on my back. We're both breathing heavily and sweat trickles down my forehead then into my eyes.

From my high vantage point, the giant snake-like creature can be observed in greater detail. Its tall spiraling horns look even sharper from up here. The same dark red coloring of its face also covers the rest of its body with the exception of its black stomach. Elaborate, jagged geometric patterns flow across its back. Sporadic rows of inky-looking spikes line its spine and a particularly large black spike protrudes from its tail. The thing moves swiftly in slithering motions. I can't find any legs on it.

Terrified to watch but unable to look away, I see the snake sets its eyes on Soll. Focusing my best, I try to aim an arrow for the creature, but it isn't close enough for me to shoot.

As I wait for it to come within my range, Saige launches one of her two long spears. The spear embeds into the side of the thing's neck. Blood spurts from the wound. The serpent hisses loudly then stretches out its face toward Saige.

Now it's close enough for me to do some good. Looking past the arrow head, my eyes fix on its stomach. I take the shot. The arrow races through the air at high speed toward my target, but the creature's tough stomach diverts it. Useless, the arrow falls to the ground.

Soll, Saige, and Laon hack at the giant thing with their swords and clubs. Their attempts prove ineffective since they can only reach its rock hard stomach. Our swords and arrows don't even faze the monster.

Finally, it manages to scoop down, almost swooping up Saige in its giant mouth. She dodges and hits the ground near Soll. As it begins to swing its head back into the air, Soll tries to take advantage of its proximity, cutting at its neck with his sword.

Meanwhile, Korun and Rifan have managed to sneak around the serpent and leap on its back. They're doing some mild damage, stabbing at its flesh.

Saige is now positioned at its other side. She's clearly trying to assess the most effective location to launch the other spear. As if things haven't already gotten bad enough, a scream rings out from below the tree I'm perched in. I look down to see Keelie has returned. Curled up in the tree's huge roots, she screams and sobs uncontrollably.

"Damn it, Keelie!" I yell at her. "Run!"

"No, I'm not leaving you all again."

There isn't time or reason to try changing her mind, so my focus quickly shifts back to the fight. The best place to aim is between the serpent's horns.

As I load up my next arrow, Rifan manages to plunge his sword deep into its back. The creature yanks its body violently, throwing him to the ground. Somehow, Korun manages to keep his grip on one of its spikes and stay mounted.

When Rifan hits the ground, the serpent whips its tail toward him, and fire sprays from the giant spike on the tip of its tail.

Rase was right. This thing isn't just a large serpent. It must be a Buyu.

Scorched by the flames, Rifan falls to the ground, writhing in pain.

Korun is still hacking at the evil thing with his axe and Laon tries to pound it with his club, but nothing is helping. By this time, Saige has thrown the other spear, but it didn't pierce the hide. Instead it has fallen to the ground.

I've now shot two more arrows at its head, but one missed and the other hasn't slowed it down.

"These things are ancient and practically indestructible," Rase urges. "We should let them distract it and run."

"Our best chance is to stand up to it together," I argue.

Soll defiantly marches straight toward the reptile and begins taunting it.

"He's insane!" Rase shouts.

For once, she's right. He's lost his mind. What in the world does he think he's going to accomplish? Using his dual swords, he hacks at its solid belly, causing it no harm or distress.

"Down here, you big worm," he shouts. "Don't I look tasty? Come on!"

The Buyu lets out another loud hiss then lurches down toward him. Its giant mouth gapes open almost four feet wide and a split slimy tongue writhes within it.

"That's right. Come and get me!" he yells again.

He crouches down as it nears him. Then he launches up toward it. The tall green-haired man leaps past the creature's teeth, jamming one sword into the roof of its mouth and the other through its jaw. He proceeds to swing himself farther inside its throat, yanking the top sword, leaving the bottom to prop its mouth open. From his new position at the back of the Buyu's throat, he plunges his sword up into its head.

The serpent still writhes about, but it wavers its head around sluggishly, trying to dislodge the sword pinning its tongue to the bottom of its mouth.

Korun and I both take advantage of the unique opportunity Soll has provided. Holding an arrow steady, I aim for its left eye. It's moving so slow now that the chances of me missing my target are slim. I make the shot. Blinded in one eye, the creature hisses angrily.

I can't tell for sure, but it looks like Soll has managed to stab it a few more times within its mouth. Despite all the damage, it still won't die.

Korun, by this time, is working his way up its back and toward its head.

"No," Rase screams at him. "It's tail. Go for its tail."

"The tail?"

"The legend says if you cut off its tail, it will die" she responds.

"You better not be lying!" I grill her.

"Why would I lie? I want to survive, you idiot."

"The tail," I shout at Korun, "cut off the tail."

He makes a quick turn and backtracks.

The snake still hasn't been able to remove the sword Soll drilled into its mouth. It's trying to bite down and swallow him anyway.

Shooting for its other eye should keep it distracted, but my arrow misses miserably. It's worth another try. The second arrow bounces off a horn. The arrows are running low. It's crucial to focus this time. The snake is moving around enough that it's difficult to predict where to send the shot. Sweat drips sting my eyes, but I shoot, hoping for the best.

The head of the arrow disappears into its other eye, blinding it completely. Blood spills from both its eyes, flowing down its face like red tears.

The Buyu jerks around spastically, somehow still alive.

"It's blind and he's been stabbing up into its brains," I yell at Rase. "Why isn't it dying?"

"I told you. The Buyu are ancient creatures. Our only chance is to cut off the tail."

"Ancient or immortal?" I retort.

She shakes her head as she starts climbing back down the tree.

"Get back here, you selfish coward." I scratch her arm, attempting to pull her up. I'm forced to fight with her. My battle should be with the Buyu right now.

Without warning, she flips out of the tree, yanking me down with her. As muscular as she is, her athletic abilities aren't surprising.

"Don't make me use those bottles!" I threaten.

"Screw the bottles. If that thing gets me, it isn't going to matter anyway." She yanks at the ropes on her wrists, trying to remove them.

"You heartless wretch!"

We fight violently as she pleads for me to let her go. Her fist collides into my cheek. Pain charges up my tongue and across my face. If we didn't need her help at the wall, I think for a moment I could kill her. She makes me so angry.

I grip tightly on a chunk of her hair, yanking her around. "I'll do it! I'll use a bottle!"

My grip on her hair has spun her front side away from me and she screams in pain. My hand pulls her head farther down, bending her backward. She struggles to gain control of herself. Swiftly, my other hand blindly searches for the liquid in my tote.

A boom sounds from the direction of the fighting.

The Buyu is sprawled across the cooled lava, motionless. Korun stands at its other end, holding up the large spike he cut from its tail. "Think it worked!" he yells at us.

"Soll!" Keelie runs toward the serpent. "Soll's still in there!"

My grip releases a defeated Rase. Pulling at her ropes, I drag her toward our companions and the giant carcass. Its mouth is still partially propped open with Soll's sword, but barely.

"I don't think he made it," I tell Keelie. "Be careful."

She doesn't listen. Her small body propels at full speed toward the giant creature's mouth. "Soll." Her petite stature looks even tinier in comparison to the Buyu. "I hear him," she yells as she gets closer to her destination.

"Okay, okay." My palm wipes sweat from my brow.

Saige has made her way around toward us now. "Keelie, no!"

Laon is now standing with her at the reptile's mouth. "Stand back," he tells Keelie as Korun, Rase, and I join them.

We all work together to prop open the enormous mouth while Korun looks inside. Soll is groaning as Korun inches across the slimy serpent tongue. The nasty smell of the Makta hangs in the air, like old lemons mixed with rotting flesh, and I notice a small snake tail lodged between two giant Buyu teeth. It's probably not a good time to let the group know the mystery of the missing snakes from the pit has been solved.

Suddenly, something Sir Riddles said to me dances in my brain.

> *Oh, but there is still something big,*
> *about which I am certain you don't know.*
> *Its brothers are a snack,*
> *and it's double a foe.*
> *A difficult thing to kill,*
> *but from its grave, a gift it will bestow.*

I had only taken his ramblings for madness, but now it occurs to me how oddly well his description fits the Buyu. *Its brother a snack?* Was he referring to the Buyu eating the Makta, creatures of a related species? According to what Rase mentioned of the legend, the twin creatures were enemies: *its double a foe.* What gift did he think this nasty creature could bestow? He must have been insinuating its death was a gift because it can no longer be a threat.

Our collective strength begins to waver as another minute or so passes. Then Korun emerges from within its throat, dragging Soll in tow. He moves Soll to safety outside the serpent mouth, grabbing the second sword as they exit. The giant mouth falls shut.

Soll points to his ribs. Moaning seeps from his lips. His body shakes in agony. Tensely, he props himself on one arm, scrunching up his face. Korun takes a few deep breaths. Then he places his hands on Soll. A few minutes pass before Soll's cries start to die down. After that, he lays his head down quietly.

"Think he's going to be all right," Korun announces. He exhales loudly and props himself against the textured labyrinth wall.

We drop to the ground, exhausted. Only the sound of our heavy breathing fills the air. Keelie is draped across Soll in tears. Saige sits beside them, an expression of disbelief on her face as she stares at the giant dead snake corpse. Laon is next to Korun against the wall, while Rase and I sit a few feet from the serpent's head.

It was a costly fight. Rifan didn't stand a chance after the serpent's flames got to him.

Soll coughs as he sits up. He looks at Saige, Laon, and Keelie with grim eyes then weakly stands to his feet. They join him. Again, they clasp their hands to their foreheads "We will remember," they say.

In some strange way, it brings a small measure of peace, like maybe somehow Rifan could hear them.

Chapter 21
Stubborn

A few minutes pass as the group attempts to regain composure and mourn the departed. All of the sweating has brought on dehydration that feels like cotton in my mouth. Cold water helps wash the dryness from my throat. It's more liquid than my body typically consumes in an entire day.

Lying back down to relax proves difficult to do. Closing my eyes to find a little peace for a brief moment, I'm disrupted by Soll shouting.

"Why do you keep looking at that?" he interrogates Rase.

"I glanced at it. That's all!" she defends.

"More like stared, eyes begging for it," Soll retorts.

"What are you talking about?" I question.

"She keeps looking at that thing." He points at the huge spike, which Korun dropped on the ground near the Buyu's head when he pulled Soll to safety. "What do you want with it?" he demands of Rase.

"Nothing, really, I promise," she defends.

Of course Rase is up to something. There's no hesitation believing Soll over her.

"Grab it for me," I tell Soll.

Rase narrows her eyes as he approaches it.

"Here." He hands it to me.

"So, what aren't you telling us Rase?" I inspect the shiny black object. It stands about a foot tall in a conical shape, its skinny end tapering at a slight angle. Dank souring smells rise from the bloody large bone and flesh within it.

She shakes her head.

"I guess in that case, you won't care if I hold on to this," I threaten. Emptying one tote, I make room for the disgusting item. Hopefully the bag will conceal its scent.

She doesn't have anything more to say about it, but she's clearly irritated. Her cheeks are flushed and her eyes narrow again.

Korun approaches us now, his arms full of our weapons he scavenged from the dead serpent's body.

My arrows are now reloaded into my quiver and the crossbow strapped to my back. Like a decoration, my dagger is still positioned in my hair. I'm ready to get going. Saige straps the spears on her back. Soll sheaths his bloody swords.

Before the Buyu attack, it seemed like maybe we were in the clear. Obviously, that was a premature assumption. How such hopeful thoughts prevail is a mystery. If Rifan were still here, I would have someone to commiserate with. He was the only one of us realistic enough to admit there would be more disaster before, if ever, we reach the wall.

"All right, the day is getting away from us. We're behind schedule, weak, and tired from the fight. I say we try to reach the hideout you spoke of and consider resting for a couple hours before making our dash for the wall," Soll suggests.

"You're right," I agree. "Come on, everyone."

Soll, Saige, Keelie, Laon, Korun, Rase, and I start back down the labyrinth path, headed for Blue. We leave Rifan's body with the Buyu.

"So, you said the legend spoke of twin Buyu." It feels appropriate to rekindle the earlier conversation with Rase. "Where is the other one?"

"I really don't know," she tells me. "The legend says they don't get along, so I would guess it isn't nearby. I had no idea what lengths Simul would go to in the event of a segment breach."

"Segment breach?" I question.

"I've said too much," Rase backtracks. "I'm sorry you don't like us, but that doesn't change what you are."

"What I am? A Mahk. Something your people created."

"You are failures," she retorts, "humanity gone wrong."

"You must really believe that to make us live in this barren labyrinth and starve us to death. And if that's true, then why are you continuing to create us? Is every Mahk batch a test and then you're too ashamed to kill us when we don't turn out like you want, so you force us to kill each other instead?"

She looks down at her feet as she walks.

Before our time together is over, I'm going to make that woman explain more to me, but for the moment, the subject gets dropped.

Segment breach insinuates many things. Clearly, a segment implies its only part of a whole. Do they define the castle break-in as the segment breach within the whole of the labyrinth? I also remember my encounter with the one-handed man. He told me to request a transfer. In the middle of the chaos, it flew through my ears and missed my brain. A transfer where? The ugly truth is the guards did chase Korun through that wall. There could be many more Creators on the other side than the ones we deal with in the labyrinth. My lungs tighten the flow of air within me at the thought. Despite the risks of getting to the other side, I'm reminded of the dangers within the labyrinth as the dried lava crunches under my feet.

Rifan's painful death replays in my head at the thought of the terror Simul is unleashing within the labyrinth. The silence as we walk is haunting. The others might have had a disliking for Rifan's dark side, but I appreciated him. His loss hits me so differently than that of other Mahk. Guilt sweeps over me looking at Saige, Soll, Keelie, and Laon.

This whole mess is my fault to begin with and now Rifan is dead because I'm leading them to the wall. The wall that they believe offers refuge. In reality, it may or may not. The closer we get, I'm beginning to fear it may hold even more trouble for us. It must offer a better place though. Korun came from the place on the other side of the wall and that alone is a sign of hope. It's a fact other people are there, people like Korun, even if the Creators are there too. Based on the interaction Korun had with the guards before they caught him, his people most likely don't get along with the Creators. Once we find them, even if they didn't have problems with the Creators before, they will when they learn of all the people dressed in white down in the Creators' prison.

Resolved to get us to the wall, I narrow my focus to our route. We walk under the upper branches of a tree. Its base that once resembled a thick, dark braid is now swallowed beneath the lava. Now that we passed the snake pit, we aren't too far from the acid river where we usually collect obsidian. That will be the toughest spot to cross, because it forces us to emerge from the labyrinth walls for a short time. The lava may have covered the acid river all together. Whatever the case, we'll deal with that challenge when we get to it.

Korun walks up beside me. "You know, it's okay to be sad," he whispers in my ear.

"What do you mean?" My arms wrap around myself as if he's tried to touch me.

"I mean, I know you have trust problems and I understand why. But I know you cared on some level about Rifan. You don't always have to pretend like nothing fazes you."

Though his gaze begs for my attention, I refuse to make eye contact. "Maybe nothing fazes me," I tell him.

"I don't think that's true," he replies.

"I spent two years running from the Creators and other Mahk. What makes you think a few days of interaction is going to change that? You don't even know these people. For all we know, they're as selfish as the other Mahk and only banding together for survival. When we get to the other side of that wall, don't be surprised if they all turn on each other," I spout.

"You don't really think that. You know they can be trusted, but you don't trust yourself." The skin of his finger grazes my arm affectionately.

He's grating on my nerves now. He even reminds me a little of Darith, but Korun's remarks are more irritating because he probably thinks he's a better person than me. At least Darith never judged me.

"Look, I appreciate your efforts, but I don't need you dissecting my every emotion. I know what I'm doing. I know who I am. I know who I can and can't trust. I've survived in a cutthroat world for two years and done fine. So don't lecture me."

"At this point, if you don't trust these people..." He pauses. "If you don't trust me, then you're beyond help."

"Help? Is that what this is all about, Korun? Am I some project for you to fix?" I shake my head. "I don't need fixing. I'm doing fine."

"I don't even want to be around to see your expression when you realize that's not true," he retorts.

Arguing isn't getting us anywhere. He's distracting me from leading the group to the river. Pursing my lips, I'm resolved to end the discussion.

"You're so stubborn," he grumbles as he lessens his pace, allowing me to walk ahead of him.

Everyone keeps telling me I'm stubborn and need to change my attitude, but they don't understand their opinions aren't of value. One foot in front of the other, I put the argument behind me and push on.

Chapter 22
Death in the River

Luckily, we don't encounter any lava or another Buyu on the way to the river and we make good time. As we draw near to the familiar location, memories of days spent on the bank of the acid river blink through my mind. Usually the place would be lined with Mahk, scrounging for obsidian. All of us spent so many hot days, searching the river bank, digging until our fingers had sores. Compared to our current circumstances, a part of me actually misses those days.

Approaching the stinging liquid, we lessen our pace. Taking cautionary steps, we try not to loudly crack the cooled lava we travel on. Peeking my head around the corner, I survey the area. The river runs over a hill, so the lava merely dried beside it, elevating the level of the ground.

The surrounding area looks clear. Not even one guard is in sight. The expanse is so quiet, it's a bit unsettling.

"Where are the Creators?" I whisper.

Soll's hand clings tightly to his weapon. "Their absence would make me feel better were it not an indication of another labyrinth attack."

"They could be dealing with Mahk elsewhere, you know?" Keelie offers a less pessimistic suggestion.

Everyone collects into a circle.

"We're going to have to make this really fast," I say. "It looks like the guards are off taking care of something else, but they could be back any minute. For that matter, they could be in hiding, waiting for someone to cross. We should probably take turns. If there's someone watching, they're less likely to spot one quick dash at a time, than a whole group at once."

No one objects to my statement.

"I'll go first," I offer, looking across the expanse.

"I can" offers Korun.

"No, I know exactly where to go from here, so follow me."

The realization that I've volunteered myself for an incredibly dangerous role as the first to go across sets in. The air seems too thin and I wonder if the way I'm feeling is anything like suffocation.

My gaze visits Rase then Soll. "If she tries to slow me down, use one of my arrows and take her out," I instruct. "She's only of use to us if she cooperates."

He grabs the crossbow which I hand over to him. "I won't hesitate," he agrees.

"Let's go." I yank at the rope on Rase's wrists.

We dash out into the open space then up the slope. Surprisingly, she keeps pace with me, choosing not to cause problems. Our threats are keeping her in line.

It only takes about ten minutes from the time we leave the group to cross the bridge and enter the correct labyrinth passage. Air scarcely enters my tired lungs as we leave the open space. When we reach the safety of the walls, I whip around to observe the progress of the others.

Keelie's coming next. She crosses even quicker than we had. She's a speedy little thing. After she makes it to us safely, Saige goes next, then Laon. Korun comes across after that.

So far, it appears no Creators are keeping watch by the river at all. If we get lucky, they may think all the Mahk are dead, so they've let up on the labyrinth attacks.

Soll is the last to dash across. Watching the muscular man try to be sneaky is a bit amusing. Just as he comes within about twenty feet of us, we hear shouting down the way.

He jumps at the sound.

"Faster," Keelie calls quietly to him.

Glancing around the corner, we see three guards emerge from the labyrinth walls about half a mile down the bank.

There's no mistaking them for Mahk in their nice maroon jackets and charcoal colored pants. Soll's still in the open for a moment, but the guards are preoccupied.

"Shut up, scum," they yell.

Two of them drag a man wearing shredded garb in chains behind them and the third follows. It's hard to discern his physical details beneath the thick heavy chains strapped around him.

"Grol and Simul feel you've served your time adequately, so now your time's up!" the tall one spits on the prisoner as he talks.

"I don't know what you're talking about," the captive pleads. For a fairly slender man, there's an unusual amount of chains wrapped around him. He doesn't look dangerous at all, so why so much precaution? He's covered in dirt. Deep purple bruises on his face and neck indicate he has clearly taken a beating.

"You wouldn't. That's okay though. The segment breach means it's time to get rid of you. No reason to let you sit around in the prison anymore when we can be rid of you," the brown-haired guard remarks. "Grol thought he could eventually get a confession out of you, but I never needed one to know the truth."

"Find some peace knowing the world is about to be a better place without you," the female guard adds, who trails behind the other two.

Soll has made it to the wall now, but none of us are ready to move forward.

"We need to help that man," Keelie insists.

"Who is that?" I turn to Rase.

She shakes her head. "You don't want to help him, Araina."

"Oh really? Because I'm thinking an enemy of Simul equals a friend of mine. You should start treating us like people and not dirt. Then I'll hear you out."

Rase grabs my wrist forcefully. "Araina, you deserve to live like this, but if you help that man, it's going to end up hurting innocent people."

"Innocent people?" Heat flushes into my cheeks. My heart rate shoots up and I'm so mad it feels like my insides might boil over. "Do you think you're innocent, Rase? Or Simul?" My wrist twists free of her grip. "You're evil is what you are."

They're approaching the river bank now but aren't heading to a bridge.

"What are they going to do?" Keelie looks at Rase with pleading eyes.

"I don't know," she tells Keelie, "but whatever it is, he deserves it."

"Help him," Keelie demands as she darts out toward the guards. Her small figure slices through the air before any of us can dissuade her.

Soll's right behind her but doesn't catch her in time. We all chase her up the bank, fearing what trouble she's about to get herself into. As we approach, two guards are preparing to dunk the man's head in the acid river.

Wait a minute. Why did Rase come along with us so easily?

Just as I turn to put my hand on her mouth, she yells, "Watch out."

I punch her in the face with all my might. It feels good to finally do that.

She falls to the ground dizzy. I stoop down with her. The others could use my help fighting, but Rase can't be trusted out of my sight. She's squirming, trying to seize this opportunity to escape. If we lose her before the wall, it's all over. She yanks at her ropes, hops to her feet, and attempts to flee.

"Stop!" Keelie shoots an arrow at the female guard trailing behind the others.

The arrow barely nicks her arm. The guard turns swiftly, launching her weight to attack Keelie.

Rase's hands land on my neck, fingers eager to choke me. Another punch to her chin knocks her off again. This time, she's drooling on herself. Yanking her arms behind her back, I roll her over, stomach to the ground. She's not completely knocked out. There's nothing nearby to string her up. The minute she's left alone, she'll probably wake then take off. I'm stuck here guarding her.

Keelie faces her opponent head on with her whip in hand. Her quick reflexes serve her well for using that whip. With a crack, it smacks the guard across the face, and she shakes her head. Soll is fast to join her, swinging his sword at the Creator guard.

Saige, Korun, and Laon approach the other two guards by the river, their weapons drawn. Attempting to extract their weapons, the guards fling the man in chains toward the river and charge their attackers. Part of the prisoner's face scathes the acid before he's able to hoist himself away from the water.

The tallest guard swings his sword at Korun. Saige comes at him with her spiked mace while Laon attacks the other.

Keelie and Soll have already killed the female guard at this point, and now Keelie is running to help the man in chains while Soll assists Laon.

The tall guard really puts up a fight. He seems exceptionally skilled with his sword, being able to fight off both Soll and Laon at the same time. Not good enough though. He gets one cut across Laon's shoulder, but Soll's dual wielded swords slice into his abdomen.

Meanwhile, the brown-haired guard swings then misses over and over, trying to kill Saige but taking a beating from her mace. Just as the guard tries to go for her throat with his sword, Korun stabs him through the back.

After the guards are all dealt with, everyone turns their attention to the man in chains, except Laon, who needs Korun's healing hand. Korun quickly begins to mend Laon's wound.

"Come on," Saige yells to the group "We need to get back to the walls before someone else sees us!"

"What's that?" Keelie cries out, looking past the man in chains and down the bank.

"We need to run, Keelie, don't worry about it." I point to the prisoner. "Let's get him and get out of here."

"No," Soll argues. "Keelie's right. I think there are people." He starts running down the black rocky bank.

Now Rase has given up her fight. Defeat wallows in her eyes at the sight of the three dead guards.

"Can you deal with her?" I ask Laon, handing him the ropes attached to Rase's wrists. I don't wait for an answer and take off after them. Saige and I follow Soll and Keelie toward the supposed people they spotted. Korun is busy helping the man in chains discard his bindings.

Keelie stops so abruptly Soll almost runs into her. They freeze like they've seen Simul or something.

"What?" I yell, still trying to catch up. "What is it?"

My fingers hurt at the sight of the acid river. Dread dances in my throat. What is wrong? Finally, I join them. My stomach turns at the horror they've just discovered.

"Fate be," Soll whispers.

In front of us lies a Mahk, his head submerged in the acid river. Lifeless, his body smells of death. Acid from the river has eaten away his hair and even parts of his teeth. His eyes are completely missing. Open wounds coat his face. The more horrific sight is the rest of the bodies lined down the bank, all dead.

Soll crouches beside the man and points at a scar on his ankle. "This is Doun. He was part of our colony."

Keelie walks a little past Doun's body and reaches another. "Reisa."

Saige follows Keelie, tears streaming down her face. I've never seen her allow so much raw emotion to surface. As she had done in the den, she starts clicking her fingers together and this time, she bites at her lip too. Again, the woman displays feelings which aren't easy to identify.

Laon has now joined us, Rase in tow. Upon seeing the atrocity, he throws his weapon to the ground and falls to his knees.

They were right that the colony didn't abandon them.

"I'm so sorry." I count the bodies. About seventy are within my view on this side of the bank and approximately another eighty on the other side.

The scene is overwhelming. Keelie's words in the den replay in my mind, that the Creators shouldn't have been able to find the den. The display before us makes me wonder to what extent the Creators can see and control the labyrinth. Could Simul have discovered the den through some tracking system within the labyrinth? It's even possible the Buyu attack was no coincidence. What if Simul knew where we were and sent that thing to us? If he knows we're going to the wall, we don't stand a chance. A deep breath courses through me, my mind burying the thought. Surely if the Creators were that powerful, they would have already killed us.

"I guess you were right, Araina," Soll says. "Simul did find the colony and they're all dead."

Shame stings my core. Sure, if Simul captured the colony, I assumed they'd be killed. But the colony was supposed to have abandoned the den. Looking out at the lines of lifeless Mahk shells, the truth is now painfully evident. Insensitive would be the kindest of words to label my behavior. "I can't tell you how sorry I am."

This huge public display of power makes me wonder if it was Darith and me breaking into the castle that caused Simul to initiate the labyrinth attacks after all. Maybe he happened to find the colony around the same time of our break-in and that was the trigger. In fact, it makes more sense that such a large group of Mahk banding together would threaten him much more than our little break-in.

Either way, it doesn't really matter now. The Creators are trying to kill us, possibly wiping us all out to start over with more Mahk.

My throat tightens and my stomach knots at the acid river of death. Mahk starving and killing each other has been brutal enough through the years. Even as bad as all that has been, or even the lava and the Buyu, retracing what these peoples' last moments were like is the worst of all. My arms flinch when my mind uncontrollably imagines the pain of acid filling the Mahks' lungs and eating away at their faces. The small sores on my fingertips accumulated while collecting obsidian always burn badly. That stinging magnified and running through my throat then insides would have been unbearable. Their last sight would have been the Creators. What a bitter reality to swallow as they died: the people who brought them into the world forcing them back out.

If we didn't need her to get us through the labyrinth wall, it would be tempting to have it out with Rase right now. She probably knew something like this would happen.

This is a defining moment in my understanding of her. I look up to observe her face. She stands quietly, taking in the scene. There actually appears to be water in her eyes: tears.

"Are you just sad you didn't get to help?" I yell at her. "I hate you!"

She doesn't respond. A moment of drowning silence passes.

Sometimes it seems like my existence is just one giant nightmare.

"And the Creators act like we're the disgusting ones." Keelie's eyes have narrowed as she stares out at the sight of her dead community. For once, she isn't screaming or crying. Whatever she's feeling, it must be the first time. Maybe it's all too much and she's numbing herself to the pain.

Soll wipes a tear from his cheek as he walks over to her, wrapping Keelie in his arms. A minute or so passes before he releases one arm to cradle around Saige as well.

"How could they do this? How could they individually kill each of them in such a brutal manner?" Soll pushes Rase.

Still, Rase refuses to speak.

The group hasn't started their usual ritual. They're so overwhelmed they've forgotten it. If they realize later, it will break their hearts, so I make the gesture. I raise my arms and clasp my hands up to my forehead then say the word, "We..." I pause for them to notice.

Then finally Keelie's tears come out as she, Saige, Laon, and Soll join me. Our hands clasped to our foreheads, we say the heartfelt words, "We will remember."

"Thank you," Soll says to me as we let our arms rest at our sides. Completely oblivious to the world, we stand quietly on the bank.

Then Keelie stretches her hand up to her shoulder, crossing her arm over her chest. "And there will be justice," she says.

Soll's hand brushes beside Saige's then clasps around her fingers gently. Never having seen him make any advances, it seemed her affections were one sided, but perhaps there's something mutual there.

I'm intrigued by their interaction but too consumed with sadness. The bodies keep drawing my gaze back to the river. Their smothered screams still haunt the air. They were the best of the Mahk, the people who treated each other right, and the Creators killed them anyway. The Creators chose to make an example of the few Mahk who might have actually been decent people. I've never been more sickened by the world, by the injustice of our existence.

It's unbearable to observe the horrific scene anymore and every minute we spend in the open gets more dangerous. Still, it's too hard to say anything to them as they mourn.

My attention tears away from the scene, unable to take it anymore. Turning away, I approach Korun. He could use some help with the man in restraints. "Are you okay?" I ask the man as we remove the thick chains from his body.

"I am now," he responds quietly as he weakly crawls away from the bank. Grunts escape him with every movement and his muscles continually tense up. It's clear he's experiencing a great deal of pain and in need of rest.

"Korun." I point at the man's wounds.

Korun nods, reaching his hands out at the man, who flinches fearfully.

"It's okay, he can help you," I tell him.

The man isn't particularly muscular or skinny. Shoulder length blonde hair falls into his blue eyes. He looks like he might be about thirty years old. The acid has damaged part of his face and eaten at one of his bushy dark eyebrows.

Korun places his hands on the acid burned portion of the face and repairs his open flesh before beginning to heal bruises across his arms and legs.

"How do you do that?" the man asks.

"Well, I'm not actually sure," Korun responds.

The man looks at him. "You saved my life." He grabs Korun's arm emotionally.

Saige, Laon, Keelie, and Soll finally come walking toward us.

My hand rests on the man's shoulder. "Let's get you up and going. It isn't safe out here in the open."

He nods. The man tries to stand to his feet but passes out in Korun's arms.

"I think I'm going to need some help," Korun requests.

Soll comes to his aid. They lift the man's arms over their shoulders, carrying him with us as we head back to the labyrinth walls.

Chapter 23
The Stranger

No one is in the best of spirits as we enter back into the labyrinth walls, working our way toward mine and Blue's spot. Soll and Korun drag the man about twenty minutes before they have to rest.

We come to a little nook in the walls, a good area to recuperate. A small curve in the wall provides some visual obstruction down the passage. Nice tall trees in the space offer a good potential hiding spot if guards were to come our way.

Soll, Keelie, and Laon sit close together, Soll with his arm around Keelie. Oddly, Saige stands propped against a tree, staring out into the passage. She doesn't particularly appear to be keeping watch but instead is lost in her own thoughts. Their own emotions, dependencies, and decisions led to this outcome, but they can't be faulted for that because it was all prompted by love. What we saw by the river was unreasonable, even unfathomable.

As much as my heart bleeds for them, there's something curious about the man we just saved. The man wears only rags that are far less intact than Mahk clothing. It is hard not to wonder why the guards were bringing him from prison.

He sits up and looks around at us. It obviously takes him a minute to remember the altercation at the river bank.

Soll's eyes are narrow as he stares at the strange man. "Here." Soll tosses his spare set of clothing at the blonde-haired man. "We'll give you a minute."

We all look away until the man speaks to us. "Thank you for this." He points at the clean pants and shirt on his body. "Thank you for saving me."

Observing Rase's reaction to the man, it's clear she knows who he is and doesn't like him. Her upper lip curls and her eyes narrow at the sound of his talking. What Mahk would she know? She can be hard to read but that looks like fear in her eyes. He may not be Mahk after all.

"Those guards were ready to dunk me under." The man sits back down with the group. "I don't know how I could ever repay you."

Soll, Saige, Keelie, and Laon remain quiet. They've reached their emotional limit for the day and aren't ready to be friendly, so I pipe up, "We couldn't leave you to their devices."

"Think we can ask for your name?" Korun inquires.

"Ah," the man replies, "they called me, Vickon, I believe. At least, they've addressed me that way before."

"Vickon," I repeat. "You don't sound so sure of your own name." He's clearly still recovering from the duress. "My name is Araina." I point to the others. "This is Korun, Keelie, Laon, Saige, and Soll."

He notices Rase was left out and points curiously at her.

"And that's Rase, but don't pay any attention to her."

"You look familiar," he says to her.

She turns her eyes away from him and remains silent.

"Is she mute?" He turns to us, confused.

"No, that's just Rase." Rase doesn't even roll her eyes. She sits quietly. "She's a guard and inherently has an attitude."

He flinches. "Why is she with you?"

Soll asked me that same question the other day. "It's a long story," I answer.

"Ah." He nods. The man surveys his body, running his finger across the skin which was previously bruised and cut. "I don't even remember the last time I wasn't full of injuries." The man looks at Korun. "And I've never seen anything like what you did back at the river."

"No one has seen anything like that," I tell the man, "until Korun came along."

"Thank you all so much," the man repeats. "I owe you for what you've done. You put yourselves in danger back there, for my sake."

"It isn't right what they do to us, you know," Keelie finally joins in the conversation. "Mahk may not be as powerful as them, but that doesn't justify their actions. We couldn't let them hurt you."

He smiles at her. She tends to draw that response from everyone with her friendly demeanor. He forgoes another thank you, but the appreciation whispers through his eyes. Then he looks around at us, puzzled. "Mahk?"

The group glances around at each other with big eyes.

"Mahk," Keelie says again.

"What is Mahk?" the man questions.

"People the Creators make," I explain.

Soll motions around the circle. "We're Mahk."

"Who are you?" Korun finally pushes curiously.

"I'm not sure," Vickon responds.

"All right, so you don't know who you are or what the Mahk are?" Soll clarifies. "What do you know?"

Overwhelmed with questions, Vickon glances back and forth at the two men. "I know they called me Vickon in the prison and that's where I've been for a long time."

"Did they give you a number?" I ask him "A Mahk number?"

He shakes his head, an expression of deep thought on his face. "No, I don't recall a number."

"He could have come from the other side of the wall," Keelie comments.

"All you remember is a prison?" I ask again, unsure what to think of his claim.

"Or he's a Creator," Soll declares darkly.

"I don't know," I defend the confused man. "Even if he was one, clearly they've disowned him now." I turn to look at Vickon. "You don't know why they were trying to kill you?"

"I've been living in the prison," he reiterates. "They barely fed me and beat me constantly. I never knew why. All they ever told me was that I deserved it and that I would never see Narrah or Kathar again."

Kathar is familiar to me for some reason, but everyone else looks totally confused.

"Narrah and Kathar?" Korun repeats. "You don't know what they meant by that?"

"No." Vickon shakes his head. "And that's all I really recall."

Kathar. Where have I heard that before?

"Think we could talk?" Korun motions Soll and me away from the group. We walk a few paces off, out of hearing range of the others. "What do you make of him?" he asks us.

"More like, what do I not think of him. I'm not sure he's trustworthy," Soll responds.

Kathar! It finally comes to me. One of the guards mentioned Kathar when we broke Korun out of the castle.

The man is now slumped over, tousling his hair anxiously. He looks completely unsure of himself, or us. It's clear the Creators used the same treatment on him they forced on Korun. And his mention of Kathar makes me wonder if he comes from the same place as Korun.

"I trust him." My interjection causes a pause.

"You trust him?" Soll replies quizzically. "Araina, the man can't explain anything about himself."

"He may not be able to tell us much…" I hesitate. "But we do know he's no friend of the Creators or Simul and that's enough for me."

Soll shakes his head. "I don't know. Bringing him with us doesn't seem to be a good idea."

"We can't leave him here to die!" My tone sharpens, but my voice remains hushed.

"She's right," Korun backs me up. "Soll, I'm not too sure about him either, but what choice do we have? This labyrinth is going to exterminate everyone. He can't save himself."

"All right," Soll finally concedes.

We return to the group.

"You must be starving?" Keelie inquires of Vickon.

"I can't take that from you," he tells her as she offers him some cheese and bread.

"You can't afford not to," Soll answers.

"Go ahead and take it." Keelie pushes it at him.

The man has obviously gone without food for a while. He chokes the meal down almost instantly. He still slouches as he eats. Bags under his eyes and shaky movements portray his need for sleep.

"Vickon, you've had a rough day. We really can't stay here for long, so maybe you should try to rest before we have to get going," I say.

He nods. "I'm exhausted."

"Here." I offer him a clothing tote. "Use this under your head."

"Thank you, thank you all." He then lies down and shuts his eyes.

"It wouldn't hurt any of us to relax a little," I suggest to the others, kicking back against the wall. My eyes wearily close, but my senses stay alert. The next few hours are going to be stressful. We still don't know what to expect when we finally reach the wall.

Thoughts of Blue make my heart ache, so relaxation doesn't come easy. We're so very close to finding her now. After the group is done sleeping, the next stretch of travel will be the last before we finally reach her.

If we had the option, we're so tired we could hibernate. But being crunched for time, the group settles for an hour of rest. Sleep refuses to embrace me during that time. My mind is too anxious.

Everyone's rising to continue.

"Remember to stay quiet. We're nearing my hiding spot and the wall, but that also means we're getting closer to Creators." We didn't get this far to mess up now. It's just not an option. "Chances are the guards never knew how Darith and I broke into the field and found the wall, but it doesn't hurt to be careful. Please, no one say anything between here and the hiding spot. For that matter, when we get there, speak quietly to one another. We're treading dangerously close to the enemy, so be careful."

My nerves are getting to me as we near Blue's secret spot. It's been over a week since she was left here near the castle, possibly even two weeks now. Hopefully she found her way back to our place. Everything is still as we travel, haunting.

Finally we reach the branch sticking through the wall. My first instinct is to call her name, but it's important to stay quiet.

"Here," I tell the group as we approach the entrance. The lava raised the ground about ten feet. The branch now only hangs about fifteen feet above us, making it even easier to access than before.

My arms motion for the others to wait. Being the first to check for guards makes sense. This is my home. If trouble is lingering, it should be mine to face. The guards would catch me, but at least there's a chance the others could get away.

Until now, I thought I would be dashing up what's left of these boulders to the branch, but I find myself taking my time. Part of me is scared.

Being only fifteen feet tall, reaching the top happens quickly despite my growing worries. As I cup my hand on the branch to pull myself up, I'm careful to avoid a Darktouch flower nearby on the wall. Concerned for the others when they follow, I point it out to them. When the branch begins to dip due to my weight pulling on it, I listen intently, hoping to hear a croak.

Nothing happens and my heart sinks. I move through the wall cautiously. There's still hope Blue will be waiting. On the other hand, there could be guards.

As I tensely crawl through, my eyes don't see Blue anywhere. Then I freeze in place and my heart skips a beat when I hear a barely audible whisper come from up above me in the tree, "We have been waiting for you."

Chapter 24
The Hiding Spot

I jolt fearfully, attempting to turn around and flee. Balance escapes me. Once again, my body falls from this stupid tree. This time, I twist my wrist, trying to brace my fall.

Someone drops from the tree and lands a couple feet away. Filthy guard boots laugh at my peril. I'm certain Blue's been dead for days and I'm about to join her.

Then a blue feather delicately floats down before my eyes and comes to rest near the boots.

I jerk my head up "Blue?"

She lands in front of me at the sound of her name.

Darith pats her head, still dressed in the stolen guard uniform.

Darith. Of course it's Darith. There was something familiar about the tone of that whisper. What was I thinking?

A wave of emotion overcomes me. Tears fill my eyes, but a smile crosses my face. Dismissive of my injured wrist, I leap to my feet and wrap my arms around Blue's neck. She croaks excitedly at the sight of me and ruffles her feathers.

"Ya got a real thing for this damn bird, eh?" Darith murmurs as he continues to stroke her head.

The moment is too overwhelming to even respond. My arms cling to Blue as my eyes spill happy tears.

Commotion sounds overhead from the tree. Korun drops down from a branch, observing our surroundings defensively. He lands with his axe prepared for a fight.

"Thanks, Korun, but you can put the weapon away. I'm okay. It's just Darith."

"Don't do that to us. We thought they caught you." He begins climbing back up the tree. He reaches the top before motioning for the others to come on in.

Wearing a smug expression, Darith taps his sword impatiently.

"You didn't eat her."

He laughs. "No, I didn't eat her. Is that what ya thought all this time?"

I purse my lips. "You disappeared!" I defend. "I didn't know what to think, Darith. You acted like you were fed up and even mentioned eating Blue. You left me there and never came back. I still don't know what to think."

"I didn't intend to leave ya," he replies as his gaze takes in my companions, who have now all made it down the tree and stand around us.

My cold stare could shoot ice at him. "You just took off while I slept and Korun was tending to Rase."

"Look, little Araina, it occurred to me that one of my supply stashes wasn't far off from where we were. I realize now I should've left it alone. There was no sense in it, but my temper had the best of me. Wasn't thinkin' everythin' through. At the time, I thought we could use some extra supplies, so I went off to get 'em."

Impatience has gotten the best of me as my fingers tap on my hip.

"It should have been a ten-minute run, at most. I planned to come right back," says Darith plaintively.

"You didn't!"

"No, it didn't work out like I planned," he admits. He quickly lifts up his shirt to reveal what looks like an infected gash on his side. "I ran into a group of guards before I even got to the stash. There were so many of them. I didn't want to lead them back to ya, so I took off. Amazingly, I outran them after a while, but by the time I got back to where I left ya, ya were gone."

My head shakes before a doubtful exhale. "So you came back here?"

"I figured ya must have been makin' really good time ahead of me. I wasn't sure what path ya took, but with your knowledge of the labyrinth, I felt sure ya were going to beat me here. I got here as fast as I could, thinking I could catch up to ya."

I let my cold stare give out. "And I wasn't here."

"Guess I did beat ya after all. Once I got here and ya were nowhere to be found, the lava flows started comin'. There was no way I could go back out to look for ya. Blue and I were safe in here though." He points at the entrance to the hiding spot. "The lava never got high enough to reach us in here. I knew ya didn't go through the wall yet, or else ya would have taken the bird." He nudges Blue. She playfully nudges him back.

"How did you know that I was ever going to make it here?" I ask.

"I didn't. But I promised ya I wasn't gonna eat the bird, so I never did. Plus, I had enough food not to resort to that. I've kept my eye on the wall, but it's been pretty heavily guarded, so really I've been trapped here. Welcome to my tiny prison."

Everyone is quiet for an awkward moment and I realize Darith has missed a lot as he surveys the group.

"Everyone, this is Darith," I say.

"Right. We know who he is," Keelie remarks with disgust.

Somehow in our time together, I started to overlook his reputation. It isn't surprising that they know who he is and would question my association with him. Unfortunately, there's a good chance he's killed some of their friends.

"How do ya do, miss?" He smirks at her, obviously detecting her discomfort and enjoying it.

"Cut it out, Darith. Keelie, Saige, Sol!" I start introducing them, pointing to them as I say their names. "Laon and Vickon. And you two know each other." My hand taps Korun.

Darith lets his gaze linger on Saige a little longer than the others. It's hard to know what he's thinking, but he looks a little baffled.

"Do I know ya?" he asks her. If that's his attempt at flirtation, it's pathetic.

Distaste clearly spreads across her face. "Do you know anyone? Don't you kill everyone you meet?"

He smirks smugly at her then shakes his head. "Thought ya looked familiar, is all." After a second, he gets over it. "I know this one too." He points to Rase, who rolls her eyes. "I'm surprised ya kept her around, but I suppose that's out of necessity."

"Exactly. We didn't have much of a choice," I say.

"I guess ya still don't remember anythin' about the other side of the wall, or how to get through?" He turns to Korun.

"Well, let's see…" Korun stares at me awkwardly. Then we both look at Soll.

"Ya don't remember anything?" Soll asks in a harsh tone, glancing back and forth between me and Korun.

"Obviously," Darith answers for us, slow to notice the tension. "Um… or not," he retracts, evaluating the expression on Soll's face. He eyes me nervously.

"Just be quiet," I tell him.

"All right, what's he talking about, Araina?" Soll demands before asking Korun, "You lost your memory. When?"

"Okay, we haven't been completely honest with you," I respond, "but only for your own good."

Lips tight, the normally cheerful tall green-haired man stares at me heatedly. He's reached the height of his frustration, having already had a bad day at the river. Learning he has been following a couple liars isn't making his day any better. He's gripping the hilt of his sword and his pale face is tight.

Korun has better smoothing things over skills than me. My shoulder nudges him, my eyes pleading for him to talk.

"Tell them everything," I say. "I'll admit up front that it was me, not Korun who chose to twist the truth. Don't blame him."

Korun inhales deeply before relaxing his shoulders. "Think we should all sit and have a long talk."

Keelie starts to sit, but Soll yanks her back up.

"I think you should start explaining yourself quickly, before I lose my temper," he threatens.

"Okay. Where to start…" he murmurs anxiously. "I guess it all started when these two busted me out of prison in the castle." He points at Darith and me. "When they got me out, they told me we had met previously that day in a field near the castle, but I had no memory of the encounter. Evidently, Araina saw the guards force me to drink something, so we guess that's why my memory was wiped."

Soll stills looks very angry and impatient, his knuckles turning white as his grip on the sword tightens.

"Anyway," Korun tries to hurry the story along, "basically they saved me from the castle and are trying to help me get back through the wall I fell through."

"So the wall really does exist?" Keelie clarifies, one hand held to her forehead in frustration.

"Sure, the wall exists. We don't actually know what's on the other side," he finishes quietly.

Everyone stands silently in a circle.

"We don't have a choice anyway," I tell Soll. "What, would you have stayed back at the den waiting for Simul to sweep back through and collect you?"

His jaw is strong and his eyes narrow. "We trusted you. We thought you were different than the other Mahk." He looks Darith up and down. "But if you've been joining efforts with someone like him and lying to us, I have to think differently of you."

Keelie stands nervously beside Laon. What they're thinking isn't clear. No one says a word for at least five minutes.

Darith starts to speak, "So what's—"

"Shut up!" Soll interrupts with a shout. Swiftly, he pulls one of his swords from its holder. "Fate be! Can't you just button your lips? I should kill you right now."

Darith flinches but surprisingly doesn't extract a weapon.

"You're not worth it." Soll lets go of his sword. "I don't want to hear another word from you. Never speak to me!" He stomps away from the group toward the wall.

Saige, Keelie, and Laon follow after him.

"Well, he's a pleasant fellow" Darith nudges my arm.

I exhale roughly, glancing over at Korun. He looks at me with an expression of utter disappointment and shame.

I reach for his arm. "I'm sorry, I just—"

He turns his back to walk away, leaving Darith, Vickon, Rase, Blue, and me.

"Makin' friends with everyone, aren't ya, little Araina?" Darith badgers me sarcastically.

"Not now. I'm tired and need rest. We can talk later. Just take her."

Darith takes Rase's ropes. I spin around and head toward my box of treasures. Blue follows me. The container is still there, untouched. After the box is open, the small treasures seem to stare back at me. Blue hunkers beside me, resting her head on my shoulder, seeming to take note as well. Everything appears to be there: a key, a little leaf pendant, a piece of white chalk, a coin, and a single small shard of obsidian.

Out of habit, my hand grabs the obsidian, allowing it to consume me with curiosity. This particular piece was the first item added to my box. The shard is smooth against my fingers. Its value is a mystery. Why is it so special the creators demand we gather it for them? It's like they have us collecting it simply as a form of labor, as a punishment. From what I can deduce, it's not used as currency. I'm sure I'll never learn if there's a purpose for the obsidian. As a Mahk, these answers will likely never be revealed to me.

Becoming frustrated with the small object that represents my suppression, I put it away. Inspecting the box's contents somehow brings me comfort. Next, my finger runs over the surface of the silver coin. Like most of the other objects, the little round shining silver object was barely peeking out of the ground. It had a flower carved on one side and some numbers on the other. For some reason, my mind named it a coin. No one ever taught me that. Its feeling in my hand was familiar, so I held on to it.

I stare at the various things for long moments, trying to understand how I know what they are and what they mean to me. This psychological game could go on for hours. The questions subside when the mystery box is closed.

My forehead begins to ache. It's been scrunched due to my frustration. Soll's reaction to our secret is still terrorizing my feelings. All this time, the dishonesty was intentional even though they would find out if we made it through the wall. The whole charade wasn't supposed to feel this bad in my gut. There were good motives behind the fib too. Knots tighten in my stomach.

All that can't consume me now, though. I finally have Blue, and she needs care.

I trace her beak with my fingers. My spirit soaks in her presence. She nuzzles next to me as we sit on the ground quietly. Everything else falls away. It's not worth focusing on the negative when there's so much positive right in front of me.

We sit together in silence and pretend like its three weeks ago before my world changed. Extracting the chalk from my box, I spend a few moments sketching on the wall. Creativity often helps me sort out my thoughts. The entire space is covered in my depictions but more always manage to fit. My arm dances in different directions, drawing what feels natural. Not allowing my mind to plan anything seems to extract the best results.

My sketch depicts a person slouched over in tears. With the creation of lines around and above her, the figure becomes enclosed in a cage.

"Guess that's how I feel." I look over at Blue sadly. It didn't take away the aching in me, but the drawing did help me figure out my emotions: that I'm trapped like a prisoner. A prisoner of the bounds set by the Creators and those I've brought on myself. After tucking the chalk back in the box, I close its lid.

I imagine no one else is in our hiding spot. It's just me and Blue. Her gold eyes are glowing with happiness as we snuggle next to the dark wall.

"At least I didn't let you down," I tell her, petting her back, "and I'm not going to."

A hint of peace finally washes over me. It's easy to dismiss the conversations taking place among the others and let my eyes close. When we try to reach that wall, I'm going to need to be adequately rested. Within a couple minutes, I'm drifting into the abyss of my own mind.

Chapter 25
Haunted or Crazy

My sleep brings me no hopeful dreams.

First, I sit helpless in that chair in the Rotting Pass again, and Sir Riddles grasps my shoulders. He's telling me riddles. This time I'm paying attention. The words of the sinister man shouldn't have any merit, but now I accept they might. Over and over, he's saying that same riddle he loved to spout.

Which little pets,
live in the penitentiary,
eat dead rats,
and have selective memory?

Abruptly, I'm no longer in the Rotting Pass, but instead for some reason, I'm face to face with the one-handed Creator and Simul.

Simul calls me, "Araina, number P329111."

I reach for the dagger in my hair, but it's missing. The crossbow on my back is missing as well.

"Convicted of treason and a double offense" the one-handed man says, "injuries punishable by death."

Then Simul dissipates into thin air.

I try to run from the one-handed man but am frozen in place. I desperately look around, hoping to see Korun, Soll, or anyone who can save me. There isn't a single soul but me and that man. Once again, he pushes me against a wall forcefully. I still can't see his eyes through his brown hair. He breathes heavily in my face. Then he lunges at me, my own dagger in his hands. The dagger bursts into my chest. Pain wakes me from my slumber.

Sweat slithers on every inch of me. Breathing heavily, I look around. That was quite a discouraging sequence of dreams right before our big dash to the wall.

Dying at the hands of that piggish one-handed man would almost be worse than burning to death.

And why Sir Riddles won't stay in the past is beyond me. What was he saying in that stupid riddle?

Which little pets,
live in the penitentiary,
eat dead rats,
and have selective memory?

As my brain boils on his words, trying to cook up their meaning, the riddle becomes clearer to me. Surely he was talking about his prisoners chained to the wall. *Which little pets live in the penitentiary.* Although why would he refer to his own house as the penitentiary? He probably really believed he was providing them a nice home.

"Selective memory," I say again quietly. The riddle isn't as clear as I want to think it is. After a good five minutes of mulling over the crazy man's words in my head, my mind finally shoves them away.

Blue's head is still resting in my lap and she doesn't stir at my commotion. Everyone else is also sleeping, aside from Soll, who must be keeping watch. He's perched high up in the tree. Maybe not, but it appears he has intentionally pretended he didn't notice me jolt awake. Speaking to him would be nice, if he was anywhere near forgiving me, but that doesn't seem likely.

I don't owe him anything. If it weren't for Korun and me, he would be trapped at the mercy of Simul.

I inhale deeply. My hand gently scoots Blue's head away.

Working my way behind the bushes brings me to the small pool of water. The cool water splashes on my face. It's a good feeling to scrub off some of the grime from traveling.

After washing away my conflicted emotions along with the dirt on my skin, I march over to the tree and stare up at Soll. "You don't have to like me. That's fine."

He scoffs, "More like hate you and I don't need your permission."

"That wall Korun came through is a short swim away now. And we don't know what other attacks Simul might have planned on the labyrinth." I look down at my feet and tap my fingers on my hip, because the next words aren't easy to admit. "I really do hope you guys will come with us."

He looks at my eyes intently, as if genuinely digesting that statement. He squeamishly starts to fidget like he wants to say something, but he stops. He's probably shocked to hear me talk like this.

"We could be the last Mahk. From the looks of it, the rest are dead. And I really did mean it when I said we could start new."

"Are you saying you need us, Araina?"

"No—" My head wavers. "I'm saying you should come. That's all. I'm not going to say it again."

He stares at me steadily, as if he's trying to uncover something unspoken.

"I'll keep watch now, if you trust me."

He drops his head in his hands. It's painfully obvious he's exhausted. He climbs down to the ground and turns before walking away. Soll props himself against the wall and closes his eyes.

He's angry with me and that's that. The reality of our situation can't be changed now. Maybe we never should have lied to them in the first place, but it's done. Right this minute, the best move is focus on where we go from here. It would be a shame if Soll, Saige, Keelie, and Laon don't come with us. Really, what alternative do they have at this point? Where else would they go? The den isn't an option. Now that we've seen what Simul did with the colony, we have to get away from him.

My eyes wander over everyone as they sleep. It would be nice if we could all sleep peacefully on the other side of the wall. It's difficult to imagine a life of going to sleep without being immersed in torturous nightmares brought on by reality.

My gaze lands on Blue. Her legs are tucked neatly under her belly, sunken into her feathers. Her head rests on her neck. She looks like a big feather ball with a beak. She sleeps so innocently, so naïve. What's she dreaming about? Does she dream? Creeping up quietly next to her, I collect my canisters that need filling.

"Squawk!" She wakes with a start at the slight clanging sound of my canisters. Her big eyes wander up to observe mine. Laughter escapes me.

"Shhh," I tell her. I didn't foresee being able to smile after recent events, but she brings it out of me.

Her feathers are all disheveled and her gold eyes big with surprise. She looks up and croaks at me as if to ask what the noise was.

"Hush, girl," I say quietly, "it's okay."

Amid the death and ashes, her company is a pleasant relief. She follows me to the puddle behind the bushes and stands beside me as I fill the canisters.

After dropping the water back with the mystery box and other totes, I crawl up into the tree. Listening intently for any outside commotion, I nestle up high in the branches. Blue doesn't come up with me, but she lies down in the roots, waiting for me patiently.

Snacking on gooey raisins keeps me busy on watch duty. Everything is still and quiet. No lava surges, no hiss of a Buyu—all seems to be well.

My scattered drawings on the walls bring back memories. I've drawn so many things, most of them from my imagination. Some are drawings of mysterious objects like those in my treasure box or items

I haven't seen in life but I've thought up on my own. Either I thought them up or the Creators allowed me to know of them even though they don't exist in the labyrinth. Among these renditions are beautiful horses and exotic butterflies. A large section of wall is covered with the cascading water from my dream world. It all brings me comfort somehow, even though the drawings are just illusions displayed on rock.

Then my gaze traces the random cracks in the walls as they ascend higher. It's impossible to determine how many miles up they actually stretch. Little white dots in the sky far past the top of the walls catch my eye. When we reach the other side, the beauty of the night sky might not be obstructed by walls and hazy smoke. Barely evident against their dark canvas, the stars glimmer. Judging by the spreading tint of pink, the sun must not be far off from rising. It finally feels peaceful enough to relax.

Then the raspy voice comes at me again, this time with a new set of words:

I've been watching you, my pretty pet,
your companions are asleep while you're awake.

I jolt from my reclined position, almost sure that the voice wasn't in my head. Quiet fills the air for a moment before it comes again.

You should never try to trick me.
I know what's real and what's fake.

My throat tightens as my eyes survey the space to see if anyone else heard anything. They all seem to be deep in sleep. Removing my dagger from my hair, I proceed to the end of the branch, observing the boulders and corridor outside the hiding spot. It's dark and difficult to see, but I don't hear anything else.

I must really be going crazy now. This time, the rhyme was not in my head. Logically, I know Sir Riddles is dead. The beating of my heart rises in my ear. My breathing naturally shallows. If Sir Riddles is dead and I'm still hearing his voice, then I'm either crazy or being haunted.

A quiet shuffle comes from the corner. Darith has woken up, if he was even really sleeping. He seems like the kind to always have one eye open, even in the night.

My relaxed position in the arms of the tree resumes quickly. Revealing the voices I'm hearing to anyone else seems pointless. Sir Riddles needs to stay in the past before insanity takes me over.

After he shuffles around a moment, Darith climbs the branches then sits quietly next to me. Neither of us speaks for a good twenty minutes. Listening to him breathe, my mind races. I am certain that at any minute, he'll pipe up with some stupid comment. Minutes continue to creep by.

Finally the silence is unbearable. "So," I whisper to him, "don't you have a million questions and smart remarks for me?"

"Nope," he replies.

"You aren't curious who these Mahk are? You aren't surprised to see them friendly with each other?"

"I'm not all that surprised, Araina. Should I be?"

"You of all people should know Mahk don't form groups. I never saw any join together until I met them."

"I'm not sayin' it's common, but I've seen it before."

"Did you know about the colony then?" I inquire.

"No, I hadn't heard of a colony. But I have seen Mahk take care of each other before. Isn't that what we started to do too?" he points out.

I soak that in for a minute "I guess so. I just—"

"Just what? That's always been your problem, Araina. Ya think you have everythin' figured out and that holds you back. Ya don't ever take a step back and look at the full picture. Ya evaluate everythin' around at face value and nothin' further."

I shake my head. "Quit acting like you know me so well, Darith."

"But don't I?" he retorts. "And don't they?" He points at the others. "Ya seem to think ya know me too. You've watched me since you were created, so ya know what I've done to survive. You've seen me kill to eat." He looks at me straight in the eyes. "Don't ya know me?"

The question is clearly meant to be rhetorical. Solemn, dark and yet inquisitive, his expression frightens me a little. I think I understand what he's getting at, but I don't want to deal with it.

"No," I respond. "You don't know me and I don't know you, not really."

He picks at the bark on the limb with frustration.

All the stars are gone, as if they sensed the tension and fled. Despite the smoky atmosphere that fills the labyrinth, pink and yellow colors of the morning are now apparent.

"I'm going to make breakfast for everyone," I tell him then start my climb down the tree.

"Our actions define who we are, Araina," he calls quietly after me, "and I've watched ya for two years. I do know ya. Ya know who I am and I know ya. The question is when are ya goin' to accept it? Admit to yourself the person you are instead of denying it."

I pause at the base of the tree as the words of the murderer sink in. I know myself because I know my mind. My actions aren't all that define me. My brain pushes the interaction away. I want to erase our words and anything they may have insinuated. None of it matters.

Preparing to make a filling meal, I build a fire in the middle of the space. The smell of burning wood is in the air and the group begins to wake. Allowing me to collect their food, they convey their preferences for breakfast. Mostly, they request potatoes or cooked rat, but Keelie insists she's only going to eat some raisins. Despite Soll's and Saige's encouragement to eat more, she claims her nerves have made her stomach tight.

The conversation isn't very lively. Darith asks questions about our travels, but no one is eager to fill him in, including me. He goes on to describe his encounter with the guards more thoroughly and finally Korun offers to heal his infested wound. They depart from the group to deal with that. That's for the best since the gash isn't a pleasant sight. Only a few minutes pass before they rejoin the circle around the fire. Evidently Korun's become more confident in his healing gift.

The smell of baked potato is enticing. Everyone is grateful to have freshly cooked food. We'll need that boost for what's ahead. Blue receives an entire cooked fish. Who knows how much she's been able to eat lately? Croaking happily at me, she laps it up in her mouth.

As everyone starts to eat, someone mentions the colony and the den, which spurs a big conversation. Vickon has a million questions about the Mahk, the colony, and especially the Creators. We tell him everything that's happened and what the labyrinth was like before Simul's attacks. The murderous nature of our people and the starvation are the worst parts to tell, yet the most relevant to share. He asks for every detail, thrilled to learn of the world outside the prison. He asks about our creation, wanting to know what it was like.

"We just woke up, huddled in a room together," I tell him. "It was cold, dark, terrifying. Despite how many of us were crammed into the space, it was lonely. But things only got worse from there, so that's one of my happier memories."

We try to tell him how hostile life was and that most Mahk either killed to steal food from one another or starved to death. This leads him to inquire why we all grouped up.

Then Darith takes over the discussion again, conveying the story of Korun coming through the wall from his perspective. "It was all Araina's idea, goin' after Korun."

My response is sharp. "I beg to differ. You were equally vested in the venture."

He raises his eyebrow. "It was good he showed up when he did. She had a giant gash in her leg."

"That you put there, I might add."

"Ya gonna let me tell this story, or what?"

Clearly he could gush on for hours. He really enjoys telling them all how he kidnapped Rase from the bathhouse in the castle. To my surprise, Laon actually laughs at that. Everyone else maintains their cold attitude toward Darith. That's understandable. In fact, my own intelligence should be in question for joining up with him.

After Darith speaks about the Blood Caves, everyone stares timidly at him.

Not that I'm a social master, but the tension needs breaking "After the first labyrinth attack and escaping the Rotting Pass, we ran in to these guys trying to get back here. We invited them to come along, only they begged us to backtrack and bring along their colony." I continue describing to Vickon how we ran into Soll and his group, barely surviving the lava as we made our way to the den.

Vickon is intrigued by the talk of the colony which leads him to ask Soll how it was formed. That's a topic our conversations haven't yet investigated. His inquiry piques my curiosity. We have all finished eating now, but I'm too intrigued by the formation of the colony to try and wrap up the talk.

We listen intently as Soll elaborates on the history of the colony. It originated years ago, among some peers on an awakening day. He wasn't among the founders, but the story goes that they initially ran to the Blood Caves, like most new Mahk do.

"The group," he says, "Saige was among them, encountered the Nabal in the caves. They entered the cave strangers but helped each other escape and find shelter."

She doesn't seem eager to talk about it and even appears to be tuned out of the discussion once again.

"It was then that they discovered the den. Of course, at the time, it was a large cave at the back of the mountain. They regrouped and got to know each other before they spent any time among the rest of the Mahk. As they began to venture out for food and water, they discovered how heartless most Mahk could be." He glances at Darith. "Ever after that, they sought the exceptional Mahk."

"Exceptional Mahk?" Darith asks sarcastically.

"Yes. Mahk who stood out from the others; that refused to kill." He looks at me. "Or were too young to fend for themselves at all." He glances toward Keelie. "Mahk who tried to reach out to others, not only fending for themselves."

"Trusting other Mahk wouldn't be easy based on your descriptions," Vickon comments.

"No, not easy," Keelie chimes in, "but worth it. You know?"

"I see," says Vickon.

Keelie looks over at Rase. "We proved that we're more than the Creators took us for; better."

I smile at her and nod. The Mahk probably aren't any better than the Creators, but I never have the heart to argue with her.

As she talks, that strange look appears on Saige's face again. Finally I recognize her expression—guilt. Why?

The conversation dies down as one by one we peel off to wash in the pool behind the bushes then change clothing.

Blue's starved for attention. My fingers stroke her long feathers.

"She's really happy now," Darith comments.

"Now?" I reply.

"Now that you're with her. She was really starting to grate on my nerves for a while. She acted so gloomy."

A grin spreads on my face. It's nice to be reminded that she needs me.

"Not to be pushy," he continues, "but I've been sitting 'round here a while and this labyrinth isn't gonna get any friendlier."

"I know." He's completely right. As nice as the rest and food have been, we can't delay the inevitable. The longer we wait, the better chance the guards find us or we're hit with another attack of some kind.

"Ya ready to finally find out what's on the other side of that wall?" he asks with a mischievous smirk on his face.

"Give me one minute alone with her," I tell him, patting Blue's head.

He walks away.

"We're going to be okay," I try to convince her, and myself. "I'm sorry we got separated. It won't happen again."

She doesn't understand my exact words, but she seems to know that she's loved, that someone's watching out for her.

It smells like singed feathers next to the fire that has now been put out in the center of the space. Sure enough, there's one at the pit's edge. It's contorted and mostly black.

It's odd to look up and see everyone's looking my way. They're waiting for me to direct, which is very strange to me. "If you're going with us…" My eyes shift to Soll. "Be ready in twenty minutes."

Chapter 26
Spraying Fire

Blue and I sit by the remaining logs from the breakfast fire, waiting for the others. Feeling at my red hair verifies that my dagger is in place. The crossbow is securely strapped to my back. It won't hurt to double check the contents of my bags and supplies. My canisters are already full. That was taken care of hours ago. The two pieces of bread I've been saving aren't going to last when we swim under the wall, so it's reasonable to snack on one and give the other to Blue. Removing the bread enables room to condense my food down to one bag and carry my box of treasures in the other.

The giant spike from the Buyu tail surprises me when rummaging through another sack. This thing slipped my mind completely. As I wait for the others, I remove it curiously; trying to assess what Rase thought was so interesting about it. It must be almost a foot long and a good four inches in diameter. Why in the world would Rase want such a disgusting thing? The black shiny object revolves in my hands.

There's nothing fancy about the tip, so I flip it upside down, ready to cringe at the nasty bloody insides, only to discover it has changed. Staring at it blankly, I'm unsure what to think. There's nothing inside it. The creature's veins and a large bone that were once inside it are gone. There's not even a drop of blood. The spike is clean and hollow. What happened? No one has touched my bags, but even if they had, why would they clean this out?

Checking to make sure my eyes aren't deceiving me, my fingers investigate around inside it, all the way to the tip. There's not even a slimy residue within it. My hand attempts to pull out but can't be removed. It feels as if something within the spike is holding my hand.

I'm squinting now, trying to peer inside to discern what's got my hand. Still there's nothing. My fingers flare around. My other hand tries to yank the thing away, but it doesn't budge.

There's no rational explanation why it won't come off. This is just strange. Fearfully, I swing my arm up in the air, attempting to throw it from my hand. As my arm reaches full extension, a line of fire shoots out the tip of the spike and into the air. The streaming flames cause all my companions to jump. Blue darts away from me, alarmed and confused.

I stand in the center of the place, trembling with fright as the hot fire sprays above me then dies out. Nobody says anything for a moment.

Harshly exhaling, once again I attempt to fling the thing off. My arm swings forcefully back down, and this time, the spike hits the ground then rolls a few feet away.

Everyone's eyes are large.

"What happened?" Keelie questions, her gaze still set on the spike.

Darith dashes for the object then picks it up. "What's this?" he asks excitedly. "And where'd ya get it?"

"Be careful!" I scream as he slips his hand into it carelessly.

"I am, I am," he retorts as he tries putting his other hand inside the spike. "How's it work, Araina?"

"I don't know." My body's still shaking. "I don't know how that happened."

Everyone else has kept their distance from it, while Darith spins it around in his hands observantly. He tries to ignite fire from it, slipping it back and forth from one hand to the other. "Seriously," he looks at me, "what's this thing?"

"A Buyu spike," Rase answers him.

We all turn and look at her. "How did it do that?" I demand.

"I can't tell you that, Araina," she replies.

"You knew it could do that, didn't you?" I press. "That's why you were eyeing it. How does it work?"

She sighs as she sits up from her slouched position. "I'm not going to tell you anything."

It's useless trying to get information out of her, so we turn our attention back to the spike.

"A Buyu spike," Darith repeats blankly.

"Yes, the Buyu we told you about. This is the spike from its tail," I explain.

After he fiddles with it for another five minutes, swinging it around foolishly, Soll finally takes it from him and attempts to make it spray fire. He blows inside it, even taking a moment to dust it out, then sticks his hand in but still it doesn't respond.

"Let's see," Korun comments, "think it may have just had one fire spray left in it?"

"No," I reply, "it's hollow inside, completely empty. It gripped on my hand. It seemed like it knew what it was doing. I can't explain it!"

He scrunches his face. "I don't know."

"Here" Keelie takes the spike from Soll. "You try it, Korun. Since you can heal people, I bet you can make it work again with your abilities."

Korun takes it in his hands uneasily. Like the others, he can't even get it to stay on. "It's not working." He carefully hands it back to me.

"But you cut off its tail," Keelie points out, "seems like it should've worked for you."

It's in my hands again. My inspection is cautious. My hand does not go in it again. Unsettling silence disrupts my curiosity. My eyes look back up to find the whole group staring intently at me.

"What?" I ask awkwardly.

"Aren't ya gonna to try it again?" Darith answers.

"I wasn't planning to."

"I think you should," Korun encourages me.

"We don't even know how this thing works or what it's capable of," I retort. "Obviously it's dangerous!"

Vickon has been observing the situation quietly but chooses to chime in now. "Exactly, Araina, if you can make that work again, it could save our lives when we run for the wall."

I hate him for it, but Vickon makes a good point.

My gaze rests on the shiny object another minute. Closing my eyes, I tilt the tip up then slip my hand back in. Again, it feels like something has grabbed me. My shoulders flinch.

"What?" Keelie asks.

Scrats, this is ridiculous! What if it won't let me go this time? My other hand yanks the thing back off instinctively.

"What happened?" Keelie repeats.

"Aw, did it bite ya, little Araina?"

Darith's teasing doesn't warrant a response. An exhale shoots from my lips. The spike has me wrapped in curiosity. Fear is subsiding. My hand slips in it, and it grabs onto me. Like a bird emerging from its nest, my arm bursts in the air again. The flames shoot up, high above us; their beautiful orange fumes marvelous.

"That's incredible." Keelie stares at it, her mouth wide open with awe.

"It's obedient to you," Rase finally comments, "only you."

My arm slings back down, and the spike releases its grip on me. My other hand catches it before it hits the ground. "What do you mean?" I ask her; amazed she has anything to say.

"That's all I'm going to tell you," she says, a frown on her face. "It's only going to do that for you. Now, will you quit acting like an idiot, flinging your arms all around?"

"Why only for me?" I inquire.

"You put your hand inside first," she relents.

She's usually no help at all, but maybe she'll tell us more. "Why is that?"

"For Grol's sake, Araina. I told you before. It's a legend. I don't know every detail," Rase snaps.

Observing the odd spike, Sir Riddles' words creep back into my mind. The last part of the Buyu riddle makes sense to me now. The fire is the gift of the Buyu.

Scrats, his rhymes were supposed to be pure fiction. I'm amazed at Sir Riddles' accuracy. Evidently his "pets" were providing him with some valuable information.

We need to get going. The spike goes back into my tote.

Everyone still stares at me after the object disappears into my bag. "So, are we ready to go?" I ask them.

Chapter 27
The Wall

Once everyone has gathered near the dark thorny bushes, I stare at Soll expectantly. "What's your big plan?"

He brushes dark green curly hair out of his eyes. "A distraction. Initially, I intended to offer myself as bait and I'm still willing to," he explains, "but now that you have that handy fire starter in your bag, we can rethink things."

I nod. "What exactly are you thinking?"

"Along the same lines as before, I'm still thinking we can create a distraction. This plan might even help ensure we create enough motivation for Rase to help us out."

She rolls her eyes at the mention of her name.

"I think the bottles are pretty good motivation," I respond, "but an extra push won't hurt."

"Right," he agrees. "Once we reach the other side, we probably need a few minutes to assess how many guards we're facing. Is there going to be an opportunity for that?"

It takes me a minute to remember, but I do recall bushes on the other side near the water. "Yes, we can hide in some bushes. We'll also be pretty far from the wall Korun came through, so hopefully they won't notice us anyway."

"Okay, so after we reach the other side, everyone run for the bushes. There's sure to be a fair number of guards. That's when you need to set fire to the field, Araina. The fire will distract them. I'm thinking we make our way as close as we can to the wall behind the cover of the bushes. When we make it as far as we can, we fight off what hopefully will only be a couple guards at the wall."

"Seems reasonable," Vickon comments.

"And you," I look at Rase, "you better get us through."

She doesn't say anything.

"All right, everyone ready?" Soll doesn't wait for an answer before he jumps in the small pool.

I dive in immediately after him, taking a large breath before my body breaks into the clear water. As I swim beneath the huge wall, the cool liquid relaxes my tight nerves. Blue comes in behind me. Just as my lungs need another breath, I reach the surface of the other side. Air pulls deep in my lungs.

After exiting the small mass of water, it's wise to dart quickly for the bushes. Soll is already waiting there and surveying the field. Pure disillusion dances in his expression as his gaze navigates the bright green grass, fruit-filled trees, and small flowers. I'd forgotten he'd never seen this place before. "Fate be! What do you suppose…" He's staring out past the field now.

"What?" My gaze follows his to see whisks of light stream from the top of Simul's castle. A large black stone object, possibly obsidian, floats atop the magical rays and mists. The sight is beautiful but dreadful. What in the world is going on? Rase is going to need to explain that.

Ringing out my hair and showing Soll the direction of the wall keeps me busy while waiting for the others, for Rase. Unfortunately, a number of guards protect it. As expected, they're heavily armed and, based on our castle break-in, probably expecting us to return.

Gradually, the rest of the group joins us in hiding. Darith drags Rase along, the last of our companions to join us behind the bushes.

"Explain." Soll points at the floating rock.

Her eyes are big with marvel, but not shock.

"Well?" I say.

"You don't stand a chance." She almost sounds worried. "They'll never let you go. If it takes all the power of the Creators to keep you here, then so be it."

What a typical end-of-the-world response for her. It's not worth it. We're here now. We've got to try for the wall.

"Why is it like that though?" Keelie's curious too.

Rase's eyes soften landing on her. "It's magic, Keelie. It's all magic, and you can't run away from it. There's no escaping."

"Watch us." I extract the Buyu spike from my bag. This thing makes no sense. It's a little scary, but it's amazing at the same time. It could backfire, but it could save us. Despite my hesitations, we need it to get through the wall.

Probably sensing my uneasy handling of the spike, Korun encourages me, "You can do this, Araina."

"All right," Soll instructs, pointing to the area of the field he wants lit. "Over there."

It's almost painful to light the one beautiful place in the labyrinth on fire, but it has to be done. Inhaling heavily, I aim the spike off into the field adjacent to the guards. My eyes close, refusing to watch. My hand plunges inside, waiting for the thing's tight grip. The sensation of its attachment is so odd, like the grasp of a handshake. As it thrusts on, orange fire shoots out its tip ferociously. The flames feed off the grass, setting the field ablaze in an instant.

Jerking the spike back off my hand, I observe the guards anxiously. After about five minutes of the fire growing and smoke thickening in the air, the guards finally begin to shout. Many of them run toward it.

We utilize the distraction to transition into other bushes along the wall, inching our way toward our destination.

"Where did it come from?" the guards yell frantically as they scatter. Some run back toward the castle as others head for the pool of water where we exited. Perhaps they think filling their personal canisters will do some good but the fire's too far spread for that.

We're very near our exit now and still haven't been seen. Our location is only about twenty feet from the wall, and there's no closer cover to which we can run.

At this point, there are only ten guards still posted by the wall. We're slightly outnumbered, but the spike gives us an advantage.

"Now, don't set those guards on fire yet, Araina," Soll tells me quietly. "We need to fight our way past them first. If you light them up now, we risk setting the grass around them on fire, cutting ourselves off from the wall."

He's right. We'll have to face them hand to hand before the spike can even be used.

Before we begin our attack, we survey the field and the other guards one more time. It looks like the others are sufficiently distracted with the growing flames, threatening to quench their lives.

I've got to do something with Rase. "Someone is going to have to watch her," I tell my companions. "I need to be able to fight and use the spike when the time comes. I can't do all that and worry about her at the same time." I hold up her ropes, offering her to Vickon. He's the best choice for the job. We gave him a sword from one of the guards at the river, but he doesn't know how to wield it proficiently.

"I can help fight," he offers hopefully with a big heart.

"We need someone to watch her," Korun backs me up. "Someone strong enough to keep control of her."

He nods willingly as he accepts the ropes I've offered him. At his size, she can't overtake him.

"Keep your hand on that sword. Don't let her mess with you or get away. We need her to get us through that wall."

"I know."

"Follow us. Try to stay out of the way," I tell him. "They don't know she's a Creator, so they're likely to come after the both of you. Just stay behind us."

"Don't worry. I only wish I could do more to help, but if this is all I can do right now, I'm going to get it right." Vickon smiles. He doesn't specifically bring up his gratitude about what happened at the river, but it speaks in his eyes.

Getting fidgety and impatient with our constant talk, Darith ignites the attack. "Kill the guards or we might as well go jump in the fire," he yells wildly as he charges out of the bushes.

Having been apart so long, I forgot how he tends to act then think. He's running now, so the rest of us also take off, close behind him.

Keelie, Korun, and I utilize our arrows as we approach, shooting one guard down dead and injuring two others. Their bodies fall like rain drops, spilling to the ground.

Darith heads straight for the bulkiest guard. He sends a trident spear buzzing through the guard's leg before he's upon him. The guard is barely able to unsheathe his sword and deflect Darith's first swing. Their swords continue to clash, and the huge guard seems only slightly set back by the spear lodged in his leg.

Meanwhile, Soll has been faring successfully against two guards, with his dual swords. The man is possibly the best fighter I've ever seen. He swoops at them hastily, comfortably fending off their attempted blows.

Keelie faces the guard she already shot in the arm. She never ceases to impress me. As weak as her small body is, she's vicious with a whip. She wrangles the guard's sword just as she begins to withdraw it then flings the weapon out into the field.

Korun has managed to take out his second guard with an arrow before even reaching the group. The guard I shot is now targeting Korun and moving fairly quickly, despite the seeping wound in his side. Approaching at an angle barely out of Korun's view, the guard draws his sword for his attack. Unable to extract an arrow quick enough, I call out to warn Korun.

Korun dodges, catching what looks like a small gash to the back of his upper leg. Not even making a sound in pain, he's turned around in an instant and dueling the guard. Axe crunched against sword, the two weapons meet a standstill. Their opponents are situated merely paces apart. The guard capitalizes on Korun's wound, kicking his injury to gain the upper hand.

My legs charge at full speed, carrying me in his direction instinctively, as if I have to know I tried to save Korun, even though nothing else good might come from our efforts. I retrieve my dagger from its spot and launch it through the air. Rapidly spiraling, the weapon lands in the guard's back, ripping like the massive tooth of a shark through its prey. Korun gains his footing as the guard staggers in agony.

As I work my way toward him, a loud thud sounds alarmingly close to me, catching my attention.

Laon's large club has forcefully smacked into the face of a female guard who must've been after me, knocking her unconscious. Another guard sends a dagger at Laon's hand, causing him to drop the club. The guard's only about eight feet from him. He won't have time to recover. It's too soon to pull out the spike. My dagger is now on the ground, between Korun and the guard who has dislodged it from his back. Helplessness sinks inside me.

Saige has seen Laon's distress. She launches the spear through the man's chest. He collapses to the ground. Life drains from his eyes. Motion leaves him as if it had never existed.

By this time, there's another guard upon me, his sword drawn and ready to kill. Breaking any proper rules of a fight, I spit in his eye, partially blinding him for a moment. Korun tosses me my dagger, nearly losing his life to his opponent in the process. The guard holds his sword strong as he swings at me, but I kick him breathless. I get a good stab at his arm.

Regardless of my efforts, he manages to gain the upper hand on me. Pushing me to my knees, he clenches my hand tightly, forcing the dagger out of my grasp. Deep hatred exudes from his pale eyes as he raises the sword above me. Pain, there's going to be a lot of pain any second!

As I brace myself fearfully, warm blood sprays from his head across my face. Saige's other spear has submerged into his head, and he falls over lifeless. A deep exhale escapes, and I regain my dagger. Keelie's at my side before I'm done realizing I'm still alive, and she helps me to my feet.

I missed some of the details during my own encounters, but our entire group is still standing. Korun's leg is injured. It looks like Laon took a fair hit too, but no one went down. Korun swiftly tends to Laon's wound then tries to begin on his own. The healer emits intense focus as he holds his hands steadily over his leg. Nothing happens.

"What's going on?" I ask him.

"Not sure," he answers. A couple more minutes go by as he attempts to heal the wound on his own leg but has no success.

"You're probably drained from helping Laon," I offer.

"Could be, but we need to hurry." He rips some material from his shirt and bandages his leg. "It's not that bad. I'll deal with it later."

He might be able to deal with it later, but the realization that he may not be able to cure himself hits me like a dagger to the chest.

Chapter 28
Fire and Ice

"Now, Araina!" Soll disrupts my thoughts. "Use the spike!"

It's hard to tear my eyes from the dead guards and burning field, but it's necessary. Swallowing down bitter emotions, I remove the inky-looking shiny spike from my bag. Guards head our way from the castle now. Even some who had been trying to kill the fire caught sight of us. For a moment, I'm overwhelmed by their numbers. There may be sixty in all.

Having no time for hesitation, I set my aim onto the field. Quickly, my hand slides into the Buyu spike. A semicircle of flames closes in around us, about twenty or thirty feet from where we stand. Some guards are burned by my flames and still charge through to us, but most are forced to turn back.

Their bodies torched, four guards dash madly in our direction, screaming in pain. Korun shoots two of them, but the other two reach us too quickly.

Leaving the fighting to the others, Rase becomes my focus. "Thank you," I tell Vickon, taking her ropes back and forcing her to the wall. "Get us through." My voice is stern. "Or you die with us." My head motions at the fire creeping toward us.

To my surprise, she doesn't even make a sassy comment. "All I want is my clothing back," she demands.

"What?" I choke out. The smoke is thickening around us.

"Otherwise they'll kill me on first sight when I go back," she answers, her brown eyes pleading. "Give me some guard clothes. You can all go first. Just let me have some guard clothes. Quickly!"

"I threw out my ruined guard clothes a while ago. I don't have any to give you. We're going to die!" My voice cracks as the flames angrily approach us.

Sweat trickles down her sooty cheeks, streaking her face. She motions her head at Darith.

"Damn it!" I scream and call out, "Darith, get over here!"

"How can I assist you ladies?" he asks in his cool manner, as if we aren't about to be engulfed in flames.

"She wants your clothes." I point at Rase. He starts to make some smart comment, but I cut him off "Now! We don't have time."

He might pretend to be immortal, but I'd rather try to avoid burning in the fire.

Everyone is with us at the wall now. The guards must all be dead.

"Laon, can he use your spare outfit?" I gesture at Darith.

Laon extracts the clothing without any inquiries and gives them to Darith. Darith removes the Creator clothing and tosses her his outfit. The swap goes quickly.

"So," I tell Rase, "get us through!" My voice is shaky. The smoke burns our eyes as the fire quickly approaches. "Now!"

"I am, I am!" she whines back, feeling along the wall.

Everyone is coughing. It's starting to look like this was all a mistake. Blue flutters beside me nervously, croaking at her loudest. She could easily fly away right now and escape this mess, but she stays beside me.

My heart can't take it when I see the despair in Keelie's eyes as she clings to Soll.

Probably about twelve feet away now, the bright orange flames are growing taller and wilder. It's becoming difficult to even see my companions through the haze, though they stand only feet away.

"Come on," I yell at Rase again even though she's clearly trying. Panic mode is bringing out my temper.

"Okay." She looks at me as she slides her fingers into a small crack "We've got it." She smiles and whispers a phrase, "Segment Two."

The bottom of the wall begins to waver then ripple. As the waves spread upward, Vickon grabs Rase's arm before she can run through. "They go first." He points at us.

The flames are at our backs now. Laon and Darith dart through first, followed closely by Saige, Keelie, and Soll. I force Blue in. Then Korun pushes me through, holding my hand as we enter the strange liquid wall.

My hand clings to his. There is only black all around us, and I close my eyes instinctively. A cool feeling provides sudden relief from the scorching fumes behind me. Strangely, the sensation isn't like liquid at all or any familiar substance. It feels almost as if we float through the wall. It's not possible to propel my body in any direction or run at all. I have to wait patiently.

We could be stuck like this forever. We could be dead for that matter. It feels like it's been a couple minutes. Even if this is the rest of my existence, at least it doesn't hurt.

Wait, it feels different now—weightless. Lacking any grace, we tumble onto the moist ground.

"Run," a voice screams.

I shake my head and open my eyes.

"Run now, Araina!" the voice repeats. It's Soll.

I force myself to my feet. As I do, I feel a sudden heat again and then my body being pushed along.

Everything is chaotic. There hasn't been proper time to take in my surroundings before Soll is speaking to me, "He got Laon!" The strong green-haired man pulls me behind a tree.

"Who? What are you talking about?"

"Simul, he got Laon as soon as we came through."

I'm blinking now, causing me to barely catch glimpses of our situation. A haze coats my eyes, making everything appear murky. Tall trees surround us, and I'm ankle deep in water.

Soll has propped me against some very tall tree with a wide base. The rough bark scratches against my skin as the smooth air fills my lungs. Saige and Keelie are with us, but I don't see Korun.

"Korun?" I shout hysterically, glancing around us.

"He's still alive." Keelie points at another tree. He's located a distance away, on the other side of the wall entrance from us. He's been further injured but is still with us. Not only is his leg bandaged, but he appears to have taken some fire damage on his upper arm. It looks terribly painful, but he doesn't show that on his face. He attempts again to heal himself, and it still doesn't work.

Darith stands beside him. I'm genuinely surprised he hasn't charged mindlessly into the swamp.

There's Laon, or what must be Laon's body. He's slouched to the ground against the wall. Blood stains and singe marks are scattered through his Mahk garb. Tears fill my eyes uncontrollably. I want to cry.

Korun's shooting an arrow out into the swamp. His actions are followed by what can only be described as a dark blue fireball whizzing into the tree beside him. Whatever is shooting the fireballs got Laon, but surely that fire didn't come from Simul?

Peeking around the tree, I spot the one-handed man, Simul, and a group of guards. I've had enough. It doesn't even matter what happens to me. I push Keelie aside before stepping partially out from behind the tree. My hand yanks the Buyu spike from my bag.

Just then as I prepare to shoot it at the enemy, the one-handed man says something that confounds me. "Saige, I know you're there."

What? I jerk back behind the wall. Soll, Keelie, and I stare at Saige with wide eyes.

234

"He said your name," Keelie comments innocently. "Why? How does he know that?"

Saige is flustered and apparently a bad liar. "He's a Creator," she responds, "They know all our names."

"They hardly acknowledge our names. We're numbers to them," Soll replies, a stern look on his face.

The Creator in black speaks again. "Were you able to see our display at the river, Saige? Did you tell your little friends the part you played in that?"

Tears collect in her eyes. "It's not how it sounds!" she insists.

"You played your part well, leading us straight to them," he goes on.

Her cheeks start to turn red, and her eyes narrow. Rage overcomes her. She charges from behind the tree toward Korun and Darith, shooting a spear at the one-handed man. It misses.

Then suddenly I realize why I recognized her voice the first time we met. She was in the castle when Darith and I broke Korun out. Saige was the long black-haired woman that piggish man was threatening after he cornered me in the hallway. I'm dumfounded, but there isn't time to dwell on the revelation any longer if we want to survive. Soll simply watches Saige crossing the swamp, looking like he doesn't know if he should be concerned for her safety or rooting for her demise. Keelie's hand is resting on her heart, her face red with anger.

Arrows and blue fire continue to fly back and forth across the swamp. The one-handed man and Simul stand with a group of guards. His hand moves in a circular motion as floating fireballs grow within them.

Resuming my attempt to attack, I once again step out from the wall, preparing my spike for the fight. Simul's putrid smoky gray eyes get wide when he sees fire begin to spray from the object on my hand. Angrily, he throws the fireball in my direction, but I dodge it.

Unable to move quickly enough, Simul's forearms and one of the guards are burned by my fire.

He and the one-handed man each motion an arm vertically in front of them. Two thick walls of ice appear, one shielding each of them.

I step back behind the tree and look around, checking on the others. Korun and Darith are still safe behind the other tree. Korun is shooting arrows. Then I realize Saige is no longer with them or with us. Has she run away? The coward probably ran off now that we know she was involved in the demise of the colony. Despite my horror at discovering her involvement, I pity her. The small encounter I witnessed between her and the one-handed man was sickening. I can only imagine what they did to force her cooperation.

I'm stepping out to attempt another attack when Vickon and Rase finally emerge from the rippling wall. They've taken an oddly long time to arrive. Bursting from the ripples, they're in combat. Rase has somehow managed to steal his sword and pushes Vickon to the ground. Her hands raise the sword directly in front of her body, and she prepares to plunge it straight down into his abdomen.

Korun sees the altercation so he's able to shoot an arrow into Rase's back in time. The unexpected injury causes her to drop the sword, enabling Vickon to gain it again. He stands to face her, his weapon in hand. Fearfully, she turns to run.

Another fireball hits the tree I'm using as cover. I've been too distracted, and it almost cost me my life. I whip my head back toward the source of the heat-emitting, deadly element. As I prepare again to shoot flames at the Creators, I notice Simul's eyes get big. He's not looking at my spike. He's looking at Vickon. Slapping the one-handed man to get his attention, Simul points at Vickon, who has now almost reached me.

Before there's time to process their response to Vickon's presence, Saige appears again. She's worked her way behind trees much closer to the Creators. It looks like she's managed to go unnoticed. I subtly point her out to Soll and Keelie.

She launches her other spear at the Creator group. It misses who she likely intended to hit—the one-handed man—and instead it soars past him and drills into Simul's chest. She then ducks behind another tree.

Simul falls into the dirty water stained with his own blood. He reaches up to the one-handed man but receives a cold response.

The man in black appears disgusted with Simul and shakes his head then turns his attention back to Saige. "You're turning out to be more trouble than I care for, Saige."

He briefly looks over at Vickon and me, mutters something at the remaining guards, and darts away into the swamp. The guards increase their heavy fire on us. Saige disappears back into the trees as the guards rain arrows on us nonstop.

"I should've done this earlier," I tell Keelie as an idea occurs to me. I aim the Buyu spike high above the swamp toward a large branch. Starting from its tip all the way to its base, fire from the spike engulfs the branch. It crackles a couple minutes before finally the branch gives. A loud swooshing sound rings in the air as the massive thing falls from the tree. Huge flames now separate us from the guards, allowing Korun and Darith safe passage to us.

Darith dashes our direction, but Korun goes the other way. He disappears behind the trees. For a minute, I wonder if he's running off. Then he reappears quickly, dragging Saige with him. I didn't see it happen, but evidently one of the many guard arrows made it into her leg. I run to help him carry her along.

We finally disappear behind the tree line bordering the swamp to discover another set of labyrinth corridors. There's no time to strategize so we pick a route and take it, leaving Laon's body behind and leaving Rase who apparently seized her chance to escape.

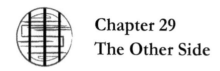

Chapter 29
The Other Side

Since we have a wounded member, the group isn't moving quickly. Soll keeps urging us to travel faster. We have put significant distance between ourselves and the Creators. He angrily hacks at the trees and moss along our path. We all know his demands are now out of rage and not for survival. He's barely made eye contact with Saige since the one-handed man called her out. It's disheartening to try fathoming what Soll and Keelie must be feeling. It was terrible how brutally their colony was destroyed, but the pain must be multiplied knowing one of their closest friends helped in some way.

A gap is starting to form, and Keelie, Soll, Darith, and Vickon have taken the lead in front of us. Korun and I drag Saige along. She begs us to run with the others. "I can take care of myself," she pleads. "Just go."

"She can't keep going like this!" Korun finally announces. "We're stopping, and I'm going to help her."

From his position in the swamp, he probably didn't hear the Creator's divulge Saige's secret, but even if he had, he would still insist we help her. We gently prop her against a wall. She's crying relentless tears and still begging us to go on without her.

Soll has backtracked now and hears her pleas as he approaches. "She said to leave her. Come on! Leave her."

Korun whips his face up, eyebrows lowered tightly.

Reading his expression, Soll defends what Korun clearly perceives to be a harsh command. "You don't understand what she's done, Korun."

"I don't care. Don't you think it's time for us all to rest anyway?" Korun reaches his hand up and wipes a tear from her cheek. "I don't know what's going on with all of you, but she fought bravely with us against the Creators. She's in pain and doesn't deserve to be left behind." He breaks the arrow in her leg and begins to dislodge it. I allow her to grab tightly at my arm. She screams with anguish as the bloody arrow head emerges from her flesh. Korun places his hands gently on the deep wound. She forces herself to hold still. Slowly the injury begins to heal beneath Korun's fingers. Saige's tears don't cease when the wound completely recovers.

"Oh, now you're going to cry so that we sit around with you until the guards show up? Is that it?" Soll yells at her. It surprises me that Soll's temper could get this bad. He's hurt, and his anger with Saige is perfectly reasonable. Still, I do feel badly for her. What exactly happened to her in the castle? And how did she escape alive? Soll's yelling interrupts my thoughts.

Korun stands to his full height, abruptly pointing his finger at Soll. "Stop! You need to stop now!"

Completely healed, Saige stands up then tries to run away down the corridor, sloshing through the mud. Dodging giant roots and ducking under hanging moss, I chase after her. The tears are still flowing heavily from her eyes, and her breathing is so rough that she can't even run fast. Chasing her through the foggy marsh environment, I think about how I have exchanged the smoke of my home with the mist of this new place. No matter what, there's always something clouding my existence. Nothing is ever clear.

"Wait," I call after her. "Saige, stop." I grab her arm and pull her around, hugging her to me. Soll and Keelie stare coldly at us from down the passage, but I don't care. None of us even know for sure what happened. Knowing her though, she never meant to hurt anyone. As much distrust as I've had in the past, my time with the group has brought me to see Mahk differently. She deserves a chance to explain herself, even if Soll and Keelie are too hurt right now to recognize that.

She's still sobbing hysterically in my arms.

"Saige," I say calmly. "Inhale slowly. Take in deep breaths."

Her breathing begins to regulate.

"I was at the castle when you were there."

For the first time since her secret was discovered, she makes eye contact with me. "What?"

"Yes. Darith and I saw the one-handed man harassing you when we kidnapped Rase."

Another tear trickles down her cheek. She winces at the mention of that man. "Grol," she responds, "his name is Grol."

"Okay. Stay calm. You're with us now, not Grol. Don't run away from this situation. We're all stronger if we stick together."

As much as I attempted to fight them off, Darith's words back at the hiding spot stuck with me. He said that our actions define us and that's how he knows me. I realize now he was right. All that time I spent alone in the labyrinth isn't because all Mahk were terrible and untrustworthy. It's because I perceived them that way. Sure, the majority probably would have killed me for a meal, but that doesn't mean everyone would have. He was calling me out because I've always been scared to be around other people. I understand his point now.

A flicker of surprise crosses her face. "Does that mean you're not leaving the group then?"

I didn't think I was so transparent, but maybe she and the others know I planned to bail as soon as we crossed the wall. "I guess I'll stick around with you guys for a bit. Clearly you can't get along without me," I spout sarcastically at her.

It would be a lot to expect a smile from her at the moment, but she nods.

"Are you ready to go back over there and tell the truth? I'll be right by your side."

A small hint of confidence returns to her icy blue eyes. She steps away, headed back toward the others. Her head gestures me to follow.

"Hear her out," I tell the group as we near them.

Soll doesn't even wait for an explanation before he's yelling again, "What are you, a Creator spy?" He's grinding his teeth with aggravation. "Traitor!"

"Soll! She's not a spy. Darith and I saw Grol threatening her in the castle. Whatever she did, it wasn't voluntary. Let's hear her out."

Everyone stands quietly. Silence grips us for a moment. Finally, Saige shatters the silence. "I was captured by the guards as I was turning in my obsidian taxes. When I told them my name and number, they escorted me away from the crowds then locked me in a castle room. That's when Grol showed up." Her breathing shallows again. "He told me they knew about the colony. There were rumors, and my name had been turned in. They knew I was a member."

I'm examining everyone's faces as she goes on. Keelie's compassion is already starting to appear in her eyes, but Soll's body language is fierce. His stance is like that of a coiled snake ready to strike.

"I didn't even speak to them at first. They didn't feed me or give me any water for many hours. I sat alone, staring out the barred window, wishing I wasn't there." She pauses, her face contorting, as if she were extracting blood from her own veins. "Finally Grol started making bigger threats."

She turns around and asks for me to remove her shrug then lift her shirt. Keelie steps back with a shriek. Vickon looks away saddened, and I think I even see some compassion in Darith's expression. Her back is completely disfigured.

"Grol started whipping me. When that didn't work, he used his fire to burn me during every interrogation." She barely forces out her words. She's fighting desperately not to cry again. I let her shirt drop and pull her back around to face us all. "I'm so sorry," she conveys earnestly. "I never did actually tell them how to get there though. After all the torture, I agreed to lead them there."

Soll scoffs heartlessly. A twinge of pain pulses through me at his insensitivity. I can't even fathom how his reaction is hurting Saige.

"I only told them that to try and make an escape. I never intended to lead them there, and I didn't. Or if I did, it wasn't purposeful. I was able to get away, but apparently someone followed me. I'm so sorry," she pleads for forgiveness.

Soll turns and walks away, pounding his fist at the wall then perching off by himself. Keelie's eyes glisten, but she holds back tears. She isn't able to verbalize an apology, but she nods silently before following him.

"Give it time." Vickon looks at Saige.

"Not to be a pain, but we shouldn't rest here long. I'm thinkin' we should find cover," Darith chimes in. The whole argument hasn't remotely fazed him, but he's right.

"You okay now?" I ask Saige.

"As I can be," she conveys.

We disband for a short time, collecting ourselves.

Small critters chirp in the tall light gray trees that lurk around us. Trying to let my feet dry, I've inched toward the wall to the driest ground I can locate. Puddles are scattered about, and portions of the corridors we have traveled have no dry ground at all. I prop myself against the ashen color wall as I sit with my legs crossed. My eyes follow small bugs dancing across the mud. They skip over the puddles nearby, barely touching the surface, creating delicate ripples. About twenty minutes pass as my thoughts replay the last couple days before Darith urges us all to get moving.

Together, we navigate this new place, absorbing humid air and fighting away pesky mosquitoes. It's anyone's best guess what the next turn will reveal or what creatures we may discover. Screeching sounds hang above us, high in the trees. My eyes shift upward, looking past the tree tops at the towering walls, the same insurmountable walls I've seen my whole life.

Our bags are still stuffed with supplies from the den. We briefly stop to eat after a couple hours. Being conservative isn't the concern it was before, now that plants and animals are all around us. Vickon asks more questions about the colony as we eat, but I find it difficult to listen, my attention stolen by the constant sounds and sights of nature.

Soll's still pushing our exploration forward, hoping to find shelter, so we're up and moving within an hour.

I hang toward the back of the group, walking alongside Saige. Her bravery and resilience are extraordinary. We have both been found out: her for what happened with the colony and me for lying about this side of the wall. If anyone here can have pity on her, it's me.

"That's incredible." Keelie's words interrupt my thoughts.

My eyes jolt up, discovering widespread open water stretching out past the labyrinth corridor in which we stand. Scattered throughout the open water are occasional bits of land, some barely big enough to hold a tree and others miles wide.

Blue happily squawks as a bird soars nearby.

Cautiously, Darith and Soll step out beyond the corridor, ankle deep in water. My gut jolts every time one of us makes contact with the water before I remember this water isn't acidic. We all wait quietly a few moments.

"We can't go back," I finally say.

"Think one of those little islands might make for good hiding? We should investigate," Korun expresses.

Soll signals us to continue into the water. We inch through. Sometimes the water is shallow enough we crouch, keeping our heads low near the surface to avoid standing out in the exposed landscape.

Blue beats us all to the first little island, her beak lapping up a fish before we arrive. We stop and rest, taking the opportunity to snack after the exertion.

"That big one." Keelie points. "Right, that's it."

Saige's spear soars through the air but misses the fish.

We eventually catch a couple. Who knew the smell of dirty water and dead fish would ever make us all so happy. A wave of tingling washes through me. For the first time, the Creators aren't controlling what we're eating.

We're only there about an hour. The island is too small and not a long-term solution for shelter. Hours pass as we continue searching the little isles. Moving from one to the next, we lose count of them. Beginning to tire, I wonder if this will be a fruitless venture.

"That one." Soll points.

"It's huge," Keelie responds hopefully.

"If that one doesn't work, we'll at least make camp there and rest," Soll says.

We reach the island, dragging our feet. Heavy wet clothes weigh us down, and a chill hangs in the air. Darith leads the way now, the only one of us still moving steadily.

"Not real pretty, is it?" He picks up a muddy turtle as we continue walking.

"About as pretty as you," Soll replies.

Keelie snickers. My left cheek scrunches, holding back laughter.

"What's that over there?" Saige asks.

Our eyes shift to see something that looks almost structural. Patches of heavy fog obstruct our view, but tall slivers of dark wood peer through. Slowing our pace, we walk closer.

"Trees," Vickon replies. "Well, roots and trees."

He's right. Giant roots protrude out of the ground, forming entangled webs beneath tall standing trees. Each thick root arches above the ground, probably nine feet in the air. The roots meet in the middle, supporting the tall trees above. Several dozen of these trees stretch out into the distance. We'd seen those trees on other islands, but none this tall or this many in number.

"This is it," Korun interjects. "Think we should stay here for now. We can't keep running forever."

Blue croaks as if accepting Korun's suggestion.

"Blue sure wouldn't mind staying here, you know?" Keelie responds.

I catch Soll glaring hatefully at Saige, as if the thought of staying anywhere with her is like poison on his tongue.

"Okay," I say before Soll says something he'll regret. I'm tired and he's right. We made it. This may not be some beautiful paradise, but it will do for now. Who knows? It might do forever.

Chapter 30
Tomorrow

I'm the second to emerge from a night of slumber within the giant roots. What looked barely livable to my tired eyes the day before doesn't seem so terrible today.

"Couldn't sleep?" I ask Saige, joining her at the edge of the brown water. Colorful dragon flies buzz around us. Even a mild breeze rushes by, breathing peace into my spirit.

"I did. I just didn't want to keep sleeping." She sighs. "Reality worked its way into my dreams where it wasn't welcome."

"The colony?" I ask.

"All of it. Grol, the burning." She rubs her back. Korun healed what was left of the open wounds, but permanent scaring remains. "And the colony."

"There's only one thing I still don't understand," I say to her. "Why didn't you tell the colony what happened when you got back to the den?"

"I don't even really know." She stares down at her own feet. "I guess I was ashamed of what happened. I didn't think it mattered that much since I got away without revealing our location. Not to mention, by that time, there were blades shooting out of the ground. I had bigger concerns."

"But they knew about the colony. Someone else was bound to get captured."

"I did think of that, but there's something else that happened while I was in the castle. There was a map," she says.

I'm nodding along as she speaks. I'm tempted to interject questions, but she's probably getting to the answers if I'm patient.

Breaking the stillness of the morning, my fingers snap apart small twigs and toss them at the water as she speaks.

"It was hanging above the bed in the room where I was kept. I only got to see it twice because most of the time I was tied in a chair facing the other direction. At first, I didn't think much of it, but then I noticed the castle. From there, I saw the field and even the wall, Araina. But it was called a gate on the map."

I shake my head as I process her words. "So you already knew about the wall before we ran into you."

"Yes, I knew. After the first labyrinth attack with the blades and the guards all mercilessly murdering the Mahk, I suggested to the colony that they send out a search party. Of course, previous to that, no one had considered there being anything outside our labyrinth. I suggested our little group go looking for a way out of the labyrinth because I already knew there was one. But who could imagine there was anything outside our world? The colony respected my suggestion and let our group go searching, but they only sent us. I know they thought it was a fool's errand. Everyone else stayed in the den, trying to hide from the Creators. I was determined to get us out. I had to find a way to get everyone to the wall without mentioning my time in the castle. Recalling the map was tricky, it being so fuzzy in my mind, so I wanted to verify I could even find the wall."

"You were going to try to save them all, not just get your little group to the wall?"

"Of course I was. And when you showed up knowing exactly how to get us there, I was so relieved. Before you came along, I didn't know how to access the wall, aside from possibly going through Simul's castle. Once you showed up, I hoped we could get the colony and get out through your secret passage." She's all worked up again, her face red as she makes large hand gestures. She's been through so much in so little time.

"I know," I reassure her. "But you don't have to hide secrets anymore and we're out of the labyrinth now. We're better off." I could tell her I'm sorry for all she's been through, but sometimes silence speaks volumes.

Her breathing settles as a few moments pass. "There's more," she goes on. "The map was huge."

"Sure, it showed the entire labyrinth, right?" I ask.

Her eyes are big as she responds, "Right, the entire labyrinth," she emphasizes. "It's gigantic, Araina. That's another reason I didn't want to tell everyone the truth. The part we came from is only a segment of the whole thing on the map."

"Segment Two," I say, repeating what Rase said before we came into the swamp.

Saige nods. "I didn't want to take away everyone's hope about this side of the wall. You made it sound so great, and I knew we couldn't stay where we were. I wasn't ready to tell everyone. I needed time to figure more out."

"What were you trying to figure out?"

"I was trying to get more details about the rest of the labyrinth out of Rase."

"I never saw you talking with Rase."

She brushes loose hair from her face. "That's because I only did it when everyone else was sleeping or busy. I was trying to put together all the pieces."

"You mean from the map?" I ask, trying to picture what a map of the labyrinth might look like.

"The map and other small things: like how Vickon had heard the word Kathar before. I saw Kathar on the map. It's a place."

"You think he's from Kathar," I deduce. "And I think Korun came from there too."

She doesn't question my reasoning for that belief but just nods. "Once I put that together, I didn't know what to do with all the information. It felt wisest to focus on getting through the wall."

"I completely understand," I agree. "That's why I hadn't mentioned to anyone that I heard the guards talk about Kathar when I rescued Korun. Where was Kathar on the map?"

"Far away," she tells me. "Our labyrinth is within two that wrap around us and ours is small by comparison. It's completely on the other side of the other two. And I don't even know for sure I could remember enough to get us there. For that matter, who knows what we'll find there?"

We sit quietly for a moment as we observe the landscape. I sigh. It takes a good ten minutes to mull it all over and decide what to do next. She's deep in thought as well.

"I don't think we should tell them about Kathar yet," I say to her, "if we tell them at all."

She nods, seeming as reluctant as I am to deal with the heavy information we have exchanged.

"To think, the Creators would have kept us caged in that dark labyrinth. Your description of the map sounds almost unbelievable." I glance around us at the muddy ground and occasional bushes. This place may not be pretty but we can hunt our own food. We have shelter. The Creators may not come after us here. There's no guarantee we'll find another place like this.

"Simul's dead now." Relief blows through me as I say that statement out loud. I look at the tall roots where the others sleep, and Saige follows my gaze. "Enough of our group perished trying to get us here. I say we explore this place and stay settled. Maybe sometime I'll talk to Korun about Kathar, but not now. We finally escaped the Creators, and you three need to mend things." I point at Keelie and Soll, who are now emerging from our shelter.

"Thank you, Araina" she responds with a slight hint of happiness in her tone. "You really are a good person."

Goosebumps rise up on my neck and arms. Never did I imagine someone saying that to any Mahk. I shrug. "If I am, then you all helped me become that way." My eyes gesture not only at her but the whole group. "Thank you."

I walk over to Blue, who has curled up beside Darith of all people. He's propped against a tree, lounging like he doesn't have a care in the world.

"I don't know what she sees in you," I tease as I approach.

"Better breath than ya, I think," he jabs back.

"I can't believe we made it," I confess with a smile across my face. "We actually got through the wall."

He nods. One eyebrow is raised like usual as he pats Blue's head. "Yep, Araina. We made it together. Ya still haven't darted off yet. I'm surprised."

"Someone told me that our actions define us. That got me thinking," I admit.

"Thinkin' what?" he inquires.

For a man I took to be a completely heartless killer, he can be extremely profound at times. "You say I should know you, Darith, but I can't actually base my knowledge of you on what I knew before because I never saw the details behind your actions. I think now I can understand the reasons for your actions and start to know you better."

He smirks. "Hmm, I guess that's somethin' for me to think on."

I exhale deeply as I settle in next to Blue. She lies between the two of us, her head still on Darith's lap. I pick at her pretty blue feathers. I would never trade the time I spent with just Blue, but I realize now that we're both happier to have found some friends. I survey the others closely. Some relationships need mending. Some of us still have much to learn about ourselves. I look at Darith then down at Blue again, and I'm grateful that, amidst all the pain and confusion, at least we have each other.

We're safe from the Creators for the moment. That is, unless they come after us again. Together, we're stronger than when we are apart. Tomorrow is another day, filled with a new hope. Tomorrow holds promise. The strings are cut; the puppet masters only a memory. I'm free and I'm ready for tomorrow.

The End

The Haunted Realm Excerpt
(Obsidian Series Book 2):

Head aching and eyes blurry, I strive to gain full consciousness.

"You've been out quite a while." A woman's voice helps to draw me out of the abyss and into reality.

"Who are you? Where am I?" I shake my head.

"The name is Zem, but don't plan on getting too familiar."

"My name's Araina."

"The Creators are on their way to take you."

"You're not a Creator?" My vision clears, and my eyes take in the blonde-haired woman in red clothing who stands before me.

"No, but they've had posters up with a depiction of you for months. They'll be pleased to get you into custody, I'm sure." Judgment rolls through her piercing blue eyes.

Ready to know what happens next?

Grab The Haunted Realm Today

Obsidian Series Books

Experience more of the adventure...

Sample Coloring Novels™ Titles:

Have you seen Emilyann's Coloring Novels™ collection?
Visit the website to see what loved stories are available.

www.bestcoloringnovels.com

Don't forget, post your colored pictures or photos
reading Emilyann's books on social media and tag
Emilyann. She tries to respond and connect.

Notes from the Author

First of all, thank you so much to my readers. Writing is tough, because you don't even know if and when someone will pick up your book. When you decided to read my book, you fulfilled my mission and dreams. Again, thank you.

Acknowledgements to the Editors

Special thanks to Nicole Zoltack, my fabulous editor. You truly did wonders to bring this work into its full potential, Nicole. I appreciate your belief in my work and the amazing touches. This story needed you to come in to its own. Thank you so much.

James Allen, Sr., thank you for your diligent work on this story. You've got a sharp eye and treated the story like your own work. The Labyrinth Wall world benefited greatly from your input.

Continued Acknowledgements

Thank you to my husband, Justin Girdner, you have been patient and incredibly supportive of my writing. Without your input and advice, I might never have been able to transport the world in my mind to paper.
Thank you to my family and dear friends. Everyone has been incredibly supportive of my work and pushed me to grow.

Thank you Mom, Dad, Henry, and James. You've all invested so much love through the years and it means so much. Henry, you are just absolutely amazing. Your investment of time and love in your little sister's writing must be some kind of record breaker. In fact, all readers who enjoyed this work should thank Henry, too. Without his honest and encouraging feedback, I may not even have had the confidence to come this far. James, you've always been a voice of wisdom. I truly appreciate every late night talk and time of laughter. I love you, brothers. Thank you, Mom. You are one of two people to whom I've told the entire series concept. Your fascination and support kept me motivated.
Dad, you were one of the first people to read the entire first draft of The Labyrinth Wall. Your encouragement spurred me on. Thank you so much. You've always encouraged my writing and kept me on track. I love you all.

To my aunt, Bonnie Varble, your work on my first novel taught me so much, which enabled to move forward to this point. Thank you so much for the sacrifice of time, the encouragement, and the wisdom you have given me.

Specifically, a huge thank you to all friends and family who read and gave me feedback on my unpublished novel or the beta version of The Labyrinth Wall: Henry Allen, Bonnie Varble, Jocelyn Kessinger, Sumar Foster, Michaela Dehning, Katie Grabowski, James Allen Sr., Tenzin Paldon Kahler, Tiffany Girdner, and Angie Kahler.

To my writing, blogging and social media friends, thank you for being constant sources of encouragement and inspiration. It is truly appreciated. A specific shout out to Rachel Morgan and Cherie Reich who have been kind mentors during my journey.

All the way back in high school, wonderful mentors and teachers gave me inspiration and confidence. I thank each of you and my college professors. You guided my creativity and inspired me to pursue my passion, not what the world would have me pursue.

About the Author

Emilyann Girdner is the creator of coloring novels and the author of Amazon Best-Seller, Dante Rossetti Award Finalist, and Reader's Favorite 5 Star rated young adult fantasy novel, The Labyrinth Wall. Emilyann's writing has appeared on websites and blogs including Sound & Communications Magazine, The TV Shield, Center for Work Life, Easter Seals Florida, MU Museum of Art & Archaeology's Musings, and Examiner.com.

She has been a guest and spoken for events with organizations such as Barnes & Noble stores, Wizard World Comic Con, MegaCon Fan Days, and AltCon. And City Surfing Orlando, Miami.com, Orlando Weekly, Street Insider, Tallahassee Democrat, Tallahassee Magazine, and WorldNews are some of the media outlets that have mentioned Emilyann. Emilyann hopes to share a love for others and God in all she does. She believes that imagination sparks beauty in the soul.

Emilyann Girdner

Photo by: Laina Mari Productions

"The more you learn,

the more you grow.

One day you will

change the world,

with all you know."

~Emilyann

Get a FREE eBook at the author's website:
www.emilyanngirdner.com

The Labyrinth Wall Glossary

(with the author's suggested pronunciations)

A

Araina

Pronounced:
A·rain·a

Araina is the protagonist in The Labyrinth Wall. She looks seventeen-years-old, but has only been alive for two years. Placed in the dark labyrinth by the Creators, her life consists of constant battles for survival. She has red hair that she wears twisted up in to a knot using the butt of a dagger, pale skin, green eyes, and is average height. Though perception is her ultimate weakness, hope is her redeeming strength.

B

Blood Caves

These caves are home to the most horrific residents of the Segment One labyrinth, the Nabal. They are located within the same mountain range as The Den (home of the Mahk colony).

Blue

Blue is Araina's pet bird. Named for the color of her feathers, Blue is a delicate and loveable friend to Araina. Her innocence sets her apart from the heartless nature of most beings in her world. She is so loved, that Araina even carved her image into her knife handle.

Buyus Pronounced: Bu·yous	Buyus are legendary twin ancient serpents. These creatures can hibernate for indefinite periods of time. They can only be awakened by the scent of the Makta. They are very wild animals that eat anything in their way. These dragons look like giant snakes, about thirty feet long, and five-foot diameter. Two giant spiral horns stick out of their heads. They have distinct dark red coloring and jagged geometric gray patterns on their backs. Their stomachs are black and have a coal texture to them. Sporadic rows of shiny black spikes line their backs as well, and the tip of their tail is a giant shiny black spike.
Buyu Spike	This object is almost a foot long and a good four inches in diameter; it's shiny black conical shape tapers at a slight angle. The spike is rumored to have magical properties.

C

Creators	The secrets of their powers are still unknown. They simply throw their creations into the dark labyrinth, then force them to fight for food and pay obsidian taxes. They are considered evil rulers.

D

Darith

Pronounced:
Dare·ith

A Mahk like Araina, Darith was created and placed in the labyrinth, but given no explanation as to his purpose. He's angry, selfish, violent and even a murderer. Witty, dark humor doesn't win him favorite points either.

Darktouch Flowers

Common within the labyrinth, these beautiful florets which are so pleasing to the eyes are far less pleasant to the touch.

Den

Commonly referred to as The Den, this place is home to the Mahk colony. It is also located within the same mountain range as the Blood Caves.

G

Grol

Pronounced:
Gr·all

He's the one-handed Creator that wears all black. His soul is darker than obsidian.

K

Keelie

Pronounced:
Key·lee

Keelie is a member of the Mahk colony. She may not be strong or even all that mature, but Keelie's got will to defeat an army. She's a speedy and courageous young lady with blonde hair that reaches her elbows.

Korun

Pronounced:
Core·un

Many mysteries surround Korun. He doesn't know much about the labyrinth walls in which he finds he is confined or even much about his past for that matter.

L

Laon

Pronounced:
Lay·on

Laon is a member of the Mahk colony. He's skilled in battle and puts up a fight for his beliefs.

M

Mahk

Pronounced:
Ma·k

These are beings brought into existence by the Creators. Their lives are spent avoiding the many dangers of the dark labyrinth and fighting each other for resources.

Makta

Pronounced:
Ma·k·ta

Small snakes found in the snake pit of the labyrinth. Their distinct smell resembles lemons mixed with rotting flesh. They are blind, about a foot long and are orange colored. They don't bite, but are poisonous to consume.

N

Nabal

Pronounced:
Na-ball

Hiding in the Blood Caves, these Mahk are the worst of their species. In a land where food is scarce, these brutes have become cannibals. Interestingly, this group mirrors the Minotaur who eats labyrinth visitors in traditional mythology.

R

Rase

She is a Creator guard, despised by all Mahk.

Rifan

Pronounced:
Reef·un

He is a member of the Mahk colony. A large boned man with a chiseled face, Rifan is known for his less than enthusiastic views on life.

Rotting Pass

More dead bodies occupy this creepy pass than live ones. If its smells don't deter visitors, its nastiest inhabitant, Sir Riddles, surely will.

S

Saber Tooth Mutts

These deadly canines live in the Rotting Pass and answer only to Sir Riddles. As their name suggests, their long fangs distinguish them from other creatures in the labyrinth.

Saige Pronounced: Say·ge	She is one of the founders of the Mahk colony. Saige's long black hair and icy blue eyes may be enchanting, but she's got secrets.

Scrats	Araina's made up word which she spouts when she's unhappy or confused. It is a combination of her two least favorite things: scars and rats.

Sikla Pronounced: Sick·la	Sikla is the one volcano in the labyrinth. It is considered by some to be a beautiful jewel against the barren land.

Simul Pronounced: Sim·all	The leader of the Creators and Araina's most hated enemy. He's got all he needs and more, but still let's his creations starve.

Sir Riddles	Gruesome goopy eyes and dog like features don't mask a warm and fuzzy interior; he's just rotten all the way through. But when one listens closely, it becomes clear he speaks rhymes of value. He makes his home in the Rotting Pass and he's known to be a bit crass.

Soll Pronounced: S·all	He is the leader of the Mahk colony. He's tall with green hair and unlike any other being in the labyrinth. But what sets him apart most is his leadership ability, which has been known to save more than one life.

T

Thorn Patches Valley	Thorn Patches Valley is rare space within the Segment One labyrinth that consists of thick, thorny bramble. Despite its prickly nature, the valley also offers rare and enjoyable herbs for cooking.

V

Vickon Pronounced: Vick·on	The most peculiar thing about Vickon is that he was kept prisoner and heavily chained in the Creator dungeon. It isn't common for the Creators to go through such trouble to subdue a Mahk...

Edited by Nicole Zoltack and James Allen, Sr.